THE SHADOW BENEATH THE WAVES

MATT BETTS

SEVERED PRESS
HOBART TASMANIA

THE SHADOW BENEATH THE WAVES

Dedication

I figure this is probably the right book to dedicate to my good friend Brian, who discovered MST3K, Robot Jox and a slew of bad movies with me.
Thanks for watching out for me.

1

Martin Taylor watched as his divers surfaced and waved at him.

"This is it," Takis shouted. "The hull is intact, just like we thought."

Cass raised her mask onto the top of her head. "It's gorgeous. Exactly what the video showed." She grabbed the ladder and climbed. Martin extended her a hand and helped her onto the deck, then did the same with Takis. The two divers sat on the edge with their feet dangling in the water as they removed their tanks.

"Excellent. I'll let everyone know we're in business." Martin climbed up the ladder to the main deck and walked toward the wardroom in the bright Caribbean sunlight. It felt good to relax and enjoy the afternoon weather. They'd been hunting the wreck of the *HMS Swansea* for nearly two years, and a lucky break finally brought them here. Some of the crew had left along the way, looking for greener pastures, but the dozen or so that were left were hardcore believers in the hunt, and would be overjoyed at the find.

When Martin opened the hatch to the wardroom, he was greeted by the shouts and cheers of the remaining crew. The large overhead monitor, recently most used as a screen for movie nights, showed the blown up image of the word *"SWANSEA"* barely visible on the wreck below.

When the noise died down, Martin spoke. "Cass and Takis say it's the real thing. And fairly intact."

"The *Eyeball* told us that days ago," Rina said. She referred to her mini sub camera that they always used to explore potential sites. "But I guess waiting around for two people to swim down and see it isn't a complete waste of time."

"He's old-school. Leave him alone." Jakob handed Martin a plastic Champagne flute full of his favorite cheap American beer. "To the *Swansea*." He raised his own glass in salute. The rest of the crew did as well, shouting their excitement again.

"To all of you. The crew of the *Adamant* has done me proud again," Martin said.

"To the *Adamant*," the crew shouted.

Ozzie Suvari, Takis's brother, came up and patted Martin on the shoulder. "My hands were starting to get prune-y from all the diving looking for this thing. If it'd taken much longer, they might have stayed that way."

"Think of all the exercise you've been getting. I've been saving you a fortune in gym memberships." The two touched their cheap glasses of alcohol together in salute and took a drink before Ozzie went over to join Rina and Jakob.

The beer was slightly warm and a little flat, but it still tasted good to Martin. They'd succeeded when everyone else had failed; where everyone else had given up and moved on. He was close to doing so himself, and would have, if he hadn't been so loud about his resolve to never quit on this search. Every interview brought up the subject, and instead of leaving some wiggle room for leaving, he doubled down on his insistence that this day would come. For some, today would be a vindication, proof he was right. But he'd depleted a good portion of his once-fat bank account. If they'd gone after some of the smaller treasures along the way, and left their options open on the *Swansea*, things might have gone more smoothly.

As Martin eyed the crew, he realized that three were unaccounted for; Cass, Takis, and Goldman. Cass and Takis were probably stowing their gear and changing still. Martin figured that Joe Goldman was in the wheelhouse, keeping an eye on the weather or some such worrisome detail.

After a careful extrication from the party, Martin went looking. He found Goldman, as he'd expected, in the cramped con room. Goldman sat in the captain's chair, surrounded by instrumentation. The original controls of the modified ship on his left, the banks of computers and new technology on his right. He was alternating between staring at a weather radar monitor and another screen downloading emails.

"Everything good? You're missing Kronenbrau in plastic."

"Does it taste better than Cronenbrau from Styrofoam cups?" Goldman didn't look up. "Cause that shit is nasty."

"Hey. Cronenbrau is an American classic," Martin said. "You seen Palmer?"

Goldman pointed to the bow, where a lone figure stood leaning on the railing. "She's been out there since they came up for air."

"Thanks." Martin turned to join her but Goldman stopped him.

"I'm having a little trouble with the wireless connection, but I have a message from S.B. that's trying to download. Seems like a big file."

"Really?" The crew knew who S.B. was; she'd provided a lot of the intel on wrecks and treasures that Martin's crew had managed to find.

She'd hacked and evaluated the race data from a Caribbean sailing regatta, and extracted a point of data no one else cared about in order to lead Martin and the *Adamant* crew to the *Swansea*. The woman seemed to never sleep, scanning maps, satellite feeds, forums and military channels for tidbits and scraps that she could build into a whole theory on the location of any given mystery. Occasionally, she creatively "borrowed" information from other treasure hunters, which never went over well. "What are the odds that she can hit a homerun twice in a row? Let me know when you get that message, though."

Martin turned and walked toward the bow.

Cassidy Palmer turned and nodded when she saw him. "You leave the party already? I thought the captain went down with the ship."

"Had to make sure the whole crew was celebrating," Martin said. "What're you doing out here?"

Cass waved a dismissive hand. "Eh, you guys have run the ball pretty far on this; I've only come on in the last six months. You all are due for a major party."

"You've worked on this too. Don't let yourself miss this. I hear they busted out the goat cheese we picked up in Bonaire." They'd been eating the goat cheese since the day they left port. "Nothing else says party like goat cheese."

"So when do we start raising the treasure and getting rich?" Cass asked.

"I forget how new you are to this. We'll probably get to bring a couple of things up for proof that we found her, and we'll go down and take a ton of cool pictures, but there's a lengthy process before we get to do much. Legal stuff, mostly," Martin said. "I didn't think you were in it for the money."

"I'm not. I'm just getting bored already and want to get moving on the next search, really."

"Well, strap yourself in; it could be a long wait." Martin patted the railing and started back. "You should really join the party." He didn't linger, and realized she'd probably stay where she was, but at least he tried. He walked up the stairs and as he passed the wheelhouse, Joe waved him in.

Martin assumed it was something party-related, but changed his mind when he walked through the door and saw the gunman standing, half-hidden by the equipment.

2

Martin kept his hands raised as he addressed the men pointing guns at him. The single armed man in the wheelhouse had forced Martin and Joe out and into the common room, where other attackers had rounded up the crew. "Look… We found this site and intend to file a claim on it. We won't be intimidated into leaving." Martin looked around the cabin to make sure his own people were calm and safe. He didn't need anyone getting antsy and getting killed.

One of the thugs stepped closer and pointed his gun at Martin's head. "Intimidated? Who said anything about intimidating you?" He racked the slide on his machine gun for emphasis. Martin noticed the man had a vaguely French accent.

"Woah. There's no need for this. You tell your boss we'll…"

"What makes you think I am not in charge here?" The man acted indignant.

"You're all wearing headsets. I saw some of them reacting to orders as they rounded us up, but you hadn't said anything." Martin nodded out the port window. "I just assumed there was someone over on your ship giving the orders." Martin had noticed the ship as he'd come into the room.

The head gunman was silent for a moment and then pointed to the door with his gun. "All of you out on the deck. Now." He pushed Ozzie with the butt of his rifle. "Go."

Martin tried to assure his crew things would be okay. "Come on guys. Let's go. Just do what they say." He led the way, his five crew members followed closely out of the room. "Take it easy." In his head, Martin was anything but calm. Two of his crew weren't accounted for yet and he hoped they were safely hidden.

They walked out into the sunshine and stumbled across the deck of the modified cargo ship, *Adamant*. Everything was in disarray from the confusion of the attack and the preparation he and the crew were making for the exploration below. Martin scanned the equipment, looking for something to use as a weapon or to signal for help, but there was nothing but rope, chord and electronics. There were wetsuits and air tanks, but no harpoon guns or dive knives, whatever good those would have done.

"Stop," the lead gunman said. He was hard to hear out on the deck with the wind picking up. They'd come to a halt near a rope ladder that must have been strung up by the attackers. Peering over the side, Martin saw a large, empty outboard boat that the men used to get over from their own vessel.

Two more pirates, Martin just decided they must have been pirates, approached from the other end of the ship. They were alone, which meant they hadn't located the last of Martin's crew. It gave him a glimmer of hope.

"Marco, Anthony—head down and start the boat," the leader said.

"Your boss want us dead now, or are we all going over to talk to him?" Martin asked.

The gunman stepped as close as he could to Martin. "If we wanted you dead, I would have killed you. For now, we're just going over to our ship, where things are a little more conducive to a discussion." He motioned to the ladder and Martin began to climb down, hand over hand on the thick ropes, followed by the others, and then the remaining attackers.

Soon, they were all standing on the deck of the smaller boat, and Martin stared out at their destination boat in the distance. He figured once they got there, they would die. These men would kill him and his crew and toss them overboard. They'd take the *Adamant*, and the treasure on board, and use the Suvari brothers' notes to find the rest of it on the bottom of the sea floor, not too far off from their current position. Martin assumed the only reason they weren't dead yet was because these attackers hadn't found those notes.

One of the gunmen leaned hard on the throttle and smacked the boat's console. Another walked over and they began a heated conversation in WAKE, a dialect that was a melding of several Pacific languages and regionalisms— some Chinese, a little Japanese, Hawaiian and some Indian. It had been the predominant language of the Circle of Liberated Territories during the war more than a decade back. Martin wasn't skilled in the interpretation of it, but some of his crew were. Rina leaned forward to tell him what was being said, but it was easy to understand without knowing the actual words. The boat wouldn't start.

The two men at the helm continued to bicker as they burned through all of the curse words that Martin knew in their language. He looked around and found that there were only five men, not counting the bickerers. Sure, they were heavily armed, but given the opportunity, the crew could overpower them. They just needed an opportunity; he just didn't know what that opportunity would be.

Seconds later, the pirates' ship exploded. A large fireball erupted from the aft of the craft, sending smoke and flames high into the bright blue sky. The blast threw the shapes of two men into the air, dropping them in the water.

Martin figured that was a sign if ever he'd seen one. He looked to his crew, who were already waiting on him to say something. Martin nodded and the crew attacked the stunned pirates, who were staring at their flaming ship. Martin and Ozzie jumped on the pilot and his companion who had stopped working to start the boat just to look at their ship. Jakob Rask, the largest of the *Adamant* crew, punched the nearest gunman and shoved him overboard before quickly grabbing another and kneeing him in the groin. Rina jumped on a man's back and punched him in the ear.

Ozzie emerged from his efforts with one of the men's rifles, and he shot it in the air. Everyone stopped and turned to see who had used the weapon. The attackers struggled to gain control of their own guns, mostly with Jakob.

"Drop your guns," Ozzie said. "Drop them now."

He meant it, Martin knew. Most of the crew had seen some sort of military service, but Ozzie had seen actual combat years ago. There was a question of whether anyone else would be willing to shoot someone. The pirates raised their hands. None were in a position to shoot Ozzie, and the majority of them were incapacitated anyway.

"The second I heard the explosion, I knew where my brother had gone," Ozzie said. "Takis tends to make a loud mess."

That was Martin's suspicion as well. He just hoped Cass was with Takis and they were both safe.

"Jakob? Head back up the ladder and you can keep guard as we send these guys back up. Then we'll sort out what to do with them." The crew brought the pirates aboard safely and watched the other boat as it seemed to slowly take on water, sitting lower in the water, especially at the stern. Gunfire erupted again as a small, motorized lifeboat sputtered off in the opposite direction, firing to cover their escape. Martin counted maybe three figures.

"Well, there goes your ticket out of here. You could try your bigger ship, but you lot may be swimming home if that one sinks any lower," Jakob said. The pirates saw nothing funny and mumbled in WAKE under their breaths.

"They said something about your mother and an oversized zebra," Rina pointed out. "No. Not a zebra..." She snapped her fingers as she searched for the words. "It looks like one." She held out her hand to stop anyone from saying it before she could remember. "I'll think of it."

"You don't need to translate it exactly. I get it," Martin said.

Loud splashing in the pirate's small boat below them brought everyone's attention. Cass and Takis threw their diving gear into the craft and pulled themselves in. They dropped their vests and tanks, and then leaned over to pull up a small sea sled. Martin assumed it was what got them over there and back so fast.

"Ahoy!" Jakob said.

The duo looked up and waved.

"Takis, what did you do?" Ozzie yelled down.

With a thud, Takis's weight belt dropped to the deck. "Did you see that?" He pointed to the burning ship. "I mean, did you see that? It was awesome."

"Yes we saw it. How could we miss it?"

While the brothers continued to yell back and forth, Martin focused on Cass. "You okay?"

She looked up, nodded and put her foot on the rope ladder before pausing. "Everything okay up there? Is it safe to come up?"

"Yeah, we have everything in hand up here." He watched her climb up the rungs and could see she'd taken off all of her equipment, except the thick dive knife strapped to her ankle. It wasn't that unusual, he'd guessed she wore it to bed as often as he'd seen her with it. He always chalked it up to her being a female on a new boat with mostly men, and he didn't blame her for being cautious. She'd made friends with everyone in the three months since she signed on, but she was still the newest crew member by far, it was hard to get dropped into that situation and trust everyone so quickly. When she got to the top, Martin gave her a hand.

"I knew Takis was crazy, but... wow," Cass told Martin.

Everyone nearby laughed.

"Did you call for help?" Cass said.

Martin shook his head. "I'd hoped to locate the two of you first. But now that we have you..." He turned and helped Takis up onto the ship. "I better go do that. We could be seeing some of the men from that ship make their way over here any time now, if they survived, and their lifeboat left without them."

"I'll do it." Cass grabbed a towel from the clothes line they'd strung down the middle of the deck and patted her face dry. "I can give them a good idea of what I saw over there."

Martin looked at her for a moment. "You sure? I mean, that could be a little nerve-wracking."

"Of course I am. Communications is one of my jobs on this bucket," Cass told him. "Besides, I wasn't the one with a gun pointed at them. I'm fine." She slipped on some deck shoes and made for the wheelhouse.

The smoke darkened over at the pirates' boat, and Martin stared at it as it rose. They'd had problems with claim jumpers and thieves before, but this was as close of a call as he'd ever want to see. He turned and watched Cass. She would be fine he supposed, but he wondered about her.

7

Rina came running up to him, a big grin on her face. "An okapi."

"What?" Martin was dumbfounded.

"The pirate? Remember?" She looked amazed that he couldn't remember. "I translated what he said about you. He said your mother has sex with fat okapis." She was pleased with herself and Martin had no idea whether she was messing with him or if she was really trying to help.

"Thanks," Martin said. "Thanks a lot."

3

Cass went inside the ship and turned toward her cabin just before she got to the *Adamant*'s wheelhouse. Once there, she locked her door and pulled aside her mattress, then opened a slat, in the floor under the bed. From there she pulled out a pair of thick warm socks, unrolled them and pulled out her satellite phone and earpiece. She turned it on and while it found a signal, she pulled on a pair of jeans, a t-shirt and sweatshirt. As she pulled her scraggly brown hair back into a ponytail, she noticed the green light was blinking on the phone. She put the bud in her ear and, as the proper tones sounded, she keyed the mic. "Chaperone Delta-One calling Blind Date Citadel. Come in Blind Date Citadel." She paused and repeated until a click indicated she'd been transferred to an actual person who'd know what the fuck she was talking about.

"Blind Date Citadel." It was a matter-of-fact monotone from a male voice.

"Copenhagen, Denver, Munich," Cass said. She'd memorized the pass code, but rarely used it. She waited for the response, which she'd also memorized.

"Miami, Tokyo, Bangor." The man's tone loosened. "Good to hear from you Chaperone. What's your update?"

Cass knew Blind Date's real name was Linden Kemp; they'd worked together on a number of ops over the last five years. He'd taught at the academy when Cass was training, and had requested that she be assigned to his command in the Navy years ago. Now, they worked together in covert ops for the Naval Interdiction Administration, keeping an eye on smugglers, terrorists, low-lifes, and, in this particular case, treasure hunters that may be of some use. "Nothing good, I'm afraid. We're still at a standstill regarding our missing item. No new information on that."

"Sorry to hear that, Chaperone."

"Me too," Cass said. "We're in a situation. The crew found the treasure it was looking for here, but the boat was attacked by pirates. We could use some help taking care of the situation without too many questions."

"Understood. Is the situation in hand?"

"Copy that, Blind Date. They seem to be neutralized for the moment, but their boat is sinking, so we can't just leave them for the authorities and move on."

There was silence before Blind Date cued back on. "You could. No one would miss them."

"Blind Date, I think our connection is garbled. Could you repeat last transmission?"

There was another pause. "We'll send a group to meet you. E.T.A... give them one hour."

"Copy. Chaperone out." Cass clicked off the phone before Linden could ask anything else. She turned it off and stuffed it back into the wool sock and shoved it back into the slat beneath her bed. She felt around inside the hole and made sure her pistol was still there, right next to the radio. She hadn't had time to get up to her cabin to retrieve it when the pirates attacked earlier, but she just needed to make sure it was there. It was comforting to know it hadn't gone anywhere.

Once everything was back in place, she made her way to the wheelhouse and picked up the radio handset. She stood there for a minute until a couple of the crew had looked up at her and noticed she appeared to be doing what she said she'd do. She waved, gave a thumbs up, and they looked away. She had no intention of sending a description of their location, for fear of more pirates and criminals using it to hone in on their position before the Navy made it.

After a few minutes, she put the mic back and took the steps back down to the deck. She approached the crew to find they'd had the pirates sit down with their hands behind their heads. "Any more of them come swimming over?" She looked out at the pirates' boat. Its bow was slightly out of the water, and its aft was nearly level with the sea. It was obvious the boat was going down any time.

"Not one," Jakob looked slightly annoyed that he had no one to punch.

"I raised some help; they said they'd be here in just over an hour."

"Ugh," Martin said. "I want to start looking at these cups you guys brought up with the wreck. You sure it's the right period?"

"Boss, I know my treasure. These cups might as well have had "Property of *Swansea*" stamped on them."

Cass laughed, but she scanned the water between the ships, just to make sure no one surprised them. The pirate ship slowly sunk twenty minutes later, disappearing below the waves, barely disturbing the surface. No one swam away from it.

***

4

Linden ended the call and pressed stop on the recorder. He didn't care about pirates and lost treasures, and he couldn't care less about any of Martin's crew, other than to find things. They were good at that. The NIA planted agents with several crews of treasure hunters and salvage operators, looking for clues to the whereabouts of an unusual treasure: a giant war machine.

The agents were tasked with seeking out any new rumors, facts, tidbits, or clues as to the machine's location or the fate of its fifteen-man crew. Linden felt Chaperone, Cass Palmer, had the best chance of finding something. That crew had a knack for finding hidden treasure in the most obscure places. As a bonus, the leader and owner of the crew, Martin Taylor, would fixate on the big prizes, ignoring other things in search of glory. And he could be baited, tantalized.

"Anything new?" Linden's assistant, Sergeant Lou Forester, dropped a folder on Linden's desk.

"No. Nothing. Cass's crew found some sort of treasure, but no new clues on the *Cudgel* yet," Linden said. He began to write down some numbers from the phone call's readout. "Sounds like they had a run in with some pirates. Can you get a rescue group sent out to these coordinates?"

"Can do," Lou said.

Linden stood and came around the desk. "I'll walk with you. I need a drink."

They turned and walked past the front desk over toward the break room and vending machines. They passed their situation room, where Lou admired the models of the missing fighting machine that adorned the wall.

"How does a giant hunk of metal like that go missing?" Lou asked. "It still baffles me."

"Don't get me started." Linden broke away from his assistant and walked to the soda machines. He dropped his change in the slot and pressed the button for a grape drink. It fell with a clunk and he grabbed it and slipped it into his coat pocket. He dropped more coins into the slot and got another soda, this time a cola and slipped it into his other jacket pocket. He grabbed a coffee cup and headed back to his office.

On the way back, he stopped in their small planning room and looked at the models of the fighting machine called the *Cudgel A-9*. He asked his assistant's question to himself. How did such a huge chunk of metal just disappear? The going theory was that it was somehow neutralized and stolen by the Circle of Liberated Territories during the war. But, when the war ended, no trace of the *Cudgel* was found on any of the captured CLT bases.

Other theories floated around, but none stuck. If the machine was downed, its emergency beacons would have been triggered. The crew would have found some way to signal for help if they'd survived. But nothing materialized.

Linden sighed. He'd inherited this mission almost two years ago, and the machine had been missing for just over eight years before that. He was beginning to fear the only way out of his post was by finding the *Cudgel*, retiring, or having a coronary incident. Unfortunately, he was in good health and only forty-two, so those options were likely out. He took one last look at the blocky white model and turned for his office.

Lou nearly ran into him. "Hey, sorry. As empty as this place is, you'd think we could stay out of each other's way." He turned, headed back to his office. "Rescue call made, cavalry is on the way to help your treasure hunters."

"Did you tell them that our people are the good guys?"

"Hmm. Can't recall. Hopefully it turns out okay," Lou said.

Linden nodded and thanked him. He stepped back into his own office and set the coffee cup on this desk. He pulled the grape soda from his pocket, opened it, and poured half of it into the cup. He pulled the cola out and poured some of it into the cup with the grape. As the fizz died down, he sat in his chair, and woke up his computer with a touch on the desk pad. He took a long drink of his concoction and pulled up the *Cudgel* maps for the umpteenth time.

5

Almost exactly an hour after Cass made her call, Martin noticed a large shadow appear on the horizon. Then a couple of smaller ones, and then some more that were smaller still. "Anyone want to hand me the binoculars?" He looked around to see Rina sitting on a deck chair with her headphones on and a MAC 93 submachine gun on her lap that she'd taken from one of the pirates. Though she was wearing a large pair of sunglasses, Martin was sure she was staring at the prisoners on the deck below.

Jakob tapped Martin on the shoulder and handed him the binoculars at about the same time Joe leaned out of the control room to point to the ships in the distance.

Through the viewfinder, Martin allowed the device to auto-focus on the large ship and its battle group. Magnified, it was easy to tell what was coming. "Cass? Who the hell did you call for help? There's a god damn naval destroyer and its support ships headed our way." Hearing no response, he looked back into the binoculars. "Jesus, they're launching troop and gunship drones. Maybe we can invite the marines to our treasure find next time."

"Is it the American navy?" Jakob asked.

It was a fair question, this far out, but the stars and stripes waved from the deck of the destroyer. "Yeah, no one else would bother with us." He handed Jakob the viewer and leaned against the rail as the drones closed in quickly. The four gunships circled the *Adamant* twice, then hovered around the ship as the two troop drones hovered over the deck while sailors in shiny blue jumpsuits rappelled down.

One of the troops came towards Rina, who hadn't moved and still had a hand on her weapon. Before the soldier could utter a word, Rina pointed toward Martin. The sailor took off their helmet to reveal a woman with short-cropped red hair and a stern look. "I think you can stand down now, we've…"

Rina interrupted by jutting her finger a little more firmly at Martin.

The soldier looked to Martin, but didn't move.

"She likes her music," Martin said. "When she gets tense, she likes a band called The Hans Gruber Experience. It's loud."

The sailor walked over to Martin, stopping only to watch the rest of the sailors spread out and take up positions on the deck. "Are you clear up here? Any more targets unaccounted for?"

"I think we got everyone."

"You think? Mind if we have a look?"

"Uh," Martin stumbled. He assumed that they'd gotten everyone, but they hadn't walked through the ship to check. "Well, sure."

The sailor mumbled into her mic and several of the others took off into the *Adamant*.

"My name is Sergeant Johnson," the woman said. "We got a call that there was trouble out this way."

Martin looked around at the hovering drones, the looming destroyer, the fast attack craft, the loaded guns, the intense soldiers covered in combat gear and hidden by helmets. Then he peered over at the pirates' ship, still slightly visible below the water, then the dozen or so captives sitting on the deck, eating Martin's crackers and drinking his water. "Yeah. Thank God you're here."

"Did any of these men say anything to you?" Sergeant Johnson asked.

"Other than 'Don't move or I'll shoot you?' No."

"Just asking," Sergeant Johnson said. "Probably just after money or any treasure you might have already brought up."

It took a second to click, but Martin realized they weren't. "That's the thing. They were going to herd us into the motorboat and take us to the ship that sank. They never even looked for treasure as far as I know."

One of the warship's attending ships maneuvered over to the pirates' ship and lowered chains and a harness down to a dive team that was already in the water. They hooked the ship up and in twenty minutes, they were raising it up alongside the Navy vehicle.

Martin watched the water drain from the charred boat as it left the water, watched it hang there above the ocean, empty and disabled. If the pirates and their leader weren't looking for treasure, what were they really looking for?

Once the captives were loaded onto a troop transport and hauled away, Sergeant Johnson shook Martin's hand. She'd spoken to the rest of Martin's crew, gotten their stories in a quick manner, then circled back to him. "Thanks. We'll be in contact if we need more information, or help with further investigations."

"Shouldn't be hard to find us, we'll be right here, hauling up our claim."

The sergeant nodded. "I assumed as much. Good hunting." She stepped onto a dangling rope and climbed up as her troop transport moved off the starboard side.

"She seems nice," Rina said, her headphones were bleeding sound out of some heavy beat.

Martin didn't bother replying, he knew Rina wouldn't hear him. He would've had trouble saying what he thought of her, really. She was all business. He still found it odd that a task force that size would've mobilized so fast to check on a claim of an attack on a civilian boat.

After the pirates and their boat were hauled off by the large warship, things got relatively quiet at the site. Tensions subsided, and the crew of the *Adamant* got to enjoy their find. By the time the warship disappeared over the horizon, the sun was well on its way out of sight. They set up a more thorough watch, with two crew members on guard together for three hours, before waking the next pair for duty. Normally, one person would take six hours alone. It wasn't much, but it allowed them some peace as they slept.

The night passed without incident, and the crew slept well on that first night from all of the excitement.

During the next day, they cleaned equipment, sent drones down to the site and did a few passes of the ship on their own. It was a little anticlimactic from the high of first finding it.

On the second night, they celebrated. There was French Champagne and Japanese steaks, German beer and individually wrapped slices of American cheese—a guilty pleasure of Jakob's. They sat on the deck in the dark and stared out at the dimly glowing buoys that marked their find. The moon was up, giving them a gorgeous view of the ocean around their site.

Martin raised his glass. "Another find of a lifetime." The others raised their glasses in salute.

"Which do you think you'll run out of first; finds or lifetimes?" Rina sipped her Champagne from a red plastic cup as she waited for a response.

Martin had been asking himself that same question in a roundabout way. He'd been doing this for nearly two decades—briefly taking a break during the war when it got too dangerous, and a portion of his crew had left to fight for the Allied Forces. As soon as the war was over, Martin started getting commissions and requests almost immediately. Citizens wanting him to find their lost fortunes buried in the rubble of a bombed-out town; corporations missing supply ships that were sunk by the Circle in the middle of nowhere, and, eventually, the military came calling. They wanted help with their own ships, their own missing persons, and their own treasures. Martin and his people assisted when they could, but the chaos of war made finding anything a true challenge. They waited until the dust settled and helped in the following years. Martin had no idea what he wanted to do with his fortune, so he put his money to as good a use as he could think of by doing all of his hunting for free when it came to war-related requests. Eventually, he got back to work finding things just for himself.

"Hello?" Rina said.

It took a moment to realize he'd perhaps paused too long in thought. "I don't know what I'll run out of first. It might be neither. Maybe I'll get bored and open a pizza shop in the San Jose area."

His crew laughed at him. They'd seen him chase one thing after another with no talk of stopping.

"Anyone need another steak?" Takis asked. He'd set up the grill on the deck to cook, and the food was delicious, even with the simple ingredients he had to work with. Some peppers, some spices. Everyone was wowed. "Come on people, there's plenty to go around and I don't want to burn these."

"Wrap mine up to go," Cass said as she stood. "I'm stuffed." She stumbled, and Martin reached out to steady her, but she righted herself without help. "And I'm a little drunk."

"Oh come on." Ozzie opened the cooler he'd been using as a footrest and pulled out another bottle. "There's still plenty of beer in here. We've barely started."

"No, thanks. I'll see you all in the morning." Cass looked better on her feet after a few steps.

Martin leaned in and put out his hand. "If she's not going to drink it, hand it over to me. I'm the one who bloody paid for it." He twisted the cap off and flung it at the trash; it hit the rim of the can, bounced off and flew overboard, into the water.

"Great. That's going to be someone's treasure someday," Jakob said. "You've just made someone in a hundred years very rich."

"We'll get the second crew to clean that up," Rina said.

Again, everyone laughed. They were drunk enough and happy enough, that everything was funny. The second crew consisted of another boat they brought in to help catalog and document the finds. They were all capable divers, scientists, and historians who chose not to live the bulk of their lives on a boat chasing treasure, instead they came once something was actually found. This unwillingness to live a wandering life earned them scorn and good-natured ribbing from their nomadic brethren. And a smaller share of the find.

Martin looked up toward the living quarters and saw Cass's light come on. He was impressed with her initiative and calm in dealing with the previous day's attack. She'd fit in well once she worked on her drinking skills.

6

The next morning was a late one for most. When Cass came down to start breakfast, Jakob was sitting in the mess hall with his chin on the table, staring at the coffee maker. His lids hung low and the bags under his eyes were deep and dark. "Did you sleep?" she asked.

Jakob moved only to blink. "No." His tone was weary and he did not elaborate.

"Stay up all night drinking?"

His right eye closed slowly and then Jakob nodded.

"Did you finish off all the beer?" She was slightly concerned about what it would do to the poor man's health, but she'd heard stories of his alcohol-consuming prowess from the time before she'd joined the crew. She'd never challenged him, he'd never challenged her, she just assumed he was the king of the boat when it came to alcohol.

Jakob's hand came up from under the table and Cass saw he was holding a half-consumed lager. He looked at it, swirled it around and then put it back under the table. "Not all of it," he said.

It wasn't Cass's turn in the rotation to make breakfast, but she decided that if she wanted to eat any time before the afternoon, she'd need to do it herself. She grabbed eggs and milk from the fridge and bread from the box and proceeded to prepare a French toast that was simple, yet delicious and hopefully compatible with hangovers. She dropped a few candied walnuts and smashed bananas into the mix and whisked it briskly, which caused Jakob's closed eyes to twitch. "Sorry," she said. "I'll stir a little more quietly."

Jakob put his head down on the table and stared at her, his expression asking her why she was doing this to him.

"It'll be over in a moment, I promise," she said. Cass stopped stirring and lit the stove, waiting for it to heat up the skillet. She looked at her pitiful friend and then at the coffee maker. As he closed his eyes, she tiptoed over and pressed the start button on the unit, causing it to begin whirring and filling.

"Hallelujah." Jakob shook his fist in the air in triumph.

The hangovers slowed everyone down. Takis and Ozzie came down together, dragging their feet and cringing at loud noises. Somehow Rina seemed overly-cheery, smiling, but she was wearing her largest sunglasses and moving gently as she sat down at the table.

Martin was last. "Good lord, what a night. Let's never do that again." He laughed heartily and winked at the mass of people staring at him. "Just kidding. We should resupply for the trip home." He slapped

Takis on the back. "You're in charge of the beer and Ozzie can handle the rest."

Cass smiled, realizing he was boisterous on purpose just to torture his crew. "Can I get you some breakfast, Martin? I've made French toast and some of that sausage we picked up. I can make eggs."

"Nah. For hangovers, I eat plain old oatmeal." Martin leaned over and opened the cupboard over the sink, pulling the box of instant oatmeal packets down.

"She's made some killer French toast, man. You should try it. Tastes like walnuts and maple." Jakob had perked up a bit as he ate and consumed some coffee. He'd complimented Cass's cooking a number of times as he shoveled more and more food into his mouth. She figured it was just the hangover talking, but she still took the compliment to heart.

Martin filled a bowl with hot water and dumped in the powdered oatmeal. "I'm good. Thanks."

They all sat around the table and spoke low and quiet.

Rina sat with her headphones in, sunglasses still on. She picked at the food, not committing to eating anything. As she watched Martin spoon oatmeal into his face, her phone on the table began to vibrate. She let it go for a moment, but glanced down to see the message. "We have a new meeting request from Subtle Bagpipe."

This got Martin's attention. "Hmmm. Maybe she has a line on our next expedition. Didn't she hint at a manifest for the *HMS Sturgeon* the last time we spoke?"

"I can't remember. When did we last talk to her?" Ozzie asked.

"Months." Jakob mumbled with a mouthful of breakfast.

Rina stabbed at a banana slice, seemingly energized. "She gave us that rumor that led to the plane in Alaska. I can check my log to see when the call was connected, if you want."

Cass felt left out of the discussion. She'd heard of their contact/informant, but never got much information. "I've been here nearly three months and I've never talked to her, or been here when you talked to her. So it has to have been at least that long." She looked around for someone to jump in, but they were all too busy shoveling the last of their breakfast. "Who is she?"

"Don't know." Ozzie threw his dish and fork in the sink. "I'll do the dishes later."

Takis followed, syrup still in the corner of his mouth. "Yeah, don't know. And he'll do the dishes later." Takis dropped his things in next to Ozzie's and took off toward the ship's 'strategy' room. It was their communications hub and the place where they all gathered to plan their day, or their week or their next move in a search. It also had a big screen for crew movie nights.

Martin and Jakob both dumped their dishes and headed for the strategy room, leaving only Rina with Cass. She was slowly eating a handful of grapes and listening to her music. She stirred her coffee with the handle of her fork—either not wanting to dirty another utensil, or too unmotivated to get up to get another utensil—and took her time. She still had on the big sunglasses and Cass had no idea what the younger girl was looking at.

"You coming?" Cass asked.

After another sip of coffee, she turned her head toward Cass. "They won't start without me. They don't know how any of that stuff works." She smiled and popped another grape into her mouth.

"I'll see you in a few, then." Cass walked toward the strategy room alone. She couldn't begrudge Rina her fun. The girl generally stayed in the background while the men did manly things, like lifting equipment, jumping off boats, fighting when needed, jumping out of planes, burping, farting, fighting, jumping off cliffs, wrestling lions—if their stories were to be believed—dancing, etc. None of which Rina wanted any part of. She liked listening to her headphones, working at her computer, and, collecting bugs from the various places they visited. She had a case with dozens of insects pinned in their own little cubicles. She had her quirks.

When Cass got to the comms room, the men were all seated around the table and facing a blank screen on the opposite wall. They all looked at Cass.

"You know how to turn this on, right?" Takis said.

Cass didn't want to respond. She knew how to turn it on, but didn't want to face Rina's wrath if something got screwed up.

"Just give it to me." Martin grabbed the remote from Jakob and pointed it at the screen, even though most of the equipment was behind him in the electronics cabinet.

"I wouldn't do that," Cass said. "Rina might…"

"What? I'm in charge here. This is my boat and my equipment. I can do whatever I want." Cass watched as he leaned in close to read the text on the remote's buttons. "Is this AUX 1 or INPUT 4?"

"Oh, I think Cass is right, you should really leave that alone." Ozzie moved his chair away from Martin slightly.

"I've seen her do it a thousand times." Martin looked up at the screen, and seeing it was still blank, he looked back at the rows of buttons on the rectangular controller. "I can do it."

It got calm in the room quickly, and Cass realized that Rina was standing at the hatch to the comms room. Everyone looked away, or stared down at their hands or cups or the table; anything to keep from looking Rina in the eyes. Everyone except Martin, who was still fiddling with the control. When he noticed the silence, he looked over at Rina and smiled before dropping the remote on the table in front of him.

"You know, after all this time you really should show someone else how all of this stuff works," Martin said. "I mean, what if you aren't around? What if..."

"Ah...ah...ah." Rina raised her hand to stop Martin.

Martin tried to persist. "But..."

"Ah." She shook her head. "If you've messed anything up... If you've fucked my bass levels again... If you've increased the tint on the projector..." Her phone began buzzing, but she refused to look at it. She just stared at Martin. "We've been over this." Rina waved her hands around the room at the equipment. "All this? Mine." She finally looked at her phone. "It's *Subtle*." Rina walked over to the chair nearest the television, propped her legs up on a bench, and began tapping away on her phone. Seconds later the projector came on, and instantly a blue box started bouncing across the wide screen with the word "Initializing."

"Wait," Ozzie said. "You can do everything from your phone?"

She nodded lightly. "There's an app for that."

"So you don't even need the remote?" Martin asked.

"No. Not at all. That's a cheap remote I picked up when we were in Singapore that time. The lights work, but otherwise it's useless."

Cass laughed. She loved how Rina could wind Martin up and still get away with it. The others were trying to hold their own laughter in, but gave up when they saw the dumb look on Martin's face, and the grin on Rina's. It was a tight-knit crew and Cass felt at ease among them. She felt bad from time-to-time in the last few months about deceiving them, lying about her true purpose, but, she'd been undercover before and she knew how it went. Still, it was going to suck when it was all over. The best she could hope for was for the N.I.A. to pull her off the boat before she had to blow her cover.

The laughter was interrupted by the screeching, hideous sounds of bagpipe music being played loudly, and poorly, from the screen. Soon, the garish avatar for Subtle Bagpipe appeared on the screen; a large cartoon bagpipe with red and pink tartan across it. Rina turned the volume down.

"I'm assuming that's you, Subtle." Martin looked at the screen. The music continued for almost another twenty seconds before dying a horrible death as the air left the bellows of the screeching instrument. "Subtle?"

"Hey Martin. What's new?" The familiar female voice scratched out through the speakers. As usual, no image appeared other than the avatar. "Miss me?"

"Always," Martin said.

Cass wondered who this informant was, and how she ever hooked up with Martin and his crew. From the sounds of it, she was crazy tech-savvy and was constantly tripping over information that was useless to most, but priceless to others. She was just good at cultivating those others, from the sounds of it.

"Look, I don't know how long we'll have this link, I've got a storm moving in quickly, so who knows what that shit will do to our little convo." The avatar dissolved and the screen changed to the image of a map of the world.

"Oh, you've prepared a little presentation for us this time," Takis said. "How sweet."

"Anything for you guys." The screen zoomed into the map to focus on the Pacific. "You all are familiar with this area, right? I don't need to explain, do I?" She hurried on before she got any response. "It's the Pacific. It's Hawaii. It's the Aleutians, and the Bering Sea. Okay. Fun." A red blob appeared and covered the areas from the northern-most tip of the Hawaiian Island of O'ahu, over to just beyond Midway Atoll and then up until the blob covered the Russian city of Palana, then over into the Aleutians nearly to Kodiak in Alaska. "Check that out. It's a massive search area that includes a ton of unexplored area underwater. Autonomous sea drones have crossed a portion of that area and mapped it, but they've barely scratched the surface." Slowly, a line appeared in the middle of the blob that appeared to form an upside down letter "C." Then above it, two eyes slowly took shape, until the blob looked like a sad face. "But don't worry, I can help."

"Wait," Martin said. The whole room had been silent until he'd spoken. The crew was hanging on Subtle's every word. "You haven't even told us what treasure you're talking about."

A black line suddenly encircled the blob's sad face. "Oh Martin. I'm embarrassed for you. You know this one."

Cass certainly knew it. She'd been briefed so many times on the area and the story of the disappearance, that she knew it by heart. "She's talking about the *Cudgel A-9*, Martin. The big prize."

The bagpipes played again through the television briefly. "Ding. Ding. Ding," Subtle said. "That must be the new girl. She gets the prize today."

"My God." Jakob leaned back with a huff. "I'll believe it when I see it. We've had too many false alarms."

Ozzie took the same stance. "Yeah, you know we love you and all, Miss Bagpipes, but we've been through this before. No offense."

Everyone turned to Martin, who had an undecided look about him. "Well, the lady was nice enough to call us. Let's hear what she has to say."

Cass took her phone out of her pocket and started the recorder app. If this woman had any real information, Cass would want to send it to the N.I.A. for analysis as quickly as she could.

∗∗∗

Martin sighed. They had been down this road before and to no avail. It was fun and exciting the first two times, but those times had also been expensive failures. He was almost relieved that the tip was about *Cudgel*, it made it easier to say no. He let her talk to humor the rest of the crew. Hopefully they would see the logic in letting this thing go without much fanfare.

"See, the *Cudgel*'s last transmission came from the very eastern portion of my blob here." There was a crackle on the line and a recording started playing from the monitor with more static in the background.

> *"Strike Base, this is A-9. Listen, we're seeing some kind of object on radar. No idea what it is. Running identifiers now."*
> "A-9, this is Strike Base. Can you get a visual?"
> *"Negative Strike Base. Not exactly. All we can make out visually is some sort of shadow beneath the waves that seems to be approaching us from the opposite direction."*
> "A-9, you are authorized to take any evasive or defensive moves you deem necessary.
> *"Affirmative Strike Base."*

"It was just a few minutes later that it disappeared from radar and no one could raise them on any form of communication. They tried sat phones, text messages, smoke signals, and everything else," Subtle continued.

"Yes, we've all heard the story of the missing war machine; it was kind of a good fairy tale for a while there. My kids loved it," Martin said. "Satellites were tasked to look, subs checked into it, drones, whatever. No one found it."

"True. But they were limited in what they could do at the time, because that whole area was a hotbed of activity from the Circle that had a base in eastern Russia." Subtle's map zoomed in to show the fortifications built at Kamchatka Krai, Russia. Martin knew that that particular island stronghold had been an important target in the war, it was all over the news waves at the time. It was close to mainland Russia, Japan and China, where many of the separatists had broken from to form the alliance.

"So when the war was over, and the area was stable, and they actually got to search for the *Cudgel*, everything was a little fuzzy and the trail was cold. It was just under a year before they even got equipment in the area. The navy, the government found nothing." The screen's image changed to a sound playback with a wave configuration displayed. "Okay. So, on May 23, 2086, two years after the *Cudgel* disappears, this happens…" There was a click on Subtle's transmission and the music player began transmitting audio. It was comprised of bubble sounds, swishing water and a low scraping sound. "That was recorded by a seismology team in the Aleutians."

Everyone looked at each other and then to Martin, who shrugged his shoulders. "Okay, what is that? Whales humping?"

"No," Subtle said. "Let me strip all the common sounds away, and let me know what you think." She played it again, and the bubbles and water were gone. This time the scraping sounds are clearer, and showed themselves to be a more regimented pattern. Two high clicks, a pause, then two clicks and a pause. "This goes on for a full minute before stopping. The scientists who recorded it thought little of it since it didn't happen again, but luckily for us, they archived it with their records."

He was intrigued and that bothered Martin. "So what do you think that is? And how does it point to the *Cudgel*?" He was still ready to pass.

"First, let me say I can't find a record of anyone recording a similar sound on that date on 2087, but in 2088, a submarine on its way to help in the clearing of mines near mainland Russia recorded the exact same sound with the exact same pattern on the same date and time. The next year, two different sources recorded the same thing, same area, same time. One was an underwater drone shooting video for a documentary on the impact of the war on certain areas of the ocean, the other was a fishing trawler using sensors to find new fishing grounds."

It was a crazy longshot and it didn't convince Martin. "The sounds happened three years in a row? Why didn't anyone else realize this?"

"Well, they were all different sources. None of them consulted with any of the others. A fisherman, an American sub, a documentary crew and an Aleutian research station, they had no reason to think about it. I'm sure the sub reported it, but I doubt anyone followed up. Each of them only experienced the phenomena once. And these are just the ones I've found. There may be more from other years, or more from the same years as these."

"So how did you get this information if no one else put it together?" Cass asked.

"Martin pays me to find him info, not to tell him how I found it."

The crew began to discuss the sound with each other, but Martin still stared at the screen where the sound wave configuration was still up. "I don't know what this proves. A sound happened a few years in a row, in the area where the thing was last sighted? That doesn't appear to be a slam dunk to me. I don't even know what that sound is. And to call it a pattern is kind of a stretch." His head started shaking before he'd even formed words for his opinion. "No. I don't see it. I don't see packing the crew up and heading back out there for this. I don't…"

"Today is May eighth," Rina said.

Ozzie and Takis smiled. Jakob looked around, confused by the statement.

"That's why I waited to tell you. You've got two weeks to get out to that site—I can give you about a ten-mile search area based on triangulating all of the recordings I found. Be there on May 23, at two-oh-six in the afternoon, local time. Set up your listening equipment and get ready. I guarantee you'll hear this."

"But do you guarantee it'll be from the *Cudgel*?" Martin asked.

The line was quiet. "No," Subtle said. "I can't. But I have this feeling."

"The last time you had that feeling, we came up with nothing," Martin said. "And it cost me nearly a million dollars." Martin sighed and stood. He walked toward the open portal, fully intent to head to his quarters and catch another hour of sleep.

"Maybe I've had a couple of bad guesses, but how did my tips on the *Swansea* turn out?" Subtle asked. "Word has it you're onto something out there, is it the *Swansea?*"

Martin was slightly dumbfounded that news could travel that fast. "We just found this wreck, how could you possibly know about it?"

"When you put out a distress call for assistance with some pirates, word gets around," Subtle said. "So matey, did ye find the booty or not?"

Her pirate impersonation annoyed Martin. "Yeah. We found it. But it's going to keep us pretty busy. We'll have to pass on the war machine." There was a slight gasp from one of the crew members, but Martin couldn't tell which one.

"Look, if you're getting out of the *Cudgel* business, just let me know," Subtle said. "I can look for a contact more willing to take risks." The feed ended and the screen turned blue.

It was quiet for a second as Martin paused at the doorway.

"Seriously?" Takis asked. "Seriously?"

Ozzie interjected. "I think what my brother is trying to ask is whether you truly intend to just walk away from this?"

"Yes. Seriously, *dude*?" Takis asked.

Jakob rolled his beer bottle in between his hands. "We've been after this for a good long while."

"But we're not getting paid to chase bubbles and underwater signals. We have an historical find out there, just lurking below the waves. All we have to do is collect it." Martin didn't sound very convincing to himself, he could only guess how he sounded to the others. "And you want to go out and waste that money on another wild goose chase?"

"I'm good with that. In fact I'm all for it," Cass said from one of the booths. "I'd forgo my share of the Swansea if it means a shot at the *Cudgel*."

The others turned and looked at her, deciding if they'd go that far in their own convictions.

"I'd do it." Jakob was generally up for anything and had voiced his excitement whenever they got a tip on the *Cudgel*, not exactly a hard sell.

A glance brought the Suvari brothers into agreement. "Eh, at the very least it's a trip to the lovely waters not far off the former Territories' home turf," Takis said.

Joe raised his hand. "I can't do it. I mean, look, I know I spend most of my time in the wheelhouse, and I keep to myself, but look out there. There's gold, there's something tangible out there. I can't chase another dream, hoping it's better than this one."

"I get that," Cass said. "But…"

"No buts. Forget the hunt, forget the find. We had guns pointed at us. Jesus, you guys blew up a fucking boat. People are dead here. I can't stand around and pretend that didn't happen. When the *Alba Varden* gets here, I'll jump over there and hitch a ride back to port."

"You don't need to go, you can work on the *Varden*," Martin said. "Whatever."

"No. I think I'm good. I appreciate it, but I need to get out of here."

Takis shrugged. "You're joking. You're a sailor. You love this shit. What the hell else are you going to do? Go back to giving Hover Duck tours in Boston?"

"Maybe. Can't remember the last time one of those was hijacked at gunpoint. Can you?"

Martin was frazzled, already at odds with himself, and unwilling to listen to the crew split the same way. "Look, you don't have to go, no one has to go. Just let me think." He left the room and plodded down the hall alone.

7

Linden Kemp listened to the recording Chaperone Delta-One had sent via satellite message, while on the phone with her. "So she didn't say where in that area she believes the *Cudgel* is?"

"No, she didn't. She was waiting to see what Martin said before she sent the information. I don't know what kind of agreement they have, but she was pushing that idea, and he wasn't having it. I like to think that I know him by now, but his whole internal process is still a mystery to me." Cass's voice sounded tiny in the phone and Linden had the volume turned all the way up.

"So what's next?"

There was a crackle and Cass's voice broke up. "I don't know. I guess we just wait for Martin to make up his mind."

"If he says no, is there a way for us to trace that contact and try to obtain the information ourselves?" Linden was already running through scenarios and ideas in his head for catching up with this contact of theirs. Treasure hunters generally don't have mysterious informants.

"I don't know. She contacts them when she wants. We can see if there's any way to trace signals that the ship receives, but it sounds like this Subtle Bagpipe is pretty savvy from what they've told me."

"Okay. Keep me posted and I'll start running down any information on this repeating sound she talks about. Maybe I can find all the military records and then start looking at the private instances. At least then we can confirm or disprove what this contact is saying," Linden said. "It may take a while, hopefully Martin changes his mind quickly."

Cass signed off and the line clicked. Linden looked at his screen and pulled up a map of the area that Cass and the recording had outlined. It was a wide area. Setting drones loose out in that expanse would probably yield some sort of results, but to be effective, they'd have to go reasonably slow and that would take a long damn time. Linden sighed, knowing that he had nothing but time at this point in his career. He swiveled in his chair and walked around the corner to find his partner, Lou Forester. After catching Lou up on the call, they both walked down the hall and got in the elevator.

"A repetitive noise? That's what's going to finally find this thing?" Lou asked.

"I don't know. Just another lead. Their weird little informant seems pretty sure of herself," Kemp said. "Who the hell knows at this point?"

They rode the elevator upwards, both reading from their tablets, both humming along to the music softly piped in through the elevator's speakers. Once they got up to the forty-fourth floor, the doors opened and they walked out into the land of the computer literate. These were the tech gods that most of the Naval Interdiction Administration relied on at this point for most of their intelligence and evidence. They were the ones that collected obscure information from the airwaves and stored it away for some sort of use later.

Linden walked up the hall to his friend Holli Edson's office, where she worked with six other analysts to identify, among other things, various auditory phenomena. Her team was tasked with such delicate projects as identifying sounds on recordings, like the make of gun that could be heard in a tape, what type of vehicle was leaving the scene of a crime off-screen on a video, and more. Generally, the computer did the heavy lifting, but it took real direction from an operator to feed it information.

As soon as he opened the door, all seven analysts looked at him, though none of them stopped typing.

"That guy over there is playing Galaga," Linden said, pointing at a random person. The analysts stared at him blankly. "Come on, that's an *Avengers* joke. You've seen the movie, right? Come on, you have to love super heroes. You're computer nerds."

One of the analysts mumbled about it being an 'old-ass movie,' only one really acknowledged him. Holli's expression was an obvious smile of pity, meant to keep herself from cringing. "Hi Agent Kemp. What can I do for you?"

"Got time to take a quick walk to talk to me? I need some help with a noise."

The other analysts turned and looked at Linden nearly in unison.

"I don't think that would be a good idea." Holli had lowered her voice and leaned in close to Linden.

"Why?"

She discreetly nodded her head toward her coworkers, who were still staring. "We are crazy swamped here. If I take on one more 'one-time' quick favor for you, or anyone else for that matter, they are going to stab me in the eye with a stylus sharpened into a shiv."

"Oh, that's not..." Linden looked up at the others, who had slowly gone back to work, but were leaning a little closer, listening. "Look. We're just trying to identify a noise that repeats over and over for a minute. We have it from various sources over a period of several years. How hard could it be?"

Holli stared at him blankly. "I'm slowly moving over to the side of the room that hates you."

"I mean, isn't all this analysis done by computer anyway?" Linden could feel he was digging a deeper hole for himself. "Not that you...don't..." He looked to Lou to help him get out of it, but Lou pretended to have a stain on his tie, and worked at getting it out.

"Just..." Holli sighed deeply. "Just send me the details," she said as quietly as possible.

"That's great." Linden started to say more, but could feel Lou grab his arm and pull him toward the door. Holli did not look happy, and turned back to her workstation, typing away almost immediately. "Goodbye."

"Thanks," Lou muttered.

"Thanks!" Linden tried to smile at everyone in the room, hoping that a smooth departure would get them all to like him more. Or even some.

"That went well." Lou pressed the button for their floor and stared forward as the doors closed.

The term 'gibbering idiot' was the first thing Linden thought of as they descended. "I could have brought them around."

"No you couldn't. You had no chance. They're still mad about the Christmas party you ruined and the fart noises you made them try to identify."

Linden laughed. "That was two years ago. Plus the Christmas thing wasn't my fault."

They got out of the elevator and walked past the closed doors to empty offices until they got to their own.

"What's next?" Lou asked.

"I guess we have to wait for Martin to make up his mind, find this Bagpipe person, or hope we can pinpoint the thing ourselves."

Lou turned and started back for his own doorway.

"Hey," Linden said.

Lou turned.

"They were manatee farts, not my own."

"Oh," Lou said. "That's much more mature."

8

Martin ascended the nearby stairs up to the deck. He stood in the cool sea breeze and looked over the web of buoys that marked the treasure on the surface. He'd seen similar sights more than a dozen times now at sea, from the small wrecks he started on, to the salvages for corporations, to these personal passion projects. He'd done finds on land from the Himalayas and New Jersey, to Thicket Portage in Manitoba. None of them pissed him off more than the *Cudgel A-9*. There was so little to go on, and many others had tried already and failed. Then, there was the whole matter of what would happen if they actually found it. Would the government swoop in and cover it up and take it away? The navy eventually gave up their active search and finally put it out there that the weapon was missing. Sure, they'd want it, but would they allow Martin's crew to get some publicity for it? Would it even make the news? It was a lot of money to throw at a project with possibly no return, other than satisfaction that they found the apparently unfindable. Personal satisfaction didn't pay the bills.

"You know you want to." Rina was standing next to Martin and he hadn't realized it.

"Want to what?" Martin wasn't on his game and the question came out lame.

"Here's my opinion."

"On what?"

Her eye roll was epic. "We're doing fine. We're getting more work than we can handle."

"Is fine good enough?" Martin looked back at the ocean and the markers over their latest find. "Is this what we do from now on?"

"Martin, there are maybe three treasure hunters in the world that people can name. One of them is you. If news heads want an expert, you're at the top of their list. But what we do really isn't the lead story on the news. Never has been," Rina said. "And that's fine, too. But, if you find the *Cudgel*? That changes, and you move up the news cycle. You're talking a book tour, museum tours, documentaries, speaking fees—hell, maybe you can even finally pay someone to build a nice website for you."

It wasn't the accumulation of money that kept Martin going, but it was nice. No, at this point in his life, he would settle for being THE top treasure finder in the world, not one of the top three. "You don't think the government will screw us?"

"How could they? We'll broadcast live via the internet as soon as we confirm what we have. The world will know before any government can come after it," Rina said. "I can send Bagpipe an email tomorrow."

"You're kind of smart for someone dumb enough to join my crew."

Rina put her earbuds in and walked away in the bright morning sun. "I question my judgement every single day."

9

The entire ship's crew stayed onsite for another week, mapping the site deep below the sea. They'd found more than just gold, they'd found weapons, and skeletons and barrels. A good portion of the ship was intact, lying on its side in a particularly deep valley on the ocean floor. After he'd done the preliminary work, posed for pictures, started the paperwork, and shook hands with the locals who'd be deciding the fate of the treasure, Martin notified his harbormaster, Ben Durant, that he'd need their other ship, *Alba Varden*, brought on site to take things over, so that the *Adamant* team could follow up on Subtle Bagpipe's lead on the *Cudgel A-9*'s whereabouts.

"Jesus, Martin. This thing isn't exactly a speedboat. People notice when it leaves and shit. I thought you were trying to keep a low profile." Ben had been with Martin since practically the beginning. They'd been on treasure-hunting legend Ed Hanley's crew together back in the day. Ben and Martin were both young and full of enthusiasm for finding lost ships, getting rich and getting famous. Every time Ed had his picture taken for a paper or magazine, he did it alone, and gave the crew absolutely no credit in the ensuing interviews.

"Look. It's not like we haven't used it before, and no one batted an eye any of those times," Martin said.

"What? You weren't here. Eyes were batted. People noticed." Ben sounded agitated to Martin; he was talking fast and in a higher pitch than usual. It was rare that Ben voiced disapproval. They'd just been in it for the fun after they left Ed's crew, but it'd become a business more recently. "I'll need to see which freelance crew are free. I can't guarantee I can get everyone we need." There was a moment where it went silent, and Martin was afraid that he'd lost Ben's signal. "Jesus, we've tried this before, haven't we? What makes you think you'll find it this time?"

"Ben, I don't know. Hell, we might lose out again." Martin paused. He'd thought about all of this, but never put it together. Money was usually the motivation. It always had been. What was the return on investment? Money in, versus money out. But it just didn't ring true with this one, and he couldn't think of the next one that money would be at the top of his list. Maybe Subtle Bagpipe was right. "I don't know, Ben. It's getting to be the time when I think about what I'm doing next."

"And that's going to be chasing the *Cudgel* for the rest of your life?"

"No." Martin was getting agitated with himself now. "Look, I need the crew here as soon as possible, and once they get here, we'll update them and the rest of us are off. This is kind of time-sensitive, so turn this around and send them quickly."

"So you've made up your mind?"

Martin waited with the receiver in one hand and a bottle of warm beer in the other. "Just send them. Full equipment." He shut off the receiver and left the communications room, just in case Ben tried to get back to him. If Martin wasn't in the room, he wouldn't have to ignore the little light that flashed to tell him there was a call.

He walked out onto the deck, where there was a small fire still burning on the grill. Rina was lying on her back on a lounger, her feet propped up on the railing, dark sunglasses on at nearly midnight. Martin wouldn't have even noticed her if it weren't for her music blaring loud enough to be heard outside of her headphones. Martin turned, not wanting to bother her and not in the mood for small talk.

"What's your favorite constellation?" Rina asked. She didn't move.

Against his better judgement, Martin stopped. "How can you see anything with those glasses on?"

"Just tell me."

"My favorite constellation?"

"Yeah."

Martin turned and looked up at the star-filled sky. "I have no idea. I don't have a favorite random pattern of stars, really." It was a silly question. The woman may as well have asked him what his favorite recipe for poutine was.

"How long have you been doing this at sea? I mean, just look up. Tough to see all of this in a city." She reached up like she was taking a handful of stars and squeezing them in her fist. "It's like someone dumped a salt shaker across the hood of a black Pontiac Firebird."

Trying to decide whether that was profound or ridiculous, Martin shot back, "Where have you ever seen a Firebird? They haven't been made since long before either of us was born."

"You find a lot on the web."

Martin turned and walked back toward the stairs. "You're a complex and wonderful person, Rina."

"Don't you forget it."

As he neared the first step, Martin knocked over a number of bottles sitting on the deck and they fell with a clatter.

Three loungers away from Rina, a giant frame suddenly flew into the air and Jakob stood up, fighting his way out of a blanket. "What? I'm up. What was that?" The blanket fell to the deck, and Jakob was left in a close approximation of a ninja pose, with his hands chopping at air and legs ready to strike.

Martin laughed and climbed the stairs to the next deck and followed the hall to his quarters. He didn't change, brush his teeth, or wash up, he got in bed, put his head on his pillow and fell straight to sleep.

10

The *Adamant* crew continued to document the wreck site deep below the ocean surface over the next few days, but they put more time into preparing for their trip to the search zone. They checked food and supply levels, checked trouble spots on the ship that had vexed them in the past-resulting in a quick patch on the bow by Jakob-they confirmed alcohol levels were at maximum, and that everything they needed to transfer to the *Alba Varden* was ready to be moved over as quickly as possible.

One late afternoon, as Cass examined the search area map on her tablet, a huge green drone appeared from near the waterline, hovered just near the railing of the *Adamant*, and then rushed forward to buzz just over her head. It was followed by another almost identical drone with a number 2 painted on its side in white. The second one had mismatched, recently-repaired red arms protruding from each side. As they both flew over her, Cass guessed they were the size of shipping containers; huge and yet graceful in their own way. Both machines turned and followed the line of the ship, dipping and rising until they had completely encircled it, then they came about and hovered next to each other at the bow of the ship, seemingly staring at Cass.

The hatch to the interior of the *Adamant* slammed open and Rina ran out, followed by Jakob. "They're here!" Rina was smiling and nearly leaping, two steps at a time, as she ran to the forward railing. Jakob stopped on the deck and pointed off toward the horizon. A large ship loomed in the distance, cutting its way through the ocean. The *Alba Varden* had arrived.

Martin came and stood next to Cass and watched the ship's approach.

"So that's it?" Cass had heard about Martin's other ship since she'd come onto his crew, but they'd never had occasion to use it, and every time they'd been to port, the *Alba Varden* was off somewhere being refitted, or painted or waxed or some nonsense, almost to the point where Cass believed the crew had been pulling her leg and the craft didn't really exist.

"That's it," Martin said. "The *Alba Varden*. Sounds like they finally have everything just the way I want it."

"It looks..." Cass looked for diplomatic words to use, but she was wildly unimpressed by the old vessel as it approached.

"Like a crappy old container ship?"

It wasn't what she was thinking, but she agreed anyway. It was large, way larger than a treasure-hunting vessel had a right to be. Cass had heard they'd remade the inside hull into amazing living accommodations on one end and a glorious research and recovery facility at the other end. Of course, she'd never seen the inside, she'd been stuck on the *Adamant* since the beginning.

"They were preparing to scrap it and I just couldn't stand to see her go. Maybe soon we can make it our new headquarters. I'll need to sign off on everything, of course. It has to be just so."

"But you've had all this work done to it. And..."

"And it STILL looks like a crappy old container ship? Yeah. That's partly by design. We wanted something big in case we needed to live off it for an extended time. We wanted to be comfortable, even at sea. But we also wanted something relatively inconspicuous. So we could stay off of people's radars, so to speak."

"And that's it?" Cass gave him a piteous look. "You got swindled if they sold it to you as a stealthy vessel. It's not. Not even a little."

Martin nodded with a grin. "I know. I just like it."

They walked down the stairs together to the dingy moored to the aft of the *Adamant* and Martin held down the button on the motor until it sprang to life with a quiet hum. Rina jumped in with them just as Martin gunned the motor and pulled it quickly away from their ship and toward the nearing vessel. A number of the crew from the *Alba Varden* had gathered along the rails to wave to their friends and fellow crewmembers. Rina waved back, but Cass barely knew any of them and just smiled at the cheering group on the humongous boat.

"How long do you think the transfer will take?" Cass asked. She didn't want to be too eager, but the idea that their quarry could be out there waiting for them made her anxious.

Martin leaned closer. "What?"

"When can we get loaded up and leave?" Cass had to shout over the sounds of the ocean, the ship, the dingy.

"Depends on whether they brought good beer or not. If they didn't, we can leave in the morning. If they did..." Martin shrugged. "Maybe a little later."

They pulled up to a lift at the aft of the *Alba Varden* that attached to the dingy and raised it steadily to a midlevel. A half dozen people gathered around to help Martin and his passengers out of the tiny boat. They hugged Rina and Martin, kissed them on the cheeks and then turned and shook Cass's hand.

One woman shook hands a little longer and more enthusiastically. "You must be the new one. I'm Caroline." She was tall and rail-thin, though Cass noticed she was muscular, probably from hauling equipment around for the *Alba Varden*.

Cass didn't realize that she might possibly be the most recent hire to Martin's team. Surely there was someone else on a lower rung. "That's me. I'm Cass. New girl."

"I study plant life."

Cass looked at her and nodded. Not entirely sure what that meant.

"Underwater, of course," Caroline said. "The plant life." She nodded and sipped at a glass of something clear that Cass was fairly sure wasn't water. "Oh, with limited or no light."

"Plant life that grows in the darkness underwater?"

"That's what I said," Caroline smiled.

They were alone, Cass suddenly realized. The rest of the party had disappeared through an open hatch without a word. "Hey, do you know where everyone was headed?" She swept her arm around the deck area to show that they'd been left behind.

"Oh." Caroline looked puzzled. "Dining hall? Let's check the dining hall." She stepped gingerly over the threshold and into a hallway lined with beautifully done woodwork. Cass thought maybe it was mahogany, but it could've been a decent fake. Mahogany was terribly hard to come by anymore. The lighting and fixtures looked similar to images that Cass had seen of the *Queen Mary*, and were surely forgeries, unless Martin himself had rescued them from the ocean floor.

It was certainly beautiful, Cass thought. She certainly couldn't see why Martin might not find it acceptable. Maybe he was nit-picky, or a perfectionist or maybe he was looking for a reason not to come in from the nomadic life.

Caroline led on to the dining area, and sure enough, the rest of the *Alba Varden's* crew was already laughing it up with Rina and Martin. Caroline joined them and Cass waited by the door, next to the coffee maker. Eventually, some of the other crew introduced themselves— Lewis, Theo, Hakim—but none lingered. They got back to the more boisterous members of the party. As the others had their fun, Cass poured a cup and loaded it with sugar packets and creamer before she even tasted it.

11

The rest of the *Adamant* crew came over, with Takis and Ozzie swimming from boat-to-boat, rather than taking the other dingy with Joe and Jakob.

As the impromptu party got louder, Martin excused himself to hit the bathroom, but instead walked up the stairs to the con room. At the controls, Ben Durant moved swiftly from one console to another in his wheelchair.

"You say hi to everyone else before you say hi to me?" Ben asked before Martin could speak.

"Do you always frantically work at steering the ship when it's anchored?"

Ben gave Martin a sideways look. "Shut up. It's a delicate machine that needs constant attention."

"You could have come down," Martin said.

"You could have come up."

It was a stalemate. They were both right, Martin figured. And both stubborn. "You didn't have to come along. You could have had someone else pilot this whale out here."

"I'm tired of sitting in the harbor and yelling at seagulls. I needed to get out." Ben wheeled starboard to the floor-to-ceiling window that curved around the wheelhouse. He stared out at the smaller boat not far off in the water. "The *Adamant* in good shape?"

"Great shape. Do you seriously yell at seagulls? Do I need to look into some sort of support group for you?" Martin laughed and looked at his friend.

Ben wheeled himself around to face his friend. "Look, Martin. I appreciate that you've kept me out of the field out of concern, I really do, but I'm bored as hell. I can get around fine, but I need you to let me get around."

It was Martin's turn to look away and turn his back. He thought he was being sly, or being a good boss or something by keeping Ben back on dry land and safe from whatever the sea could do to him. He wasn't so sneaky apparently.

"While I was waiting for you to get your ass up here, I've been filled in on all the gossip."

"Rina's been up to see you?"

"She says Joe Goldman is out. Doesn't want to go on this little escapade of yours anymore."

Martin nodded. "True."

"Thought about what you were going to do for a pilot?"

"I thought maybe Jakob could fill in."

Ben sighed. "You thought?"

"Not like I had a lot of warning."

Ben rolled closer. "I'll do it."

"What?" Martin could understand Ben captaining the research and recovery vessel, but the *Adamant* was a whole different animal. "That's…"

"That's what I want. Or maybe I walk, too."

"Jesus. That's how it is?"

"That's how it is."

Turns out they brought wonderful wine, bourbon from Kentucky, and vodka from the old Soviet territories that could knock you on your ass, but no beer. They prepared to shove off in the morning.

Ben joined the expedition, along with Caroline and another researcher named Lewis. They came over and Joe agreed to temporarily stay on as the pilot of the *Alba Varden* as they researched the *Swansea* find. Once the *Cudgel* expedition was over, they'd take him back to port. Cass was surprised he was the only one, as she'd sat at the fringe of a number of conversations at the party; she'd heard whispered tones about the attack from Rina and Ozzie. Takis boasted about his role in the whole thing and how he'd had a plan all along, but she'd been there with him, swimming to the boat and rigging that leaky line, and she knew he was just as freaked out as anyone. The *Alba Varden's* crew sounded alternately impressed and terrified at the prospect of being accosted by pirates or whatever those men were.

Everyone said their goodbyes after loading up on supplies and the *Adamant* set off at a decent rate of speed.

12

Here we go again. Linden dropped the phone back on his desk and sat back. Maybe the information would be good this time. It would take a little while to find out. If this noise they were talking about happened when they said it would, they had five days to wait. It would take the *Adamant* itself nearly three of that just to get in the general area. *If they were right.* He rolled his chair to the doorway and shouted toward Lou's office. "They're on the move."

"Headed for the *Cudgel?*" A shout came back.

"Allegedly."

Linden heard his cohort snort back laughter.

On his desk, Linden had the transcripts of the recording open on one monitor, and a map of the general area open on another. He reached into his desk drawer and pulled another flexiscreen out and attached it to the first two. After it was paired, he displayed all the information he and Lou dug up on drone maps, sub sonar returns, corporate fishing information and whatever else they'd thrown in. He took the maps and displayed them in layers. Each source added a little more to the picture of the sea floor in the area. But it really wasn't enough. There was so much open area and even private mapping efforts hadn't managed to reach that far out. It was simply too much area to cover.

He added an additional layer--the satellite records of the *Cudgel's* last flight path. They did take the robot close to that area, but it was off by a couple hundred miles to the north. Not entirely out of the question, as no one knew what happened after they lost communications, and their last directive was to pursue the 'shadow' they'd seen in the water.

Linden put all these factors into the program and hit enter. He looked in his empty mug and took it to get coffee while the program did its thing. The coffee maker was empty, so he opted to be a good guy, fill it, and start it again. He stared at it as it whirred and ground the beans. It whistled and brewed for a few more seconds before Linden got bored and headed to the conference room to see if the computer had finished rendering his simulation.

In the dark room, a blue button flashed on the keypad. Linden logged in and started the simulations. The computer ran through all the possibilities that Linden had asked for and more. It showed the shadow as a whale, as a school of fish, as an oil slick, and a garbage patch, all of which shouldn't have confused the *Cudgel's* sensors. One of the likely scenarios was that the shadow was an advanced submarine for the Circle, with stealth or jamming technology. The *Cudgel* and this mystery ship engaged and the sub bested the *Cudgel*. But what happened to the sub? One of the simulations suggested the opponents destroyed or disabled each other in the fight.

Lou knocked at the door. "You coming to the game?"

"Game?"

"Football at the Duplex? Remember? Argentina and Mexico in the lower deck, USA versus Canada in the upper? I got good seats for Argentina, but my Canadian seats suck," Lou said.

"Nah. I've got too much going on here." Linden nodded to the simulations that were still playing out. For fun, he had asked the computer to work in an iceberg like the one that sunk the *Titanic*. The animation playing before him put the odds of that scenario at nearly zero percent, showing the *Cudgel* deftly avoiding the iceberg with no trouble.

"You do look crazy busy," Lou said. "Emphasis on crazy. This'll be here tomorrow. Come on."

Sports had never been a big draw for Linden, and the crowds would be insane. "I'm going to pass. Thanks, though."

"On that old ship of theirs? It'll take two days to get there, right? Two days. You just going to stare at maps and simulations until then?" Lou pulled on his suit jacket and fixed the collar.

"Maybe."

"Fine. Adios," Lou said, as he walked away. After a minute, Linden heard the faint ding of the elevator that came to pick Lou up and whisk him down to the ground floor.

The most recent simulation ended, with the computer declaring the chances the *Cudgel* was abducted by a UFO to be in the six to ten percent range, which made Linden laugh. He watched the three dimensional computer rendering again, to see a swarm of saucer-shaped objects swarm up around the *Cudgel* and carry it off.

"This looks important." Linden turned to see Holli in the hall, staring at the simulation. "Is this for another case, or are you still trying to find the *Cudgel*?"

After a couple of taps, Linden hit the right button to make the images go away. "It's for the same search. Just eliminating possibilities."

"Okay." Holli gave Linden a small smile. "I don't have a whole lot of time before I have to be back upstairs to the office."

"I was thinking of going to the coffee shop across the street, just to get away from the awful stuff here. Why don't you come with me?" Linden took his ID and his wallet and started out the door past Holli.

"No. I need to get back."

"Come on. Fifteen minutes. They won't miss you for fifteen minutes." Linden tapped the down button on the elevator repeatedly. "Let me buy you coffee, just to make it up to you."

Holli held up the coffee cup in her hand that Linden hadn't noticed when she walked in.

"Fine. Let me order you a scone or something with pumpkin flavoring in it," Linden said.

"I despise pumpkin anything; let's just get on with this." She lifted her cup and sipped, all the while staring at Linden. She handed a file folder with a thin disk inside. "This took no time, really. It was pretty straightforward once I cleaned up the audio and removed the ocean sounds, and various other crap."

"Other crap?"

"Whoever made these recordings also had a lot of ambient noise in a lot of them—ship sounds, mostly, the screws on a sub turning, the creak of a rudder or old sonar array, nothing big… Well, one thing that was big, but we'll get to that." Holli pulled her paper-thin laptop open and turned it around to show Linden. "See it took a while to figure out that each instance was slightly slower than the last, so I had to speed each recording up a little depending on when it was made."

"And?" Linden looked at the screen to see a graph of some sort, showing what he assumed were the years of the instances, and how much they'd slowed.

Holli tapped the screen and the picture advanced to the next slide, which showed an advertisement for a wristwatch.

"Do you have pop-up ads for your debriefings now?" Linden was confused by Holli's inclusion of this in her research.

"Click on the part of the ad that says 'More Information.'"

He did as he was told and the browser switched over to the website for Connery and Sons Watches. "And?"

"Now click the link for 'Unique Alerts' in the middle of the page."

Linden rolled his eyes. "Just fucking tell…"

"Humor me. I'm doing this for you out of the goodness of my heart, at least let me have the thrill of revealing what I've found," Holli said.

Fine, Linden thought. *If she was going to continue doing me favors, might as well let her have one.* He clicked the link and a low-pitched alarm sounded in long beeps.

"Again."

Linden clicked it again, but this time the alarm was different. It was very close to their sound, but not quite. "I don't think so."

"Listen, I've changed its speed to about the same as our annual mystery beep and put them side by side, removed the background junk and matched the speeds." Linden played them at the same time, and it was hard to tell the difference. "And according to the site, this is a reminder sound, and, unless someone stops it, it goes on for exactly one minute."

"Just like our sound."

"Just like our sound." Holli drank some more of her coffee, and sat back. "It's a watch with a dying battery."

It made sense to Linden. Someone on board had a watch set to go off once a year. "And this can be picked up by sonar?"

"If the sonar is sensitive enough and close enough, sure."

He stared at the ad on the computer until something caught his eye. "Wait. The features on this ad say it has a battery that will last a lifetime." Linden pointed at the page. "Guaranteed."

"Yeah, I saw that. I'm having trouble figuring that one out. If I'm right and it's the watch, I don't know what could cause that," Holli said. "But maybe the same thing caused the *Cudgel* to disappear?"

13

The two days it took to reach the site seemed much longer. Cass spent the majority of the time helping ready equipment for the hunt to come. They had air tanks filled for the divers, sea sleds charging on deck, and the drones were tested and retested for secure connections and maneuverability. Takis and Ozzie took them through their paces by racing the large machines against each other both underwater and in the air. Rina checked out Eyeball, the underwater camera she'd used at the *Swansea* site only a few days ago. It could operate entirely on its own, focusing in on whatever she told it to, or automatically focusing on any action or movement. The drones had cameras as well, but they weren't quite as sophisticated as Eyeball.

The rest of the time was a waiting game, and Cass took the time to get to know her new crewmates, Lewis and Caroline. Turns out Caroline had taught at the Centre of Marine Sciences in Lisbon. CCMAR was one of the schools that Cass had considered applying to, if she ever found time for higher education. They discussed the excitement of living in Portugal, and the hazards of chasing an unknown species deep into the abyss. They ended up passing the time together the first night by watching old shark movies in the communications room. Caroline pointed out the unrealistic behavior of the Great White in the series, but still jumped when the beast attacked the fishing boat.

The other transfer to the *Adamant*, Lewis, was a little more tight-lipped. He tinkered in the small room left open for the scientists on the boat. He set up equipment, aquariums, trays and instruments with the idea that there would be sea life at their position that was worth studying. When Cass visited him, she found he had a background in oceanography as well, but also one in animal husbandry. He minored in theater, according to the copies of his diplomas he put on the wall in the lab room. He also taped up a picture of Albert Einstein, which seemed at odds with an ocean-studying actor, but Cass left it alone. Cass helped Lewis unpack a few beakers and sample slides, securing them in cabinets to keep them from breaking when the ship hit rough seas. Finally, she watched him pull out a small, potted tomato plant with tiny green tomatoes on it. "Just making it home," he said. "We could be here for a while, why not make it nice?"

Cass agreed with the possibility that they could be on the ship, and at the next site, for a good long while. However, she was not exactly sure how much time Martin would give them. With his initial hesitation, he might be inclined to leave if they didn't find something immediately. The *Swansea* site held a sure thing, but the *Cudgel* site was a fairy tale.

The trip was relatively uneventful for the two days; a storm started toward the end of the first day, nothing terrible, drizzle and a little thunder, but it was enough to drive everyone inside for most of the trip, forcing them to either ride it out in their quarters, or socialize in the comm room, or dining area. Rina started a marathon of pirate movies and episodes of some obscure Chinese superhero series, which kept most of the crew amused. Cass stayed in her room, reading everything she could on the *Cudgel*, its fifteen-person crew, and the past search attempts. She forgot to eat the first day, because she was so intent on what she was doing. It was dark all day from the storm, so time passed in stealth mode. She only realized how late it was when she heard Lewis vomiting in his room due to the rough seas.

She rapped on his door. "You okay in there?"

"Fine." She could hear him spit weakly in the room. "I should know better than to eat stew on rough seas."

"Stew is not your friend when it's rough?"

Lewis coughed and cleared his throat. "Actually, pretty much everything is a bad idea except bread or crackers. Anything more and I'm in for it."

It caused Cass to think, but she couldn't remember anyone else on the crew that had trouble with seasickness, even on worse seas. She supposed that they'd all managed to put their time in on the sea, and that very little slowed them down anymore.

In the old navigation room, Rina was taking a break from her movie theater duties and was setting up large monitors and other equipment.

"Need a hand?" Cass asked. She stepped into the room, helped place the first monitor on a table.

"Thanks, these are all for controlling those drones. Once they're set up, they can be simple to control, but..." Rina clicked the monitor in place and stepped back to look at the boxes and equipment. "All this crap is a pain in the ass until then."

"I'll bet."

"Good thing you're here. They have you controlling the newer drone during the expedition, at least at the time that the beeping is supposed to go off." Rina tore open a box and removed the three tiny hard drives within, setting one on each of the tables. "I'll control the other one. Should we be back-to-back, or next to each other?"

"Maybe next to each other. Just in case I need some help." Cass wasn't worried about controlling the machine; she'd driven deep-sea drones on a number of missions for the NIA in the past, she was more concerned about being able to look over Rina's shoulder to see what she was seeing, she wanted a front-row seat in case Rina made it to the *Cudgel* first.

Once everything was set up, Rina and Cass booted the computers and loaded up simulation programs to practice with the drones. If the simulators were true to life, then the dumpster-sized machines would be tough to handle. "Wanna arm wrestle?" Rina asked.

"Can we do that in a simulation?" Cass asked.

"You can do anything with a simulation. Would you like it to look like you have giant boxing gloves?" Rina tapped away at her keyboard.

Suddenly, in Cass's screen, the collector arms blinked, then came back with realistic-looking boxing gloves covering their four pinchers. The custom controls that made them reach out and slowly grab delicate objects now were changed to allow the drone to jab at the open air. "Holy crap, forget arm wrestling." Cass made the machine punch a one-two combo at the air on her screen.

"I've got money on Rina," Jakob said. He was leaning into the room and staring over the women's shoulders. The others looked as well and laughed at the idea.

"Can we watch this on the big screen in the comms room?" Takis asked.

And so was born the drone boxing craze that swept the *Adamant* for the fourteen hours before the ship reached their destination.

14

Cass took the remote for one of the large drones, while nearby Rina sat at the controls to the other. Takis and Ozzie were already in the water, both of them with small motivators that could move them quickly to the site, if the sound actually occurred.

A crackle over the radio, and Rina spoke. "I would like to name my drone *Champ*, since we crushed everyone in the World Drone League playoffs. Maybe later, if we get time I can paint it on the side of the drone in big pink letters?"

"No, no," Martin's voice came through Cass's headphones. "We're not using codenames on this one, there's no reason to."

"Yay! I want a codename as well," Cass joined in. "My drone is big and boxy and ugly. Maybe it should be *Ogre*." She was beginning to see why Rina loved to tease Martin so much. He was an easy mark.

"No, no," Martin said. "I already said we're not painting anything on the drones. Let's just pay attention."

Takis tried to talk through his own laughter. "What should mine be? Something to do with water I would guess. How about *Sea Snake One*?" He chuckled more, before turning his mic off.

"I'm positive there's no way I'm going to say *Sea Snake One*, how about *Tadpole One*?" Ozzie said.

Martin came back on. "Guys? Just shut up and pay attention. Nobody gets a code name, let's start gearing up to move, and maintain radio silence."

"Well, maybe he should be *Ogre*," Takis said. "He doesn't seem to be too pleasant."

Cass ran through her controls to make sure everything was responding. "Yeah I want another code name if he's taking mine."

"Down to about six minutes," Rina said "Make sure everyone's in place and ready to roll just in case we actually hear something."

"Oh, we're going to hear something this time I think," Jakob said. "I can feel it." He was already up on the deck waiting to see what would happen. From that position he could also jump in the water quite easily and grab another motivator for himself.

The rest were in a direction that would be advantageous to discovering the ship, or at least finding out where the sound was coming from. All of them were already in the water and watching what would happen next. Cass scanned the horizon and checked the radar to make sure no one else was around to horn in on their search, and so far, no one was. As Cass looked down at everyone getting prepared, she kept one eye on a tiny view screen at what her drone could see as it was floating just below the waterline and prepared to move in any direction necessary.

Rina messed around with her drone, making it turn in circles and flip end-to-end. She was impatient, waiting for a signal to indicate the location of the robot. She finally leaned back in her chair and looked over at Cass. "What do you think you would change your code name to?" Rina said without keying the mic. "I think it's imperative to stick Martin with '*Ogre*', so what else can we give to you?"

"I don't know..." Cass hadn't really thought about code names, other than the one the government gave to her.

"Big and green? You could go with Godzilla, but that seems a little on the nose. Hulk? Let's see, Grape Ape? That's an obscure one. What about something random like Mister Punchy, or Droney McDroneface? Or..."

"I like that one. I like Mister Punchy." Cass looked from her control and smiled at Rina. "He may have lost the drone boxing playoffs, but he'll be back."

"Mister Punchy it is."

"Getting close to go time. I need a status from everyone," Martin's voice broke the radio silence.

"Affirmative, *Ogre*. *Mister Punchy* and *Champ* reporting," Rina said. "Everything is..." she looked over at Cass. After a quick glance at the screens in front of her, Cass gave a thumbs up. "Everything is A-Okay for go. All of the sonar buoys we dropped all around are operating as needed." On the way in, they'd dropped a number of sensors around the area in the hopes that linking them all together would allow them to triangulate the sound if it occurred.

This should be interesting, Cass thought. If Martin doesn't have a coronary over all of the money flying out the window, he might have one over Rina's constant badgering.

"*Ethel Mer-man* squared away, five-by-five," Takis said.

"*Albatross One* checking in." Ozzie's breathing was heavy in Cass's earphones as he laughed.

"Just check in, please," Martin said.

"*Red Five*, standing by," Jakob said. He waited a second and clicked back on. "That was from *Star Wars*. The first one. Well, the fourth one chronologically, but the first one that came out."

"You people are weird. I think I know now why we don't mix crews." It was Ben in the wheelhouse. "Things are ready here."

"All right let's start a countdown to the supposed time the alarm goes off," Martin said. "And don't just put it on the screens, I want to hear it."

Rina agreed and got them started. "Okay. Let me synch things up. Here we go. We've got the clock counting down from ten...nine..."

Cass kind of wished she could be in the room with Martin, just to see how he reacted when the time came. He had so much put into this, and it was such a labored decision in the first place.

"Six...Five..."

A few feet to Cass's left, Rina cracked her knuckles once or twice while she did the count. A small, thin monitor next to her larger one displayed nothing but the numbers as they ticked down.

"Three...Two..."

Cass gripped her controls and stared at the world underwater through her view of *Mister Punchy's* camera.

"One..."

Everyone's mic went silent as they all listened for the sound—any sort of vibrations or noises coming through their headphones, other than the pings of the sonar array floating just below the ship. There was the occasional bloop of bubbles and whoosh of waves. But beyond that, there was no repetitive noise that came close to the recording. Cass wondered if that was why Martin had put himself in another room; so people couldn't see his anger or his disappointment at finding nothing, again.

They waited a full two minutes and still it seemed that their timing was off, or the place was off. Or maybe the noise didn't have a thing to do with it.

"Takis? Ozzie? You want to swim down a little deeper? Might as well look around since we're here anyway." It was Martin and he sounded defeated.

"Yeah. Who knows? Maybe we'll get lucky and find it. Or maybe there's a lost Viking ship just hanging around we can discover," Ozzie said.

At the next chair over, Rina blew her hair out of her eyes and leaned back in her chair. She held the controller in her lap and dreamily moved the *Champ* through the sea.

As Cass waited, she moved her drone around a bit too, getting used to the controls a little more and using the drone's camera to have a look around for any sign of life, or the glint of metal. On the screen, she noticed Jakob slip into the water off the starboard side. He'd geared up and slid into the water to look as well. After five minutes of waiting, everyone was getting bored and anxious. In one way, Cass felt relieved;

she didn't have to call a full-scale alert and bring in Kemp and his government team. She'd started to like being on the water with Martin's crew. She looked over at Rina, though she was a few years younger than Cass, they'd developed a comfortable bond, partly borne of being the only females on the regular search crew, but also for a genuine affection.

Rina suddenly slammed her chair forward. "I have something," she said to Cass.

"What?"

Rina opened her mic up for everyone to hear. "Guys? I'm getting the same sound we heard before. It's just slower, drawn out."

"Where?" It was Martin.

Rina focused on the screen in front of her. "I'm trying. It sounds like it's fairly deep."

With a flip of a switch, Cass made her drone dive down toward the ocean floor. The machine's arms automatically folded in to make less resistance. Her screen showed a huge grouping of rocks below, part of a formation that stretched on for what seemed like miles.

"It's echoing around off the rocks, hard to pinpoint," Rina said.

"Call it out, Rina. We only have a minute. Tell everyone where they need to be," Martin said. His voice crackled out on the last word and static filled Cass's ears.

"Hello? Anyone? This is *Mister Punchy*. Can anyone hear me? Over?" Cass called into her mic. No one responded.

"I can't hear anything except static. Take your drone down toward the larger rock formation." Rina said to Cass from across the room. "This is the *Champ*." The static suddenly grew louder for a moment then stopped in the headphones. Cass heard Ozzie finishing a sentence.

"...the hell is going on?"

The interference was intermittent. Someone's sentence suddenly ended in the middle, or consisted of few words that made no sense on their own.

Rina switched her small screen from the countdown to a visual representation of their communications. "Some bullshit down here is interfering with our signals. It happens. Could be something in the composition of the rocks, or a natural phenomenon." Rina talked more out loud to herself than into the mic. "There's a deep canyon between the larger groups of rock and coral beds, I'm sending *Mister Punchy* to check it out," Rina said. "Ozzie and Takis need to head that way too. Follow the drone."

"How much time do we have?"

"The sound is slower, so I hope that means we have more time," Rina said. "If so, we still have just under a minute. If not, we're down to fifteen seconds or thereabouts."

Cass turned the joystick to move the drone lower, but it didn't respond immediately. The camera image remained steady, pointed at the bottom of the sea. "I'm having trouble getting Mister Punchy to move…" Cass could hear her own signal cutting in and out over the headphones.

She tried again, and the drone moved this time, slow and skittish at first.

"Our sleds are cutting in and out, as well." Takis's voice came through clearly. "Hold on. I think we're back in business."

Cass plunged her drone downward as fast as she could. The controls still stuttered a little, but she was able to wrestle it on a course for the rocks.

"Signal's fading, but still going," Rina said. She grabbed the controls for her own drone and sent the huge vehicle deep under the water. She checked the triangulation of the sonar array with each of the vehicle's receptors. "*Mister Punchy* seems to be closest. I'm tapping into that drone's navigation system to see if it can get a fix…"

Cass watched Rina out of the corner of her eye. The woman was slightly manic, as she tried to control one drone, listen in on another, trace the sound from the *Adamant*'s equipment, and keep everyone in the loop about what was happening.

"Rina? We need some information here," Martin said. "We don't have time for…"

"It's gone. The signal's gone," Rina said flatly. "It stopped." She turned off her mic and turned to speak to Cass. "Stop your drone right there. You had the best signal where you were."

"Got it." Cass was supposed to be watching the crew on their mission so that they didn't damage or disturb the *Cudgel*, but their enthusiasm was contagious at times.

15

"This is a big old roller coaster, isn't it?" Ben said. He wheeled over to the window of the observation room, where Martin was standing and watching the water outside. "It's all happening underwater, what are you looking at? Can you even see anything out there?"

When the whole thing started, Martin could see Jakob out on the deck, but now that he'd gone in the ocean, all that was visible was the ship and the water. "No. Just habit, I guess." He nodded to the large screen at the end of the room that showed images from four different cameras, all showing underwater scenes and each glitching and going dark intermittently. "Those show me all I need to know anyway." Martin picked up his glass and took the last sip of scotch. He'd gone through three so far and he was beginning to wonder whether he'd be conscious should they ever actually find something. He turned to Ben. "What brings you up here?"

"Seriously? You have the best seat in the house, and…"

Martin filled the glass with ice and poured more scotch. "And?"

"Well…" Ben averted his eyes from Martin. "I was worried about you. I mean, if this thing doesn't happen with the *Cudgel*, that's a lot down the drain."

"You think I went to another room to off myself in private?" Martin would have laughed if he wasn't so disturbed by the idea that a good friend would entertain that thought. "I'm a little depressed that this might not work out, but I have a lot of wrecks to find before I check out."

"I didn't think any such thing. I just know you don't like being on the losing end of a deal, and you hate being so close to a treasure and not being able to find it," Ben said. "Plus, I always figured you'll die in some weird sex thing."

Martin did laugh this time. "My days of 'weird sex things' are pretty much behind me, I'm afraid. But thanks for the vote of confidence." His radio squelched and Martin grabbed it. "Yes?"

"I think we have something." It was Rina.

"What?"

"Too early to say. But Cass's drone is moving in now to get a closer look, the Suvari brothers are swimming in right behind." Rina paused. "I'm putting the *Champ* behind them to light up the area. They're pretty far down and in somewhat of a tunnel or cave."

Finally, some action. It was hell for Martin to sit and watch everyone else do the work while he kept his thumb firmly up his ass. He grabbed the remote and got rid of all of the images, except for the one feed from Cass's drone. It was still dark, even with all the lights that were moving into position. "Seriously, what was this 'something' we saw?"

"I was watching the video and thought I saw our lights glint off of something," Rina said.

"A glint?" It wasn't the exciting pronouncement that Martin had hoped for. "Jesus. *A glint*? A glint could be anything. It could be a fucking lantern fish for Christ's sake."

"There," Rina said.

"Where?" It was Cass in the background.

"Back a little to your right."

Martin could see the video of Cass's drone slowly move to the right, taking in more rocks, more plant life, more coral and more of the same dark and blurry crap they'd been seeing since they hit the water. And then, he saw what Rina saw. An almost blinding flash of light. He grabbed his mic. "There. Go back a fraction. Go back."

"We see it, *Ogre*." Rina sounded happy again.

The camera nudged backward slightly and stopped with the brilliant light reflecting off of something among the rocks. Martin began to cycle through the cameras, trying to find the one with the best view of whatever they were seeing. "Be careful, but let's get in there." His manic scroll to find a good angle halted on Rina's drone, the one furthest from the object. He determined that it was, in fact, some sort of shallow cave, with a high and wide mouth in the deep water. There was some unusual plant life dotting the cave inside and out. "Can anyone tell me what those plants are? I can't see the color on this monitor."

"I'm near some, Martin," Takis said. Martin switched to Takis's feed and watched as the diver pointed to some. "It looks like most of it is acropora coral, sort of a lilac hue. Usually around for the beginning of a reef. It does have some sort of odd coloring to it, but nothing too far off its normal color."

"What are the dark bits in among those?"

Ozzie jumped in as well. "Plumose Anemones, it looks like. But again, the color is slightly off. They're black, with sort of red lines, almost veins all the way down into the rock and coral." Martin switched to Ozzie's channel and could see him put his hand next to one, revealing the size of each anemone to be larger than his fist. "Usually, these sort of tentacles, would grab and stun fish for food." Indeed, to Martin it looked like the anemones had long shocks of hair that flowed with the tide, back and forth.

"That's... kind of fucked up," Ben said. "Think there's something going on in that cave that's messing with the environment?"

"How would a missing battle mech cause that sort of mutation?"

It was Ben's turn to laugh. "Didn't all those things have nuclear cores? I mean that was why disposing of some of them was such a catastrofuck, right?"

"I would think a leaking reactor would kill off the fish, not change them."

Ben poured a glass of Martin's alcohol for himself and plopped in some ice cubes. "I don't know. I just park boats."

There was another rip of static on the radio before Rina's voice came through clearly. "You guys are looking at the wrong damn thing."

16

Cass moved *Mister Punchy* closer. Ozzie and Takis were using her drone to steady themselves and rest as they looked on. Buried in the anemones, coral, and dark rocks, they'd found the surface reflecting their lights; it was the viewport of the *Cudgel*'s head unit. As they drew closer, Cass felt like they were looking into the weapon's eyes, and seeing its despair and longing at being out of action for so long.

"Do you see anything inside?" Martin asked.

"We certainly aren't going to find any survivors, if that's what you're asking." Ozzie replied.

"I don't expect survivors, but there has to be some sign of them. There has to be some evidence of them."

"It's too dark, and the port is tinted. Can't really see much." Takis could be seen on screen in his dive suit, peering into the *Cudgel*.

"What're those rocks? More coral, or is it some debris from the cave?" Rina asked.

"We can't really tell. They aren't rocks; they're stuck to the hull like glue. They don't seem to be coral because they have unusual spikes on them. They're almost a couple of feet long. We'll see if we can pry a sample loose and bring it back." Takis's hands appeared on Cass's screen holding a dive knife, which he tried to slide under the strange formation.

Soon, Jakob was swimming with them as they began to examine the giant government weapon that had been missing for so long. Rina used her drone to take pictures of the area around the 'head' and then took wide shots to further establish their find. It took them a while to extrapolate where the machine's body was hidden among the natural plant life and other things around the cave. It appeared the legs were locked together, and the arms were spread eagle. A thick sea grass had grown to cover the feet and part of the legs. Coral was everywhere.

Rina sent the map to everyone.

"So this thing was just crucified on the rocks there?" Martin asked.

"Kind of looks like it, but…" Jakob said. "I doubt it. I mean, where are you going to get nails that big?"

Cass shook her head. It was hard to tell if Jakob was kidding or not sometimes. She forwarded the pictures of the *Cudgel* to her personal email account. Later, she'd send them on to Linden with a message that they'd found it, and that a cleanup team is needed to seal off the area and begin the recovery operation. They'd found it.

"My god, it's just enormous," Martin said. "I knew the dimensions, but wow."

Cass hoped that the monstrous robot would prove a worthy find for Martin, for as long as he had it in his possession. He'd done the work over the years and it had paid off for him, but it had also paid off for the government to place someone on his crew, just in case.

"What's beyond the *Cudgel*? Is it just a wall of rock, or what?" Rina asked.

"Let's see." Ozzie's camera began to pan around the head unit. "I don't know. There's too much of this coral and other stuff covering it. We'd have to clear it off."

His brother spoke as well. "Yeah. I'm down by this thing's crotch, I think. And I can't even see the hull at all. I occasionally see a swath of dark blue paint, but man, I can't see what's beyond the bot."

"Hey. As long as you're checking out crotches…" Jakob said.

"Stay away from me, Jakob."

"You'll get lonely at sea eventually," Jakob laughed.

Rina keyed her mic. "Why would you naturally be the first he came to if he got lonely at sea?"

"I think it's some kind of law of the sea," Cass said. "Leftover from pirate times." She gave a weak chuckle, but couldn't take her eyes off the little bit of uncovered head piece of the long lost war machine. That uncovered chunk of forward window was immense. Cass had grown up in New York City in an apartment that faced the Empire State Building. Every morning she'd look out the window and marvel at the building's style, and how immense it was. There were other buildings that were taller and had their own unique styles, but the Empire State held a soft spot in her heart. Maybe that's why she was so fond of the *Cudgel*, *A-9*. It was larger than the Empire State Building by a good fifty feet, sported some of the same colors, and, when she looked at the *Cudgel*, she thought she could see the same style of lines in the battle machine's arms and legs, the front panels across the chest were reminiscent of the windows on the building, and certainly the unfinished one hundred and second floor landing looked like a big influence on the head's viewport.

"What should we do now?" Ozzie asked.

Cass held her breath a moment to see what Martin would say.

"Put a marker there, so we can get back easier. Cass, bring your drone up for recharging. Rina, keep yours on station and get footage of every inch you can. If you get tired, switch with Cass. Guys, start heading up, take your stops on the way. Don't want anyone getting the bends." Martin's feed was silent a moment. "Good work everyone."

Cass began to bring *Mister Punchy* back up to the surface, but stopped partway up. "You guys need something to hold onto for your breaks?"

Jakob answered her. "That's not necessary."

"But we'll take it," Takis said. "Why make it tougher than it has to be? Plus, I'm super lazy."

Cass slowly brought the drone up, pausing for the men to acclimate to the new depths, then moved up to the next level, and continued until they all surfaced.

"Everyone take thirty minutes to get back on your feet, eat something, and then we'll meet in the dining hall for debrief, discussion and high fives." Martin didn't sound thrilled when he said it. Normally, if they'd found a treasure, they'd be whooping it up or shouting with glee. Today, they seemed somber and dark.

Once she helped everyone get aboard and locked down *Mister Punchy* on the deck, Cass stood and patted Rina on the shoulder. "I'll see you in a few. Need anything?"

Rina was still using her drone to collect images. "I'm fine."

Cass left the control room and walked down the hall to her quarters. She locked the portal behind her and pulled out the satellite phone. As she began putting in the passwords to access the line, the light in her cabin went out. She made a note to get a new bulb and raised the phone to her ear. It too had stopped working. Cass pressed the power button on the phone, but it wouldn't come back on. She wrapped the phone back up in the wool sock and shoved it into the hiding place she'd located on this new ship, at the back of the small closet.

In the hall, she heard the brothers shouting about the power. As they passed her quarters, she stepped out. "What the hell?" Cass said.

"I know, right?" Takis said. "Where you right in the middle of a Super Mario level too? I was kicking Ozzie's ass."

"No proof," Ozzie replied. "Power went out, didn't save it. No proof you were beating me."

They met everyone else in the dining hall – one of the few rooms that had good lighting coming in from the windows. "What's going on?" Cass asked.

"No idea," Rina said. "I was still getting the last of the photos of the *Cudgel* and suddenly lost control of the *Champ*."

"What'll happen to it?" Ben sat at the end of the dining table, drinking coffee from a mug that read *"Divers do it Underwater."*

"The drone? If I don't reestablish a connection, it'll ascend to the surface and deploy its flotation devices." Rina shrugged. "It won't get lost or anything."

"Where's Jakob?" Cass asked.

Martin walked in the room. "I asked him to look at the problem and get the back-up generator going."

Lewis and Caroline came in the room and dropped a large aquarium in the middle of the dining table. Inside were the two large spiky amoebae that the Suvari brothers had removed from the *Cudgel's* hull, half-covered in water.

"Ewww." Rina slid her chair away. "Is this really the best place for that? Don't we have a big-ass research area downstairs?"

Despite Rina's objections, everyone else gathered closer, and put their noses close to the glass. "Could it be some sort of barnacle?" Ozzie asked. "It kind of looks like one… From the right angle."

Caroline shrugged. "I don't even know yet if it's alive. The outside is like rock, but this spike on top is almost like cartilage. It's extremely flexible." She stuck a long pointer into the aquarium and used it to knock the spike back and forth. "But look, we just got it. We haven't done any sort of tests on it yet; we haven't had a chance to use the computer for research, since it just went down. No clue what we have here."

17

Linden stared at the model of the *Cudgel* as he gathered his tablet and notes. It was an audacious machine, to be sure—bright white and blue, large, and the control room was housed in a nearly-rounded head that looked a lot like a hangman's hood, probably not by accident. It made the British and Western Russian machines look tame in comparison. Those units had disappeared as well, though not by accident or disaster, those went into mothballs once the war was over. No real need for them in combat now. Though Linden wondered if they would come back out should a conflict arise again.

A knock from behind him brought Linden out of his thoughts. "Your appointment is here." Lou leaned into the room.

"Appointment?" Linden checked the calendar on his tablet quickly. "I don't have anything today."

"It's Thursday," Lou said. "End of the month?"

It hit Linden that he'd forgotten to renew a standing appointment on the calendar. He met with Major Henry Braun about the *Cudgel* every last Thursday of the month for five years now, since Braun had taken over the search project. Braun was a career military man, who was always kind when he spoke and Linden usually looked forward to speaking with him every thirty days or so... until he started making the huge cuts to Linden's department. Usually, the two had a good meal and Linden officially reported that he had nothing new to report.

At least today that would be different.

"Thanks. I'll be right out." Linden stood and straightened his suit. He fixed his tie in the reflection of a monitor and checked his face and hair as well. He wasn't military anymore, but he still liked to follow the military expectations and make sure he was put together as best he could.

In the hall, he could see the major standing straight as a rail near the secretary's desk.

"Did I interrupt a nap?" Henry asked, he held out his hand and Linden shook it.

"Actually, we may have something to talk about. I was busy the last few days."

The major looked surprised. "Well, then. I can't wait to hear." He pushed the elevator button and looked up at the floor indicator above the doors. "How have you been? Staying fit?"

He didn't want to admit he was skipping some of his workouts lately, so he lied a little. "Still at it, yes sir." He and the major stepped in when the doors opened.

"Greg, down at the base gym, says you haven't been in lately. Says you missed a physical therapy appointment or two. Everything okay?" The concern was almost fatherly in tone.

The elevator automatically began to ascend at a rapid clip. "Sure. Yes. I was travelling and just didn't get around to rescheduling those," Linden said, lying again.

"See that you do. I'd hate for you to be on sick leave with surgery or something else you could prevent."

The elevator came to a stop three floors from the top and the men exited and briskly walked by the Major's staff. He gave each a nod, but he'd trained them not to stand up and salute every time he walked in a room. They did it each morning and as he left each night, but he told Linden he'd grown tired of the tradition every god damn time he went to the bathroom.

"Did you get the messages from General Thornburg and the quartermaster's office?" Braun's secretary asked.

"I did, Jerry. Ignored 'em. I'll check them out after lunch."

"Understood," Jerry said. He picked up a small briefcase and handed it to the Major. "You're not here?"

Braun took the case and kept walking. "No, I am not."

It was always interesting to Linden to watch Braun interact with his staff in a casual way. If that were the type of experience Linden had had, he might have stayed with the ordinance division. When he was put in charge of the *Cudgel* task force, he tried to make the environment as open and loose as he could, but it didn't work. Many of his staff had just come from the military and the war, and needed structure, even if it was saluting and tight creases on their uniforms. The NIA was a tough transition, though. A federal agency reporting to a military agency confused a lot of them. They saluted when they didn't have to, they 'yes, sir'd' a little too emphatically, for what was essentially a civilian job. In the end, many transferred back to the army, or whatever branch they'd left, which started the downsizing of his staff.

They stopped at the double doors on the west side of the building. Here, the Major did salute, and he showed the two guards his identification. They saluted back, nodded, and pressed the button that unlocked the door. They proceeded through, and then out onto the garden terrace outside. There was no one out among the gorgeous trees and flowers that were waving gently in the breeze. They continued to their traditional spot and sat at one of the small tables there.

The terrace offered an amazing view of the city and the bay from seventy-six stories up, with glass walls on all sides except the building itself. Linden never asked who built the terrace or what its purpose was, but it was a wonderful place to have a quiet lunch without being interrupted, or overheard.

"Let's see." Braun opened up the briefcase and pulled out the contents. "I think you'll like this." He placed two large containers on the table and opened one. "This is a peanut butter and... wait..." The major paused. "You're not allergic to peanut butter are you? Have I asked you that?"

He had, at least a dozen times in the last five years. "No sir, I'm not."

"Great. It's a peanut butter and jelly sandwich, with raspberry jelly and a thin layer of chocolate on thin-sliced Italian bread. It's one of my favorites." Braun pushed the container over to Linden and opened the other for himself. "Now, what's this news you have?"

As he unwrapped his peanut butter sandwich, Linden made sure to word his answer carefully. It seemed like a slam-dunk, but the treasure hunters could be wrong. "It looks like a crew may have located the *Cudgel*."

Braun looked up, mid-bite. "What? Why didn't you tell me?"

"Just unfolding. I'm waiting on confirmation that the intel is good, but it sounds good." It felt nice for Linden to be able to tell Braun the news in person, after all that time. However, he was not so happy that he was proceeding on unverified information from an unknown source.

"Where?"

"A good deal south of the Aleutian Islands."

The general swallowed a bite and looked up as he thought. "Remind me. That's the group Palmer is imbedded in?"

"That's right sir, Cassandra Palmer is our plant with this team. She's overseeing the site at this time," Linden said. He took a bite of the sandwich, thinking of what else to say. He had so little to go on, and didn't want to mislead Braun, but it was the first big possibility they'd had in years.

It was silent as the two ate, and Braun appeared to contemplate the possibilities. His eyes grew wide and he flipped open the case again. "Damn. I forgot to offer you a bag of chips. You like sour cream and onion? Honey mustard?" He held up two small bags of snacks.

It wasn't like Linden expected him to get weepy or shout with joy, but he'd expected more of a reaction. "I've never had honey mustard. I'll give them a try."

Braun handed the bag to Linden and opened his own. "That's good news about the *Cudgel*. Let's hope it's true. Good news."

"Yes, sir."

"Think about what you'll do when it's over?"

"Excuse me?" Linden asked.

The major put his crusts back in the container. "Once we find the *Cudgel*. What will you do then? This has been your job for years. Do you have a career plan for what you'll do next?"

He didn't. He'd been the lead on this for so long, that he assumed he'd be doing it for the foreseeable future. "I figured since I knew more about this thing than anyone, I'd still be needed to get it back into fighting shape."

"Fighting what? Fighting who? We're not at war with anyone. Did you think they'd deploy it to the cities to stop shoplifters and jaywalkers? Besides, it's a military vehicle, you're not military anymore." Braun dug his hands into the chip bag, crinkling and crunching. "Besides–I understand it'll be a museum piece anyway. Would you want to travel the country, giving a speech at every stop about how much it weighs, how tall it is and what it did for the war effort five times a week?"

"Museum?"

Braun nodded and opened the briefcase again. "Shit. I forgot the sodas. Aw, damn it."

The idea of going through all of this searching just to mothball the *Cudgel* stuck in Linden's mind. What good was it then? Why bother finding it? He swallowed another bite of peanut butter and vowed not to be a tour guide for anyone.

18

Martin stood at one end of the table and waved for everyone to sit down. "Look. Great work. This is a momentous occasion. We've been chasing the thing for years, the government has been chasing it for years, the world has been after it for years. And WE found it. We did." He decided he wouldn't get all mushy on the crew just now. Not while they were stuck out in the middle of the ocean with no navigational capabilities, no communications and no computers. Everything was dead, even the engines, though he figured they'd only gone out because of a computer glitch. They should be easy to get back on line, computers or not. "Jakob is looking at the power problem, I'm concerned that it was some kind of electromagnetic pulse that knocked everything out, but I don't know where one would've come from, unless there's another ship relatively close by."

"Have we detected anything?" Cass asked.

"Not the last time I checked." He looked at the creatures in the glass case on the table, and then at the people assembled. "Rina? You're our computer and electronic maven, do you want to go down with Jakob and see if you can help in any way?"

"I'm on it, *Ogre*." There were chuckles from the group.

Martin looked at his watch to see how much daylight they had left. It appeared to have stopped when everything else did. He raised it and shook it and tried to wind it again, but it wouldn't start moving. The others in the room checked their watches, cell phones, music players and other personal devices, but they'd all stopped or wouldn't power on. That made Martin even more concerned that it was a pulse of some kind. "Once we restore power, it looks like our main concerns are getting a call out for the government to come claim their missing giant action figure, get our bearings again." He looked over at the things in the aquarium. "And get those ugly-ass things off the table. That's why we have a lab, right?"

Caroline nodded affirmative at Martin.

"So we're just going to turn this thing over to the feds? Not cool. I wanted to really explore it before that happened…" Takis said.

"We'll contact them, it'll take a couple of days to reach us, and we can look all around the outside all we want while we're waiting."

Cass raised an eyebrow. "A couple of days? You really think it'll take them that long to get here? This is a big deal, a major weapon."

"They're all the way back on mainland America. They'll send a ship or two out here, probably full speed, but that's still a good distance," Martin said.

"Don't forget, the military actually has up-to-date equipment. They use hover ships, and manned drones. Those things move a bit faster than, say, an old refitted cargo ship from the last century." Ben patted the wall of the room. "Don't get me wrong, I love the *Adamant*, wouldn't say a bad word about her."

"And you never know, the government could be closer than you think, Martin." Cass gave him a concerned look and continued. "I'd just hate to break the government's regulations regarding this sort of thing."

"Without power, it doesn't matter," Caroline said. "We can't contact anyone anyway."

Lewis nodded and spoke low. "And without lights, I can't look at those things down in our wonderful lab."

Martin nodded. "Well, we've got a couple of hours of daylight left. I suggest you hang out on deck and enjoy it. The cooler out there is pretty well stocked and at least you can see up there." He looked around at the crowd and nodded. "Thanks again. I didn't think we'd do this. Not in a million years." Martin picked up his scotch and took a drink. "Well, maybe a half million."

19

As everyone filed up to the deck for food and alcohol, Cass made her way to her cabin and found her phone's hiding place, this time in the closet of her quarters, and pushed the startup button, which didn't react in the least. The phone didn't power on, the battery icon didn't flash, nothing. She dug the power chord out of the closet and plugged the phone in. She stared at it, waiting for something to happen, but it was futile. She left the phone plugged in and put it on the bed, covered with a pillow. It was risky to leave it out, but she wanted it to start charging as soon as the *Adamant*'s power came back on. She closed the portal behind her and headed up to the deck.

On the stairway, Cass saw Rina headed up from the lower decks. "Any luck getting things going?"

"Yeah, it's strange, it's like something just drained all of our power. The solar cells up on deck had charged the batteries, but all of that energy is gone-wiped clean. It looks like they're charging just fine now, but it'll take time to get them back up to a usable level," Rina said. She wiped dirt and grease from her brow and shoved the cloth into her back pocket.

It took a second, but Cass realized it was the first time she'd seen Rina without her headphones. "What about the diesel engines and generator? Shouldn't they give us some power while we wait for the main batteries to charge?"

"You'd think, but all of our electronics were knocked out. Jakob is trying to manually get those engines going, but without the computers right now, we can't bring anything on line."

"That sucks."

Rina nodded. "Big time." She nodded and continued on toward her own quarters.

On deck, the rest of the team leaned against the railing and stared off the port side at the marker buoys they'd set to indicate the location of the *Cudgel*, far below the surface. "Beer me," Cass said as she found her own spot to stand.

Takis reached into the cooler and passed one down to her. "We're bored, Cass."

It was understandable. The crew was used to being excited and celebrating when they found something, and here everything had been truncated. They couldn't explore the find any further, there wasn't any power to the ship, they couldn't let the world know what they'd achieved. "Me too. Guess we'll have to drink."

Ozzie nodded and tapped his bottle of beer against hers in agreement.

"We could still go down and look at the thing. I mean the air tanks work, right? We've got glow sticks. And we could tie some kinetic flashlights to our legs and charge them on the way down. That is how they did it in the old days, isn't it?" Takis was serious suddenly. Cass guessed the alcohol was an influence.

"That's true." His brother agreed.

"Count me in." Jakob stepped onto the deck and joined them. "I've got the engines back on line, but the ship's power won't kick in for a while. Even then, it'll be low power all night. The solar panels won't charge as late as it is, the sun won't be around enough."

"Guys? Seriously?" Cass looked around at the group. "We've all been drinking, we have no modern equipment, no lighting; it's got disaster written all over it."

"You don't have to come with us," Ozzie said. "We're just anxious and ready for some kind of action. Stay here. Hang out with Rina."

Takis ripped the Velcro apart on his vest and tightened it around an air tank. "Seriously. It's just a deep night dive. No big deal. Back in half an hour, maybe."

Once Jakob extricated his wetsuit from the locker and pulled it over his nearly six and a half foot frame, everyone was getting giddy.

"Look, let's wait until morning," Cass said. "We can leave at first light." She was beginning to wonder how far she should go to discourage them. It wasn't like she'd notified her team leader that they'd actually found the thing.

"Let's go," Ozzie was already headed down the stairs toward the dive ladder. His brother chugged the rest of his beer and followed.

It wasn't really what Cass wanted to do, she'd rather rest and wait for her phone to charge and get on with calling in her backup. But she also needed to keep an eye on the divers, and since the communications didn't seem to be up, the only way to do that was to go with them. And a chance to see the *Cudgel* close up was something she couldn't pass up. Just to positively confirm its identity, she told herself.

As they pulled on their swim fins and checked their tanks, Caroline approached them, already set for a dive. "Hope you don't mind if I tag along. I'd love to see where that weird-ass anemone came from."

"More the merrier," Ozzie said.

In a matter of minutes, the five of them were in the ocean and descending. Cass followed at the rear, a feeling of dread weighing on her.

20

Martin entered the kitchen to find Rina eating an apple and listening to her music. "Where is everyone?" he asked.

"Diving," Rina said. "Left about ten minutes ago. They all wanted to try to get one more look at the thing before nightfall."

It sounded like trouble to Martin. The sun was going down soon and they'd have trouble finding their way back if the ship didn't have any running lights. "What about the *Adamant?*"

"Jakob got the engines online; the ship should have low power overnight. Could come on any time now."

That was good news, at least. "Ideas on what happened? Some sort of EMP attack?"

"No ideas yet. When the computers are up, we'll see what we can figure out," Rina said. She spoke with one earbud in and the other out, and Martin wondered if she was still listening to the music while she talked.

There was a crash from below decks and a shout of anger from Lewis.

"What the hell?" Martin said. He wondered if the man had managed to injure himself in the darkness. Martin headed toward the stairs with Rina close behind. They rounded the corner and stopped at the lab entrance. "What's going on?" Martin asked. The lab wasn't in disarray, no fires, no blood that Martin could see. The only thing he noticed out of place was the metal tray on the floor with its contents spilled near it. There were scalpels, a needle and gauze, the rest of the stuff was covered by a small towel.

"Who the hell has been fucking around in here?" Lewis demanded. "Who in the hell has been fucking around?"

Rina stepped in the room. "I don't see a problem."

With his right hand, Lewis pointed at the aquarium on the table at the center of the room. He continued to jab at the air with the finger until both Rina and Martin were looking at the sample inside.

"What?" Martin asked.

"Where's the other one? There were two. Now one is gone. I want to know who moved it or took it." Lewis was pissed and Martin quickly got angry as well.

He didn't mind the horseplay, the joking, the comradery, but when his crew messed with artifacts, treasure or samples from a dig, or a find, he drew the line. He wanted to keep each site in as pristine condition as possible. And this was worse-absconding with an unknown variety of sea life would be a potentially terrible idea for his ship. "What makes you think someone took it?"

Lewis's disbelief was evident. "With all due respect, Martin." He pointed at the aquarium that held one creature, half submerged in seawater. "But do you SEE the other one? This one hasn't moved, so what makes you think the other just got up and wandered off?"

"Just take it easy. I see the same things you do," Martin said. "Did you look around? Maybe Caroline moved it somewhere to experiment or some shit."

"I could check her quarters," Rina said. "Could she have moved it in there?"

"They're too heavy for her to move on her own. Plus there aren't any smaller containers missing." Lewis gestured toward the row of small aquariums and tubs that were secured against the wall by metal bands that kept them from falling off the counter in a storm.

"Wait." Rina pulled the other earbud out and held up her hand to get everyone to stop talking. "Listen."

At first, there was nothing. Martin heard only the common ship sounds—the engine turning over, the sea hitting the hull, the wind—but then there was another, more ominous sound. He thought it was tapping at first, like Lewis was clicking out a code with his finger nail, but both of Lewis's hands were in full view. "What the hell is it?" They all stayed quiet for another moment and the pattern of the clicking slowed.

With a whir and click, the generator on the *Adamant* kicked in and the lights buzzed on, but not fully, leaving the room in a half-light that provided just enough illumination to show the thing in the aquarium was wobbling.

"Shit," Rina said. "Is it just the movement of the ship making it do that?"

"Nope." Martin was no scientist, but the motion of the *Adamant* was definitely not the cause of the motion. "What's going on?" he asked Lewis.

The thing sounded like eggs being cracked for an omelet. Eventually it started to rise, moving slowly upward as long skinny legs forced their way out of the bottom of the creature and into the water of the aquarium, the coral-like portion rose nearly a foot when the flexible fin at the top began to split into four parts and droop down over the rocky black body. The rubbery appendages felt around to touch its surroundings, slowly at first, sluggish.

"Jesus." Lewis was transfixed. "It's amazing."

Martin felt Rina's hand on his shoulder, pulling him back toward the door as she spoke. "Lewis, let's leave and lock this door until we figure out what these things are."

"Figure it out? That's what *we* should do. We'd be famous, discovering some new species. Imagine if you found the America's missing war toy AND discovered a new species of sea life? We could name it after you," Lewis said. "This is a great moment…" As he spoke, long shadows reached out from beneath the table and took ahold of his shirt.

The other creature had somehow stuck itself to the underside of the table and had shot its upper tentacles out to pull itself onto Lewis. As Lewis punched at the thing, the other from the aquarium leapt onto Lewis's chest and knocked him to the deck. Martin stepped forward to help just as the first creature skittered on thick crustacean legs, further up Lewis's body and stopped at his neck. Lewis screamed and flailed at it, but his hands bounced off the hard shell. The creature reared up, showing a mouth like a Venus Flytrap, with long rows of thin, needle-like teeth. It clamped down on Lewis's throat, teeth sinking in deep as blood began to seep out. It kept closing, until both sides nearly met in the middle. Martin tried to kick the beast to stop it, only to be blocked by the other one, which began moving in Martin's direction.

Martin turned to run just in time to see Rina come into the room with a fire axe from the corridor. She shoved Martin out and swung the axe like a golf club at the creature. The pointed end connected, but glanced off the hard hide of the advancing monster. It was enough to send it backward though, and possibly stall it a moment. Martin left the room, looking back just in time to see the creature sever Lewis's head from his body.

Rina retreated and slammed the portal. She turned the outer latches, sealing the room shut. She leaned her back against the wall across from the lab and held onto the axe.

Martin fell to his knees and vomited.

21

The team dropped through the calm sea, using an anchor line with decompression stops marked with bright red ribbons at the appropriate intervals. It was weird not to be able to talk to each other. Usually the Suvari brothers would have made six fart jokes by the first marker. But now they had to give thumbs up, or nod or point when they wanted to convey something. But it was not so much of an inconvenience once they approached the cave with the *Cudgel* in it. Cass could feel her heart race as they approached it. Even in the low light of the individual flashlights and glow sticks, it was majestic, even though it was hard to see. Having watched the video feed didn't help her fully make out the lines of the vehicle, it was so covered with coral and other plant life.

The group stayed close together, exploring as a unit, so as not to lose one another. They got close to the robot's chest and started moving up toward the exposed viewport in the head.

Cass looked up close at the plants and coral that the others had mentioned, as well as the hard rock specimens that had been brought back to the *Adamant*. The closer she got, the more a strange network exposed itself. There were thin, almost threadlike lines that ran among the plants, connecting some of the larger bits. Cass looked up and saw the web of lines continued up toward the top and then back down toward the legs. She motioned for Ozzie to come look, but he was too interested in moving further up the thing to come back and see what she was waving about.

She followed, not wanting to be left alone, mostly out of fear of losing sight of the others. As she brought up the rear of the ascending group, she heard a high squeal in her headset. "Hello?" she said.

There was a chorus of greetings that she recognized as the rest of the divers coming on line in her headset. "Everyone have comm signal now?" Takis asked. Each of the divers checked in, indicating the affirmative. "*Adamant*, are you online?"

Ozzie tried too. "Come in *Adamant*, Martin? Ben? Rina?" He looked around at the divers with a look of semi-concern. "Anyone?"

"Probably beer O'clock," Jakob said. "Everything likely came on at the same time back on the boat and they have to deal with figuring out what to do first. They might not even realize the radio has come on line."

Ozzie's voice came next. "Let's check the cockpit again, see if we can get in."

"We tried that, and we're not supposed to go in anyway." Cass felt like a school ma'am, repeatedly telling the kids to stay out of trouble. She was afraid it was going to blow her cover before it was time, and made a note to tone it down. If communications were working in their helmets, maybe she could get a call out to Kemp and get the whole thing over with when she got back topside.

They stared into the forward portal of the *Cudgel* as if they could see inside. The portal was tinted a light red that allowed the *Cudgel's* crew to not be seen from the outside anyway, but Caroline and Jakob swore they saw shapes inside. Cass had been briefed, like all the other baby-sitters that the NIA had planted with salvage crews, in just about every aspect of the *Cudgel*'s capabilities. She had memorized all the weapons, flight stats, limitations, entry points, emergency capabilities, dangers, failings and crew biographies. For a time, they thought one or more of the crew had defected to the Liberated Territories and taken the *Cudgel* with them. The government surveilled the crews' families and friends, waiting for some sign of communications to back that theory up, but none materialized. They never gave up that possibility, but the idea that it was lost at sea always stayed at the forefront of the investigation.

"I'm going to check the *Cudgel*'s storm moorings," Cass said. "I have a hunch that's what has it stuck here. Someone want to come with me?" Jakob responded, and together they moved down the machine's right arm. They followed it to the wrist and stopped, where Cass pulled her dive knife and carefully began to clear the undersea life from around it. The arm was as wide as the length of a tractor-trailer truck and she needed to clear a path to where the truck met the rock wall. She pried a few of the strange coral pieces away and set them on the arm, but as she kept going, it was obvious that the things were thicker where she believed the *Cudgel*'s hurricane moors were imbedded in the rock.

"We have about five more minutes until we need to head back, just to be safe." Ozzie's voice came through the headphones. "We need to start decompressing."

Cass looked at her gauge to mark the time.

"What can I do?" Jakob asked.

"Come over and pry some of these away from the other side of the wrist, right in here." Cass pointed around where the rod and anchor should be, and Jakob dug in, though not quite as gently as Cass hoped.

"Is this what we're trying to find?" Jakob called Cass over. He had uncovered the thick bar that anchored the machine to the rock. Cass knew that the *Cudgel* had been given the capacity to aid in the event of disasters, in addition to their war-time duties. In case a storm got too intense, they had the ability to use these bars to anchor in their bases, or, if they were caught out in the storm, they could extend the bars into the ground, or solid rock to keep them from becoming victims of the storms themselves. Anchored correctly, they could withstand winds of three hundred miles per hour. Each of the appendages had storm anchors; there were two in the torso, and one in the back of the head.

But here, the rod was deteriorated. The middle of it was almost completely worn through.

"What the hell happened to that?" Jakob asked. "Did it just rust down here? I mean it's been underwater for over a decade."

She wanted to tell him it was highly unlikely—the *Cudgel* was made to never rust, with alloys that could withstand anything nature could throw at it. Something had disintegrated the rod, a two foot thick anchor rod that never rusts and Cass had no idea what it was.

"One minute to rendezvous at the mouth of the cave," Ozzie said.

Cass looked over at the things she'd removed from the wrist. They seemed slightly different from the ones that had been brought aboard the *Adamant*, these had a dark blue streak up the flexible fin on top. In fact, all of the creatures around the anchor point had the same coloring. She approached the pile they'd made of the creatures. Was it possible these things were secreting some sort of acid or solvent that was corroding the bars?

"Time to go," Jakob said. "They're gathering."

"I can't figure this out. The whole situation is just fucked up."

"No shit," Jakob said. "But we need to leave before we run out of air."

She knew it was true, but a few more moments to check out the rest of the storm anchors would reassure her somehow.

A crackle in her headphone hurt Cass's ears and a voice came through just as loud. "Can you hear me?" It was Rina. "Lewis is dead. Those creatures attacked us and killed him. We have them trapped in the lab."

"What?" Caroline shouted.

The others headed for the anchor line to head back up, but Cass turned as a new sound caught her attention. It was a loud thumping sound, that got louder as it went on for two, three, four times. Each time it happened, a handful of the creatures fell off the arm of the *Cudgel*. She looked up at the cave entrance and saw the tiny creatures that had been waving with the tide had begun to quickly recede into the rock around them.

"Let's go, Cass," Ozzie said.

She stared at the *Cudgel*, unable to look back at the group. She could see the machine's body bow out slightly with each thud. The fifth thud turned into a rumble as the arm she'd just been examining came loose from the wall and swung out. There was another surge, and the leg and waist on that side also suddenly broke loose sending the machine outward, held fast only by the rods on the other side of its body.

The group turned then, toward Cass and the calamity that was unfolding behind them.

22

The *Cudgel* exploded outward, as though it was on hinges; the left portion of the machine was still attached to the rocks, the right swung free. Rocks, debris and the bubbles of trapped air floated freely through the water in the space where the *Cudgel* had been.

Static filled Cass's earbuds as she caught bits of voices from Jakob and Ozzie, but the set went dead again. She looked over to make sure the group was still safe, they looked shocked and frightened, but they hadn't been harmed by any debris that flew out with the *Cudgel*.

When she looked back, she could finally see what was behind the long-lost giant machine—a long but thin crevice, maybe twenty-five foot wide, by one hundred foot tall, which the *Cudgel* had managed to completely cover with its thick metallic frame. As Cass stared, some of the darkness of the crevice began to leak out. At first, it looked like only a shadow, but soon more shadows began to slither out like fat octopus tentacles, more and more came, squeezing themselves out until the mouth of the opening was filled with twitching, writhing darkness.

The rest of the divers began swimming toward the anchor line, with only Jakob hanging back to try to pull Cass along. She grabbed his arm and braced herself as the appendages fell along the edge, and wrapped themselves around outcroppings and jagged protrusions. Once they'd found something to hold onto, a blob emerged from the center, slowly getting larger as more of it came out. Soon, the creature pulled itself free and out into the cave entrance, bumping and jostling the *Cudgel* like it was nothing. Once it had spilled out, it got larger, inflating itself to a size that rivaled the *Cudgel* itself. This patch of writhing darkness moved forward toward the minimal light that filtered down from above. The light was enough to bring the thing's features into better focus for Cass. It seemed smooth and dark along the tentacles, but its body was covered in long thin strands of white fibers, the anemones that had been poking out on top of the rocks, in places, it was covered with thick patches of the coral-like lumps like the ones they'd taken back to the *Adamant*. Cass felt light-headed as her mind tried to make sense of what she was seeing.

The creature stopped and rested on the ocean floor, stretching and expanding, absorbing more coral and rock from the cave. The tentacles extended and the thing rose until it appeared that it was nearly as tall as the *Cudgel*. A head became evident as it moved its legs to keep stationary in the sea. The body was similar in shape to a walrus, but instead of flippers, the entire lower half seemed to consist of thick tendrils that reached out in all directions. The smooth, bulbous head had enormous black eyes like an octopus, that allowed it an incredible field of vision on the front and sides. A mouth opened and closed, partially obscured by smaller tentacles and tusk-like protrusions on either side.

It slowly made its way forward to leave the cave, and the strange dizzying sensation left Cass's mind and she dragged Jakob in the opposite direction of their crewmates, afraid cutting directly in front of the thing would only draw attention to themselves. Instead she and Jakob swam to the edge of the cave and did their best to stay out of sight. It moved on, ignoring the others as well. It swam like a squid, propelling itself ahead with the help of the tentacles and the relatively thin shape it had made itself into. It took a few slow strokes, seemingly getting itself acclimated to the open space again, before it suddenly took a few heavy strokes and jetted into the distance and quickly out of sight in the darkness.

Cass motioned for Jakob to accompany her back over to their crew and he sluggishly followed. Takis and Ozzie's faces were both frozen in shock and surprise-eyes wide within their facemasks-moving their bodies only to keep themselves buoyant. Jakob lifted his gauge and pointed at the needle in the red zone that indicated he, and everyone else, was dangerously low on air. The group moved together to make it to the anchor rope, and they held hands to make sure no one made a frantic swim to the surface that would surely give them the bends or worse. They surrounded the rope in a circle and ascended to each level. At the halfway point, Takis motioned to his brother and dropped his own regulator to his side. For the rest of the way up, the brothers shared Ozzie's mouthpiece, drawing air only from what was left in Ozzie's tank.

They finally reached the surface and dropped their mouthpieces to breathe fresh air, and to scream in horror.

"What the fuck just happened?" Caroline said.

"God damn, that thing was bigger than a fucking whale. I've never seen anything like it," Takis said.

"Bigger than a Goddam whale," Ozzie whispered. "What the fuck was it?"

Cass started swimming toward the nearby ladders to get back onto the *Adamant*. As freaked out as she was about what they'd seen, Martin was in danger as well. "We need to make sure everyone else is okay." She slid off her fins, and dropped her tank and vest on the deck and stepped into her deck shoes as she got to the ladder to the upper decks. She could see Jakob stepping onto the bottom rung as she reached the top. "Rina?" Cass made her way to the control room first, and found no one there. She nearly slammed into Martin as she left the room. "You're okay?"

"Me? What the hell happened to you guys down there?" Martin asked.

"You first. Where is Rina? Is she safe?"

"Yes. She's in the kitchen, sitting down. Shaken up, but who isn't?" Martin started walking toward the ladder from the diver's platform to check on everyone else.

"We're... I'm..." Cass had trouble explaining how she felt, and just what happened. Luckily Jakob was more eloquent.

"Fuck," Jakob said. He grabbed Martin by the shoulders and held him fast. "I mean, seriously... Fuck." He let go and moved toward the kitchen.

The rest of the divers came filing up and headed straight for the kitchen, passing Martin without a word. By the time Cass met up with all of them, everyone had a drink, or a bottle in their hands.

"What happened?" Martin asked once some time had passed and everyone had stopped breathing heavily.

"The *Cudgel* was blocking something. Had it trapped. And whatever that thing was just escaped," Ozzie said. "It was massive. I can't even explain it..."

"But it was nearly as tall as the *Cudgel* and much more massive. And it wasn't something I fully understood," Takis added.

"Seriously? How did it get into and out of that small hole?" Jakob didn't wait for an answer, just chugged his beer and pulled another out of the carton.

"I don't understand," Martin said.

Cass tried to find a way to explain that he probably wouldn't understand, couldn't understand until he saw it. Up to that point, it would only be a strange fish story that someone told him. "I was frozen in fear that this thing might look my way."

"Did it have eyes?" Takis asked. "I didn't see eyes."

Cass was panicked to the point that she couldn't remember eyes either, but she could remember feeling the thing gazing around the area and getting its bearings. Maybe it did have eyes, she just couldn't see them. "I can't imagine what that was."

"I don't want to imagine."

Caroline had been silent, and refused anything to drink. "Lewis? You said that those smaller things killed him?"

"I'm afraid so," Martin said.

"Where is he? I want to see him," Caroline said.

"You can't do that. We locked the lab doors to keep the things trapped. His body is in with them."

"I have to see him. I can learn about these things from him. I can help with everything. You just have to let me see him and help him." She reached for a glass of water, but her shaking hands wouldn't let her pick it up. "I can help."

"We can't get him out without facing those things again," Rina said. She stood apart from everyone else.

"So how do we get help?" Cass looked around at the ship and found the lights were out again, and it was getting darker outside. "The radios?"

"Out since we lost contact with you," Martin said.

Before anyone could continue, there was a sound outside like a massive wave in the distance and they all moved out onto the deck to see the calamity. All they would need was a sudden rogue wave to hit the ship to add to their problems. On the horizon, a massive shadow broke the surface, and continued to show the length of its body as it moved on and fell below the waves. The lighting was too poor to make out details, but the thing's size was evident. As it disappeared under the sea, it was outlined in a sudden flash of blue, like lightning, and then it was gone.

"I take it that was your creature?" It wasn't a question for anyone standing nearby, it sounded to Cass more like a question Martin was asking himself or even possibly the sea itself.

"We're fucked. Even if we bring the engines back online, we won't have any electronics until the solar collectors get to work in the morning," Takis said. "What if that thing comes back and attacks us?"

Jakob pulled a flashlight from his back pocket. "I got the generator working last time. I can probably get it going again. That's some light, at least. I pull the plug on any parts of the ship we don't use, and that should help everyone's quarters and the navigation, hopefully."

"Fuck. Did you see that thing? Do you think this old cargo ship will get away from it? Seriously? I mean, excuse my language, but *fuck*." Takis ran his hands through his scraggly long hair.

"The way it took off, I'd say it wanted to get out of here," Cass said. "What about the other things in the lab? Are you sure they're not going to get out?"

"I just saw a creature with tentacles as large as a skyscraper," Martin said. "Forgive me if I'm not positive of a whole lot right now."

"Do you have any guns?" Cass wasn't quite sure she could blow her cover just now by grabbing her own gun, seeing as she was all alone with the crew. Certainly she wouldn't have any backup. But she also considered that her gun could make a difference if they got in a fight with anyone or anything.

"Yes."

"How many? What kind?" Cass asked

"I always have a shotgun and a revolver on board, but after the pirate attack, I had Ben bring more with the *Alba Varden*," Martin said.

"Anything that wasn't used in World War One?" Jakob asked.

23

A new sound began to repeat and for a moment, Linden thought it was more from the computer, but realized after a moment that it was just his phone. The caller I.D. showed Forester was calling. "Yeah Lou?"

"Hey, this might be a temporary thing, but our radar has lost track of the *Adamant*," Lou said. "Thought you should know right away."

"Lost contact? Do we have a satellite watching the area yet?"

"Not yet."

Linden thought about it a moment. It wasn't uncommon for radar to lose contact during a storm, a solar flare, or other problems. "Weather?"

"Clear as a bell from what we can see."

He looked at Holli, who was already standing to leave. "Okay, I'll be back in a few." He hung up and replaced the phone in his pocket. They'd decided to get coffee at the shop nearest their office building to review the latest round of data they'd pulled. "Do you want a coffee to take back to the office? A scone, something?"

"I'm good. The extra-large should hold me through the next hour or ten. You *can* explain what that call was all about on our way back." Holli grabbed her coffee and started walking.

On the way out the door, Linden dropped five dollars in the tip jar at the counter. When he'd caught up with Holli he started to explain the situation as best he could. The more he'd thought about it, his department was huge after the war, but now it was literally just Lou and himself, along with a receptionist and... well, that was it. Surely the government wouldn't mind if the department commandeered a key asset for an important lead in the case...

"See, we may have finally found the *Cudgel*, but the people who located it? They just went missing."

"Jesus. When you get a lead, you get a lead."

Together they crossed in the middle of the street, dodging traffic, other pedestrians, and immense puddles. The previous night's rain had made most of the area a wet nightmare. Linden wondered if the storms had somehow messed with the sensors locally and caused them to lose track of the *Adamant*.

They headed upstairs, stopping at Linden's floor. He noticed Holli had practically chugged the tall coffee she'd brought with her. "Late night?"

"Every night is a late night. We've been busy figuring out some recordings from a gunfight on the African coast between..." She looked at Linden with a sudden realization. "Yes, late night."

He gauged her look as an indication that he wasn't supposed to know the details and didn't ask any follow up questions.

They dashed to Lou's office, swiping their badges at every door.

Linden and Holli looked over Lou's shoulders as he brought up all the information he could on his computer screen.

"We could go in the conference room. No one is in there," Lou said. "I mean, all that equipment and just us to use it. Seems like a waste." He waited for the satellite info to download. "No? Okay. We'll stay in my office with you both breathing your coffee breath on me."

"Sorry," Linden said.

"No, it's fine. I didn't want anything. Thanks for asking." The video came up on the screen and Lou pointed with his pen. "See there they are. They're pretty much all alone, except for this…" He tapped another ship on the radar image. "It's about fifty miles southeast of your crew."

"What direction is the other ship headed?"

"It wasn't. It was stationary," Lou said. "Also, we have that battle group that helped the *Adamant* with their pirate problem still on station just outside of the *Adamant's* radar range to the east."

It was a couple of hours away, but those ships could move in to assist if they were needed. Linden crossed his arms and stared at the screen. "Okay. What next?"

The video went into motion. "Nothing unusual, until just about ten p.m. our time. Watch."

The image showed the two ships sitting in the positions that they started in. After a few seconds, the *Adamant* disappeared from the screen, only to reappear a second later. "That's it?" Linden asked.

"Wait."

The ship disappeared from the screen twice more, then the third time, it stayed gone, and didn't come back on the video. "This was taken earlier in the day. They are off of radar for a total of three hours."

"But they're back now?" Holli asked.

Lou looked up at Linden quizzically. "You can trust her. We all work in the same building," Linden said.

"Just not the same floor."

"Now you're worried about security? Halfway through the stash of secret info?" Holli laughed.

"You were quiet. I forgot you were there," Lou said. "Yes they came back on, but watch what happens. They reappear just as the other ship disappears." He played the video a little further and barely a moment goes by before the *Adamant* comes back onto the screen before the other ship goes off it. "And no, that one hasn't come back on radar yet."

"No communications?" Holli asked.

"None."

"Shit." Linden pulled his phone out of his pocket and thought about what calls he needed to make, and whether it was time to make them. He had no idea what Cass was dealing with there. Maybe her cover was blown and she was out of commission? The crew would be angry if they discovered she was an agent, but none of them seemed terribly violent.

"Get this together and prepare for a meeting in the conference room in an hour," Linden said. "And keep watching both ships. I want to know when it reappears."

Linden walked out of Lou's office and down the hall. He dialed his superiors and pled his case for retasking a satellite, but to no avail. They weren't budging until they had better intel. He'd heard the same crap since Cass left on this particular mission. They wouldn't pay to follow her around like a child.

He dialed one of his friends in the naval quartermaster's office. "Billy? Linden."

"Hey Linden," Billy said.

"Look, sorry to be abrupt, but I'm trying to get something done, and getting shit for help over here. Do you have any ships operating near the Aleutian Islands? *Anywhere* near there?"

There was a quick tapping of keys. "Hold on." The tapping continued. "We have a cargo shuttle that just took off from Sea Base Alpha and is headed to that general vicinity. Why?"

"Well, we're out of contact with a couple of ships and just want to see if there's an explanation or if something's gone wrong. If that shuttle could just do a fly-by, anything, and verify they're okay while we're sorting it out? We're working on sending our own craft out."

"I take it you want me to contact you directly with any news?" Billy asked.

"That would be correct," Linden said. "Thanks, I will buy you a bottle of anything you want next time I see you."

"Not the cheap shit this time."

"No."

"And make it a case." Billy hung up.

Linden turned to Holli. "So, we have someone doing a quick flyover to see what's what. Then we'll see where to go from there."

The men's room door opened and a tall man with a bad mustache came out. "Holli? Where have you been? I thought you left for lunch like..." He checked his watch carefully. "Like two hours ago."

"My fault. You must be Holli's section manager. We haven't met; I'm Linden Kemp, the director of the project down the hall. I'm so sorry.

Holli was helping analyze something for us and I kept her too long." Linden held his hand out to shake the manager's hand and waited.

"Linden, this is my manager, Gary Matthews."

"You're the director of that project?" Gary asked. "I wasn't aware that anyone still worked in those offices. In fact, I put in a request to annex a good portion of that space just last week."

"Well, I'm sorry." Linden smiled and shrugged, finally dropping his hand. "We're still there."

Gary continued to walk back to his offices. "That's strange; they said it probably wouldn't be a problem to get the space we needed."

"Want to transfer to my team?" It was directed at Holli—a none-too-thought-out question that spilled from his mouth before he could stop it.

Holli patted him on the shoulder and started walking after her boss. "You don't have a team." They got in the lift and disappeared.

It took a moment for Linden to accept that she was right. "Well, Gary, if you didn't think anyone worked on this floor, why were you using our bathrooms? Gross."

24

Martin followed Jakob down toward the engine room with a flashlight in one hand and his revolver in the other. His companion was similarly equipped, except his handgun was a brand-new Ruger forty-five with Taser under-attachment and a twenty-two round clip. It was big, and it was heavy, which is why Martin didn't want to carry it. For Jakob, however, it wasn't much of a problem. The handgun was more common with law enforcement and military police, as it allowed for both lethal and non-lethal means for dealing with an attacker.

There were emergency lights all over the interior, but they were dim. It was hard for Martin to decide if the lights were defective, feeling the effects of the strange sudden power outages, or if they were doing their job exactly right. They'd literally never been used in the whole time Martin had owned the *Adamant*. He did know that the shadows they cast scared the bejesus out of him.

"Down the corridor and left at the junction," Jakob said.

"Just keep leading. I don't need directions."

"Unless something happens to me. Hell, it's confusing in the dark down here," Jakob said.

It wasn't reassuring to Martin. He had volunteered for this so he didn't have to stay so close to the hysterical Caroline above decks. He felt for her, she'd been working with Lewis for years, but if he had to be near her now, he'd lose control of his own shit and he didn't want to do that in front of the whole crew. "Fine. Don't let something happen to you."

"It isn't an option I was considering."

They came to the junction and turned left, as Jakob had said. He opened the hatch to the engine room and entered. Jakob reached up and grabbed two head lanterns from a hook near the door and gave one to Martin. They then proceeded down the short set of stairs to the generator on the other side of the room. "Man, it's quiet down here. Usually you can't hear yourself think in this area because the engine is going full blast. Now you just hear those waves against the hull," Jakob said.

Martin wasn't in the mood for an existential analysis of their current situation. He wanted to get the engines roaring, and sail off in the opposite direction of the beast they just saw in the fading light of day. "What do you need me to do?"

"Well, when you had them retrofit this old thing, they didn't do the best job of marrying the old and new tech. So you need to flip that switch..." Jakob pointed his light at a yellow switch in a junction box on the far wall. "Right there." He turned back to the generator and began hand-cranking a dial on the top of it.

"Now?" Martin put his hand on the switch.

Jakob jumped away from the generator. "No! Not yet. Waitwaitwait."

"Jesus, I wasn't going to flip it." Martin held his hands up as if he were being arrested.

Jakob turned back to the generator and shined his light into the mechanism. "I'll tell you when."

It smelled of oil and the fuel mixture that ran the generator, and some other terrible thing that Martin couldn't place. It was filthy, he could tell that, even in the pitiful light. "You're right, this place is a shithole."

"I never said that. Not exactly," Jakob grunted as he worked at the machine.

"Maybe if I'd put some money into it, we wouldn't be in this situation. You were right. I need to be a little freer with the money from time to time."

Jakob stopped what he was doing and turned to look at his boss. "Did you just talk about spending money? Are you okay? Are you still in shock?"

Martin tried to smile, but the situation weighed too heavy on him.

"We'll get out of this. Maybe we'll head for Tokyo and ride out this whole thing." Jakob turned back to the generator. "We'll make it."

The words were hollow for Martin. He couldn't see the bright side, not after one of his crew was dead. He sighed and leaned against a support beam. He was about to offer to help again, when a ticking sound caught his attention. At first he was concerned that the ship or some pipe was leaking and he was hearing a drip from somewhere. He should have let Rina come down. She knew electronics, so maybe she also knew plumbing. He called himself an idiot for making that equation and took a step toward the sound of the leak. He bent down to check a nearby pipe which he was unfamiliar with. As he did, the dim glow from the emergency lighting in the outer corridor dimmed further. He admonished himself again for being so cheap, but as he turned, he realized the light was being blocked by one of the creatures from the lab coming between him and the light. He could see its legs lifting and falling on the deck as it moved and made the noise he was looking for.

"Martin? Go ahead and flip the switch," Jakob said.

Martin went hoarse, but managed to whisper a reply. "The door. Look up at the door."

Jakob whirled and saw the thing as well; it had spread itself out, extending its legs to their full length. It was easily four feet tall as it danced back and forth like a crab in the tide. Martin raised his gun and aimed. "Why isn't it attacking us? It's just moving back and forth for some reason." To Martin it looked like a kid that had to pee, dancing around until it found a bathroom.

"I don't think it can make it down those stairs. They're narrow and steep, not like the stairs from the next level," Jakob said.

"A monster whose weakness is stairs? That's a pitch for the lamest horror movie ever." Martin took a deep breath, feeling slightly better. "We should probably still shoot it, right?"

Jakob looked like he was considering it when the creature moved back into the corridor.

"*You better run away,*" Martin mumbled.

"We need to warn…" Before Jakob could finish, the creature came charging back into the room and, as it got to the stairs in question, it threw itself awkwardly over the railing that blocked it. It tumbled when it hit the deck and rolled itself into a ball, pulling its legs back inside.

"Holy shit." Martin backed up and looked at Jakob. "Holy shit. Is there another way out of this room?"

Jakob shook his head no.

The creature came to a halt and unrolled itself. It looked like a turtle, trying to right itself and get back on its feet, but having a terrible time of it. The thing's six long legs swung about in the air, trying to twist and push off the deck to turn over. The long tentacle-like stalks on its head were smashed, pinned to the deck, but they were writhing, trying to help the effort. The thing's underside, now fully visible, consisted mostly of a large mouth surrounded by thick black bristly hairs. As it struggled, it let out a cry and exposed the rows of thin teeth as it opened its jaws.

Martin saw what he was afraid was his only chance fading before his eyes. He moved closer and fired his revolver straight into the beast's open mouth until the gun ran out of ammunition, then he moved back. The creature was flailing and shaking, moving itself in a widening circle, all the while letting out a terrible wail. One of the long, whipping legs caught Martin across the chest, and he shouted in his own pain.

He was pulled back by Jakob, and they both hid themselves behind the backup generator for safety. Martin pulled his hands from his chest to see a trail of blood suddenly pouring from beneath his torn shirt. The look of concern on Jakob's face somehow made the pain even worse.

With a wet gurgle, the thing stopped moving and Jakob approached it with his own gun drawn. He walked around it. He kicked it with the toe of his boot.

"Jesus, get something and stab it or something if you're not sure if it's dead, don't poke at it," Martin said.

Jakob backed up to a work bench and pulled a pry bar off. He lifted it over his head and brought it down on the mouth, causing a gross, but satisfying, crunch. For good measure he did it again, but the crunch was slightly wetter. He set the prybar down and returned to Martin. "How bad is it?"

Martin took a deep breath and assessed his condition. It hurt. "I'm going to be okay."

"You're losing a lot of blood."

"I'm going to be okay." It was a mantra now, more for himself than Jakob. "We just have to get me upstairs and get this wrapped up, that's all. I'm going to be okay." Jakob helped him stand. "What we need to do to get this fucking ship lit up again?"

Jakob helped Martin to one of the metal beams and pointed to the fat switch to his right. "Just push that up when I tell you and we should be able to change over to the generator. The additional wave collectors will deploy and help charge overnight."

"Got it."

"We were almost ready to go before we got interrupted, just give me a second." Jakob disappeared, but Martin could still hear him tinkering. "Seriously, when we get home, *I'll* give you the money to upgrade this ship. Even if I need to take out a loan."

"I have money."

Something clanged to the floor. "You don't use it though. Christ some of these parts are decades old. It costs more to repair than buy a new one at this point." Jakob stood back up, and wiped his hands.

"Always after me to buy new stuff. I like the old stuff." Martin was getting a little dizzy as he spoke.

"Okay. On three?"

Martin nodded.

"One…"

Martin wondered why couldn't just do it. He was afraid he might not make it to three."

"Two…" Jakob put his hand on a similar switch on top of the generator. "Three…"

They both moved as one, and the emergency lighting flickered as the dual generators slowly creaked to life. The petrol-fueled portion would get the lights and whatnot working in a few minutes, while the secondary generator, would slowly gather energy by harnessing the tide and the currents as they flowed along beneath and next to the boat, which would build up a reserve.

"That's got it. The damn thing's moving again." Jakob handed Martin his gun and picked up the pry bar. They carefully climbed the stairs, and when they got to the top, Jakob pulled a flannel shirt from the same place he took the head lamps. He took a moment to ball it up and hand it to Martin. "Keep pressure on it," he said. "Isn't that what they always tell you? Keep pressure on it to stop the bleeding?"

"Yeah. I think that's what they say." Martin did as his friend said. It hurt to do, but he hoped it would help in some way.

As they moved to the hatch, the sound of gunfire and shouting emanated from the corridor around the corner.

"Jesus. We can't catch a break, can we?" Martin pressed harder on the shirt and hoped for the best.

25

In her room, Cass stared at the closet for a moment. "Fuck it," she said. She opened the door and pulled out the gun and tucked it in the waist of her jeans. She pulled a jacket on to cover it. As she left, she remembered she had plugged her sat phone in on the bed to charge. She glanced and noticed it was still dead.

She left the cabin and moved toward the deck where nearly everyone else had gathered and lit candles for illumination. "Have Jakob and Martin come back yet?"

"Haven't seen them," Takis said. "And the beer is already warm."

"You're thinking about beer, now?" Cass walked over to the nearest chair and sat tentatively.

"There are other things that I'd rather not think about right now, so I'm thinking about beer. I'm actually trying to catalog beers in my head from best to worst," Takis said. "You know, rather than thinking about whatever that was."

Ozzie and Rina were lying on lounge chairs, reclined all the way back and looking up at stars. Between them, Rina's music player was on a towel, and each of them had an earbud in one ear. As Cass neared, she could hear music emanating from them. "Wait, you have power for that thing? How?"

Rina raised her sunglasses and looked up at Cass. "I have a mini solar charger for it. It managed to catch some of the last rays of the day. It'll probably conk out any second."

Cass nearly drooled at the idea of having a power source, and kicked herself for not bringing a solar charger or planning ahead.

A sound on the deck above the control room drew Cass's attention and when she looked up, she saw Ben negotiating his wheelchair around the thin walkway. He was practiced at it for sure, he'd been involved with the ship for years, but now he seemed to have difficulty. He was looking out to the sea and not at the area in front of him.

"How long's he been up there?" She looked to Takis for an answer, but the sounds of gunfire below decks silenced him. "Martin?" Cass turned and ran for the corridor that led to the stairs down to the engine room, with the others right behind.

As they ran down the dimly lit hall, some movement ahead made Cass stop and hold the others up as well. The hatch to the lab was open and there was something lying in the doorframe, half in, half out.

"Caroline?" Rina ran forward to check on her, but was stopped by Ozzie.

"Jesus, stop. We don't know where those things are," Ozzie said.

They found out quickly as one of the creatures came skittering around the corner at the end of the hall. It rocked itself back and forth, swaying with the light roll of the ship on the waves. The long stalks on the top of the thing seemed to twitch as they pointed to Cass and the others. Cass thought about their surroundings and examined the group's options; the lab door was open, they could jump in there, but they didn't know where the second creature was; they could back out the way they came, but there was no telling if they'd make it, and that would probably send the creature down toward Martin and Jakob; Cass could pull her gun and see what happened.

She abruptly decided on the last idea when the creature began to run forward on its long boney legs, directly at the crew. With one hand, she yanked Takis behind her, and drew the gun with the other. She brought her hands together and fired two shots in rapid succession, both of which hit the thing in the center of the body and bounced off, ricocheting into the wall and then down the hall. The creature flinched and slowed.

"Shiiiit," Takis said, though it was hard to tell if he was dismayed at the ineffectual shots, or shocked to see Cass pull a gun and shoot like she did.

The body resembled hardened lava at this point, but the crab-like legs were much thinner, so Cass aimed for one as the beast in front of her moved back and forth in a semi-circle, closing in a little more cautiously this time. When it paused, she aimed at one of the joints or knees on its six legs and fired again, this time her bullets shattered a part of the leg, causing it to fall over due to the sudden imbalance. It panicked and flailed trying to right itself, hitting against the bulkhead before standing again. It backed up to the doorway to the stairs. After shaking itself, it retracted its stalks and reared up, letting out a high-pitched screech that made Cass flinch.

"Let's go, Cass," Rina said.

Cass looked back quickly to see the others had already made it outside. The creature saw it too and began to charge as best as it could with the wounded leg. Ozzie and Takis yanked Cass out with them and slammed the portal shut and cranked the lock. A second later, there was a clanging sound as the beast rammed the door. And then another, louder clang as it tried again.

Ozzie put his back to the door and slid down until his butt hit the deck.

"How do we get to Martin and Jakob? How do we help them?" Rina asked.

Cass checked her gun, making sure she'd controlled her shots and not wasted rounds with panic fire. "There has to be another way to get to them," she said.

"No," Takis said as he sat down next to his brother. There was another bash on the door and he leaned away, startled. *"Fuck."*

26

Martin rested against the bulkhead where Jakob left him. The blood seemed to have slowed, but the shirt wrapped around his torso was nearly soaked. He was dizzy and wouldn't be standing if it weren't for the ship's beam.

Jakob peered around the corner, still holding the long, heavy pry bar with both hands. He pulled back and nodded, indicating the other creature was in the corridor. Jakob came back and helped Martin along—holding him up with one arm, carrying the pry bar in the other. "Now's our best chance. It's distracted trying to get out, and once it loses interest in that, it'll come back toward us again."

"I can barely walk, and my gun is almost empty," Martin said. "How do you expect me to help?"

"Well, I suppose you could be bait. That would be an immense help."

They got to the corner just as the creature rammed itself into the closed door again. Martin could see part of a body sticking out of the door to the lab, but couldn't make out who it was. He felt more lightheaded and slipped from Jakob's grasp. "I can't help you, we can't do it." He let himself slide to the floor.

"We have to."

"No," Martin said. "Let's go back to the engine room and lock the door. We'll be safe there until they figure this out. The others are okay as long as they don't open the door. Please, let's go." His wound began to throb and he did his best not to cry out from the pain. He watched as Jakob grabbed the pry bar with both hands and looked around the corner again. When another thud came from the end of the hall, Jakob disappeared from view, running down the corridor.

There were several footsteps and Martin pulled himself along the wall to see what was happening. He got to the corner just as Jakob got the creature. It paused as it heard the approach of footfalls on the metal floor and turned just as Jakob came to a halt, sliding the heavy bar along the floor and under the screeching creature. He pushed the bar up and pinned the thing against the door as best he could, but he appeared stymied as to how to let go and grab his pistol from his waistband without freeing the monster. The long legs clawed for Jakob, the tentacles stretched to try and make him stop his assault.

Martin pulled his revolver and aimed toward Jakob and the trapped monster. His vision blurred and he could barely tell one of them from the other. He opted to aim high, maybe startling the creature and giving Jakob the upper hand somehow. Even as the strategy started to make sense to Martin, his eyes drooped shut and his muscles relaxed. Before he passed out, he heard two shots and wondered if he'd fired them or someone else had.

27

With Jakob's help, they carefully carried Martin into the observation room and set him on a blanket on the conference table. Ozzie came in with the medical kit, and Takis brought a shitload of bandages. "The fuckin thing slashed across his chest pretty good."

"Yeah, the cut's not too deep, I can seal it up without any hand-stitching, I think. Staple gun will work just fine. He's just lost a lot of blood," Ozzie said. "We don't really have anything to give him a transfusion with." He wiped the wound with antiseptic and cleaned it as best he was able.

"What do you think?" Cass asked. "I mean, do we need to get him to a hospital?"

"That's an exceedingly good idea. Though with our power cutting in and out I don't know if anyone would come for us, or where we would go."

"We managed to get the generators going, and the engine's slowly powering up to ready." Jakob washed his hands off in the bar sink and dried them on cocktail napkins. "We just won't have much power yet."

"Radio?" Cass asked.

"No idea yet. We got distracted with all of this just after the generator got chugging."

"We better check." Cass left the room and headed for her own cabin. If the phone was plugged in and charging, she might be able to phone Linden. He needed as much of a heads up on this as he could get. She turned the sat phone on and waited for it to power. She was thrilled to see the green light as it came on and started the login procedure. After a full ninety seconds, the earpiece was filled with ringing on the other line. There was a click and silence.

"Chaperone Delta-One calling Blind Date Citadel. Come in Citadel."

The other end clicked again and Linden's voice came back. "Chaperone Delta-One this is Blind Date Citadel. Good to hear your voice. Where have you been?"

"Long story. Things got out of hand here in a hurry. We have two crew member fatalities and Martin is injured." Cass couldn't remember being happier to hear a voice on the phone before.

"What? Pirates again? What's the nature of the casualties?"

She took a breath and started telling the story, starting with the power outages and the communications difficulties. She continued to explain about finding the *Cudgel* and the aftermath. "Something escaped.

It looked like the *Cudgel* had it trapped and somehow it got out when we arrived."

"Wait. What got out? What do you mean something got out? Chaperone Delta One, please repeat," Linden said.

"There was an enormous creature that burst from a crevice behind the *Cudgel*, knocking the *Cudgel* partially free. It was black and greyish, protuberances…"

"Protuberances?"

"Uh… tentacles. Its main means of locomotion seem to be tentacles that it uses like an octopus or squid." Saying the whole thing out loud made Cass feel stupid, it sounded ridiculous, but it was what it was, and if anyone would believe her, it was Linden.

"I…" The line was overcome with static for a second. "I see."

"Honestly Blind Date, I know what it sounds like…"

"You do? Good…" Linden paused and Cass was afraid the line had kicked them off. "Anything else?"

"There are these sort-of coral-covered smaller specimens that fell off of the larger creature. They sprout legs and smaller tentacles," Cass said. "They're responsible for the casualties to our crew."

"I copy that."

"Jakob and Martin discovered that they're vulnerable on their undersides, in or near their mouths."

"I copy that."

It wasn't common for Linden to be so short with his responses. Cass grew concerned. "Look, Blind Date. I know this is hard to believe. We've all struggled here. Believe me we have. But this creature was headed in the direction of the mainland when it left. You need to get some sort of defense going. You need some sort of plan happening. I'll send you the rest of the data and pictures we have, but they're all of the *Cudgel* and the smaller dead monsters here on board."

"I'll be waiting."

"I'll send some notes I jotted down about the encounter and my thoughts."

"I'll contact you with my analysis and thoughts ASAP." Linden was curt again.

"Blind Date, if this thing was trapped by the *Cudgel*, it was likely during the war. You know that, right?"

"I know that, Chaperone. Blind Date Citadel out." The line clicked and went dead.

It took a second for Cass to recover from the call. She couldn't figure out if Linden was under pressure on his end, or if he really didn't believe what she was saying. She clicked off the phone, went to put it away when she noticed she wasn't alone. Rina was standing in the doorway, headphones around her neck, pistol in hand. "Rina, I didn't see you there."

"I guess you didn't," Rina said.

"How much did you hear?"

"Enough to know you're working for someone else, they don't believe you, and they're not sending help." Rina left the room and ran down the hall.

Quick to grab her phone and gun, Cass followed. "Look, I'm doing whatever it takes to help Martin."

Rina stopped. "Now you are. Now. What were you doing before? Who the hell are you?"

The hall was empty and quiet for a moment and Cass caught herself trying to think of lies and covers and stories. It wasn't the time. "I... I'm an agent with the NIA. My section is tasked with finding the *Cudgel* and making sure it doesn't fall into the wrong hands."

"Why are you with this particular ship? Why us?"

"There are other agents with each of the most promising teams of searchers out there: Kingsley, Murdock, Generro. They all have someone planted. I just got lucky, I guess." Cass left and continued up the stairs toward the kitchen.

"Were you ever going to tell us?"

The answer was the same as she'd told herself time and again. "I kind of hoped we wouldn't find it and I could leave as a friend, to be honest with you." Now she had no choice. She had to tell them. And she had to explain the plan she'd thought of.

Jakob, Takis and Ozzie were sitting at the dining table, talking. Each looked beaten and exhausted. They mumbled low about options. Ozzie was the most experienced in medicine and surgery, and his tone was grave. "We won't make it to the Aleutian Islands. Not even if the *Adamant* could make it to full steam the whole way. Just too far."

"Any chance we could rig something up with one of the drones? They're big enough to carry him," Jakob said.

"Nah. Nice thought, but he wouldn't survive that, and the drone would fly out of our control range." Takis shook his head and drank some water. "We could set coordinates, but what if the thing went dead like the *Adamant* and our electronics? It would plunge into the sea with Martin onboard."

Cass waded into the group. "The radio is back up."

"That's great, but I'm not sure we can get supplies here fast enough," Ozzie said. "Has anyone tried to raise nearby ships."

"I'm with the government." Cass put it bluntly, pulled her identification from the phone case and tossed it on the table. "I was supposed to make sure no one stole the *Cudgel* or sold it off to some foreign power or any of that shit." She felt tired telling her story again. "I just called my superiors to tell them what happened here. They're not onboard with my version of everything just yet. They're looking into it." She stared around the table, not sure what they were thinking, but they didn't look thrilled with her.

"Jesus," Takis said. "Who cares? How are we going to help Martin? If none of your friends are coming, what can we do?"

Cass looked again at the skeptical faces around the table. "I have an idea."

28

When Linden entered the break room, Holli was stirring her coffee. "Don't you have your own break room on your floor?" She poured another drop of liquid sugar into her cup.

"Yes, but all of our agents are in the field, and it's really quiet down there. Plus, Lou hasn't come in yet," Linden said.

"In other words, Lou is the one who makes the coffee?"

Linden's coffee was for shit, but Lou brewed a sweet, smooth blend every morning. "I think he grinds his own beans, maybe."

Holli dumped in a few more drops. "I'm not coming over to work for you."

"I know. But I might actually need your analytic skills for this one." He looked around and lowered his voice. "I got a call from my agent on the *Adamant* and she says they found the *Cudgel*."

"That's great." Holli seemed genuinely happy for him, but not terribly shocked. "So what would you need me for?"

"Well, she also claims that they released a giant sea monster of some sort, so I might need you to confirm some sounds that vessels in the area have recorded before going dark."

Holli stuck a lid on her coffee and walked for the door. "Fucking hilarious. Thanks for thinking so highly of my skills." She walked briskly and disappeared into the office.

It was a long minute before Linden realized she'd taken the last of the coffee in the pot. He walked back to his side of the building with his empty mug and waited next to the coffee maker for Lou.

When his phone rang a few seconds later, he answered to an admiral's assistant asking, rather insistently, that Linden head for his communications room and log in to a conference-in-progress immediately. In a matter of moments he was online and waiting to be logged in for the discussion. His main screen lit up and went through protocol screens before satellite images began to appear.

"Thanks for joining us, Agent Kemp. We received your intelligence on the potential discovery of the *Cudgel A-9*." A voice came across the line. "We need to speak with you about a few of the details."

I'll bet you do, Linden thought. *Speak to me about a straightjacket and some medication, I'll bet.* "Yes, sir."

"This message says that your agent reported a large creature escaped from a cave or something when the *Cudgel* was discovered?" The voice didn't sound terribly incredulous.

"And that it disrupted power and communications?" It was another voice, a woman. "Then headed approximately due east in a straight line toward the American mainland?"

"Yes. Why?" Linden noticed they didn't ask about the *Cudgel* itself.

The screen changed slightly in front of him. As he reexamined it, he noticed Lou walk in and set a coffee on the table and sit down with his own. Linden nodded and looked up at the screen again.

"Your operative was here," the man said as a dot appeared at the location of the *Cudgel* and the *Adamant*. At oh-four-twenty, our people lost track of a naval supply drone that passed that imaginary straight line." A dot lit up on the screen with the time above it. "Two hours and thirteen minutes later, the aircraft carrier *USS Ellis* went off radar, along with two escort ships, the *Wallens* and the *Mitchell*. A drone flyby twenty-three minutes later found all three ships sinking."

"Were there survivors?"

"Yes," the woman said. "And they all talked about the power going out, communications disruptions and a giant sea monster."

Linden sat staring at the map and bouncing the words around in his head. The same sort of details that Cass had used.

"And since we've sent a battle group out toward that position, we thought it prudent to ask if you had anything to add to this report."

"I gave you a full accounting of what our agent told us, I don't know..."

"You could start by telling us what it is."

Linden looked at Lou and shrugged. "No idea."

"None?" It was the woman again, and she sounded shocked that Linden hadn't formed a hypothesis.

"Our agent reminded me that this all happened during the war, so maybe it could be manufactured by the RLT during the war, but that doesn't..."

"Great. That's a place to start. Find any living scientists with the RLT and find out if they know anything. And be quick about it. That battle group will make contact in a few hours. We can use all the help we can get," the man said. There was discussion between the two on the other end and then the line clicked off.

There was a deep sigh and then Lou laughed. "Find a living scientist? Uhhh... I think there are maybe four big name scientists from the war that are still around, right? The others were killed in bombings, disappeared, killed themselves."

"Two. One was executed last year and another died in prison of old age," Linden said. "So that leaves two. One of the top dogs, a guy named Nicholai Androvney, and a low end tech named Tsui."

"And which do you think we should visit?"

Linden was sure that one of the top guys in the RLT science division wouldn't roll over too easily, but the little guy was probably privy to some good stuff, even if he wasn't directly involved. "Get your shit; we're off to prison to meet the low-life tech guy."

They grabbed their coats and other necessities and made for the elevator. Standing next to the buttons was Holli. She did not look happy.

"Hey, we were just leaving," Linden said. "I won't get in your way for a while."

"No shit." She stared at Linden.

Lou pushed the down button, and they all stared at each other until it opened. The trio stepped in and Linden pushed the ground floor. "What floor can I push for you?"

Holli's frown increased. "Let's just stop. I know you got me transferred to your team for this fuckery."

Lou and Linden looked at each other. "What are you talking about? We literally just got off of the line with the admiral and he didn't say a damn thing about bringing you along." Linden was wondering if Holli was carrying a weapon, because he felt wildly unsafe when she stared at him.

"Don't bullshit me."

"No bullshit," Lou said.

It was quiet except for the ding of the elevator passing floor after floor.

29

They finished putting on their gear and sat on the edge of the dive platform.

"The *Cudgel* has a medical bay. They gave out supplies in emergencies and were well stocked with durable goods," Cass said.

"But it's been a decade; nothing is going to still be viable." Ozzie kept putting on his fins despite his own objection. "Ten years, Cass."

"The war was the dawn of the HBOC's. Basically, powdered blood that just needed to mix with the right reactant. It doesn't go bad. It's all there on the *Cudgel*. It'll take us an hour to get down there, find it and get back."

"Look, I know about HBOC's, I used them in the field during a number of conflicts. They weren't a solution, just a temporary fix," Ozzie said. "We didn't use them much, because they weren't always a reliable match."

"Better than waiting for help from the navy, right?" Jakob said. He looked around at the group one by one. "No, seriously. I have no idea. This is better than the navy, isn't' it? This is the play to make, right?" He looked at Cass finally.

"We have no idea who or what is going to show up for us, or when." She looked up at the window to the radio room, and assumed that Rina was still on the radio trying to get someone to come and help them. Takis told her that if help came while the rest of the group was down below, she shouldn't hesitate to let them take Martin, if they could save him.

Off the side of the boat, *Mister Punchy* bobbed on the waves. Takis had loaded the drone's hold with explosives, in case they needed to blast an area around the *Cudgel's* hatch to get in. The plan was for the group to descend with the drone, Cass controlling it manually through the proper stops on the way down. They'd use it to enter a maintenance airlock somewhere around the *Cudgel's* torso on the left-hand side. "Let's go," Cass said. "If we're going to do this, we can't dick around about it. Martin's life depends on it."

They nodded back at her one at a time, ending with Ozzie, who seemed the most reluctant. They slid on their helmets and slipped overboard. Cass swam to the drone and rechecked the controls, powering the propellers on and engaging the steering. She dove with *Mister Punchy* as soon as she was able, watching a monitor from the back of the machine. The sunlight cascading down from above made the cave a little less foreboding than it was the last time they'd come. Immediately, the team noticed the differences; all of the tiny amoebae were gone, leaving narrow shafts in the rocks and coral where they'd protruded. The black creatures that had attacked the crew were gone on both the outside and the inside of the cave. As the group neared the *Cudgel,* they found it was easier to see, the things that covered it were gone. All of it was either a part of the creature, or had been knocked loose when it escaped. As the giant robot hung askew from only the bolts on the left side, the group got a look at more than just the front portal, they got to see the whole 'head' unit which resembled an executioner's hood draped across the broad shoulders of the main body. A large rectangular protrusion jutted from the chest, and the thick legs ended in wide 'feet' with sharp angles all around.

They all swam with *Mister Punchy* until they reached the torso. Cass kept a running clock in the corner of her screen to make sure they didn't get low on oxygen. "Let's head around to the thing's port side and get cracking on this hatch." One by one, they all acknowledged and stopped gawking at the skyscraper-sized behemoth before them as best they could. This was the tough part, the part that concerned Cass: How to actually get into the *Cudgel.* It was airtight, locked down, and built to keep the crew inside safe. It had been trapped with a creature for a decade which hadn't managed to crack the hull. Cass had several security codes in the back of her head that she believed could work, though none were meant to be used specifically on the *Cudgel.* It was a guess, really. It was yet another shot in-the-dark on top of wishful thinking, with a big fat cherry of hope on top. And she hadn't told the others just how tough it could be. She also didn't tell them about her backup plan.

"We're here, Rina," Takis said.

"Copy." The answer came through the static.

Mister Punchy came to rest on the hull and clamped on with the touch of a button. Nearby, the hatch for supply load-in was certainly big enough for each of them to swim through with no problem. Once it was opened.

Ozzie pulled the kit from the drone and attached it to the outside of the sealed keypad, then plugged the wire in to a nearby jack. They both waited to see if the wire would still work with the jack. If the *Cudgel* had any power at all, it should seal the area and allow Cass to use their kit just like the keypad below it. It took a second, but the light on the kit turned green and its number pad lit up blue. It was a small victory, but meant absolutely nothing without codes. It was just a means of punching in numbers.

"We're hooked in," Cass said, trying to sound cautiously optimistic. She took a moment to get her head straight and removed her right dive glove to better punch in numbers. The first code was one that was a general maintenance code that the builders had installed to work around security so they didn't have to log in every time. She'd read about it on the web, on a *Cudgel* bulletin board that had been running for years.

She punched 8-8-6-4-2, carefully and then waited. She looked from the hatch, to the keyboard twice before the keys turned red for a few seconds, then changed back to blue, then the ready light turned back to green. Strike one.

"Hey, do we get so many chances before it locks us out? My phone only gives me, like, ten or something," Takis said.

Cass realized that the others were opening the storage compartments on the drone already. She turned back to the keypad and thought about the other codes. She tried 1-2-3-4, just for the hell of it. The lights turned red.

Cass looked back at the others, who were pulling bags out of the drone holds and distributing them to each other. They swam off in pairs.

"Where are you going?"

"Just keep us up to date on your progress and our countdown clock," Ozzie said. "We're just implementing a backup plan."

It was obvious that some thought went into their plan, what they were doing wasn't spur of the moment, it was orchestrated beforehand. There was only one thing that they would be doing with all of those bags. "You're not considering raising the *Cudgel*, are you? Jesus, I only suggested this to get to the medical supplies. We're not supposed to disturb it any further."

"Look, if you can't get that hatch, we're going to run out of air and have to surface without the medical supplies," Takis said. "This is just insuring we still have the opportunity to get at those supplies."

"We have to leave it where it is," Cass said. "So the NIA can examine it."

"Sorry, they can examine it floating on the surface," Ozzie said. "After we get those supplies."

"Guys, you have maybe nine bags and they can raise, what? A ton each? And that's stretching it. How are you going to raise this thing? It certainly weighs a lot more than nine tons, I assure you." Cass shook her head. *Let them waste their time.* She turned back to the keypad. There were more codes to try—she knew one from the hangar where the *Cudgel* was stored.

"Cass?" It was Rina's voice.

"Yes?"

"Your phone was ringing again, so I answered it."

"What?" Despite Rina's justifiable anger at Cass, she had no right to use government property like that. "Why would…"

"Chaperone? This is Blind Date Mobile," Linden's voice came through Cass's headset.

"This is Chaperone. Be aware this is an open line and my cover…"

"I assumed your cover was blown when a civilian answered your phone," Linden said. "Listen, things have changed on my end as well. The higher-ups are starting to come around to your report. We've had at least one major incident, and we're investigating others. There are reports of a giant creature destroying a battle group east of you."

"How many?"

"Three ships down," Linden said. "They have me following up on the possibility of it being a remnant of the war; I'm heading to Sacramento Bay Prison to interview a member of the science team."

There was another voice, Jakob this time. "Look, I don't know what we unleashed, but we have bigger problems, now. When can we expect help? Martin is dying."

"Look, I can't get any military craft to you anytime soon. They're all being either sent back to their bases, or rerouting to converge on this… thing you guys encountered. I'll see if we can get any civilian craft involved or a drone to deliver something, but I can't promise anything."

"Blind Date," Cass said. "I'm at the supply hatch on the *Cudgel*. I don't know the code. I know there are medical supplies inside that might still help us."

"Shit, Cass. That's a highly sensitive piece of military equipment. You can't go in there. You know that. Jesus, you know that. You've been briefed about this. Your job is to keep people from doing what you're suggesting."

"I know, but Martin…"

"Like I said, I'm sorry but we can't send help. And you can't go inside. Look, the VTOL is landing outside. I need to go," Linden said.

Cass had nothing to lose, as far as she saw it. "Look, get the code for me and I'll quit. I'll leave my job. I'll take full responsibility. No one here will ever tell who gave me the code. I'll pay for any supplies we use. Whatever. I'll say I found the code through our source or the Obsidian Web."

"This isn't right."

Cass agreed. "This whole situation isn't right. Come the end of the day, do you think giving me the code is going to make headlines over a giant monster attacking our fleet?" She paused and listened to the static in her earpiece. "He's going to die."

"I'll give you a three-hundred year old gold doubloon I found off the coast of Cuba... and a big hug," Jakob said.

"Heck, he'll give you two hugs," Takis said.

The line was silent for a while, until Linden came back on the line. "Fine. I'll give you the code. But this conversation never happened, and when you get back, I'll expect your resignation."

"Fair enough." Cass thought about it and was sure she was doing the right thing. She was saving someone's life, and that was what was important.

30

Martin looked around and blinked at the bright sunshine that streamed through the window of his room. He felt dizzy with every movement, so he decided not to move at all.

"You're awake, I guess that's a good sign." Ben wheeled himself around the bed and closer to Martin. "Let me get you some water."

"I..." Martin tried to talk, but his throat wasn't cooperating. "I..."

Ben leaned a cup closer and closer to Martin's face until the straw met Martin's lips. It took a good few seconds before Martin could even open his lips to draw the straw in so he could drink.

"They're diving down to the *Cudgel* again. They think they can get some supplies to help you from down there," Ben said.

It was crazy to Martin. Anyone going to those lengths to help him, hell, he didn't need saving, he'd be fine. Just fine. "That's stupid. I'm going be okay." He felt his throat rebel with each word.

The light got red and brighter and he closed his eyes until it passed.

31

Inside the Sacramento Bay Prison visiting area, Linden and Lou sat and stared at the white walls and hard-formed plastic tables and chairs. It smelled like bleach or some similar cleaning fluid. Linden noted that the place seemed clean enough. The walls were bare except for signs admonishing visitors to not touch the prisoners, and that all packages had to go through the guards and pass inspection.

He reflected on the call with Cass's team and wondered if he'd done the right thing. Was the life of one man worth it? What secrets would they find, what would they see that they shouldn't? Hell, he didn't even know if the code was going to work. It was in a training file that Linden had gone over and over in his quest to find the *Cudgel*. It was a note made by one of the pilot/operators on her tablet.

"You really think Tsui is going to tell us anything valuable?" Lou asked

"Long shot," Linden said. "We don't even know if he or the Alliance had anything to do with it." It seemed a good bet to Linden that the Alliance knew something, even rumor. The *Cudgel* goes down near their territory during the war, it was likely they at least caught wind of it.

There was a buzz and an electronic lock clicked open on the other side of the room. Two guards walked in through the slowly opening door, followed by Tsui and two other guards. Tsui smiled as he walked, either thrilled to be out of his cell, or happy to see two Americans in suits.

"Hello," Tsui said. "I wondered who my guests were. The guards were... vague... to say the least." He looked around at the empty room. "You're also the men who pissed off a lot of inmates who were expecting to see their families today."

"We'll make it up to them. Maybe we'll bring them all ice cream later," Lou said.

The guards helped Tsui sit down, and then coupled his cuffs to the electromagnet on the table. Linden nodded so they'd step away, enabling as private a conversation as they could have.

"I cannot imagine what you would have to speak with me about." Tsui leaned down the table and ran his hands through his short, dark hair, as his cuffs would only allow him to raise his hands so high. "I've been in this place for so long, I can't possibly have any more secrets to reveal. I complied with every accord in the Alliance's surrender."

"Yeah, that was the accord that required you to disclose all you and your science ministry did for the Alliance in exchange for life in prison, rather than the death sentences your superiors received." Linden began to dig in his coat pocket for the papers he'd slid in just after the guards okayed it.

"That's right, and I've given my knowledge freely. I've answered all the questions." Tsui held out his hands as best he could and waved them around. "I've complied."

"Yeah." Linden dropped the folded papers on the table, but didn't mention them. "True, but I think you may have left something out."

The smile didn't fade from Tsui's face. "What's that? I think I was very thorough."

Linden was faced with the need to lie, and in that lie he'd have to reveal information about the monster attack. "These papers are a transfer order. We're moving you to Oregon State Prison; it's a newer facility up on the northern Oregon coast. Beautiful, actually."

"It's a military facility near the Tillamook Western Grid Operations, where most of the military command centers are located for the region," Lou said. "There's also a pretty large power facility in the area, that stores and provides energy for the region," Lou added. "It's a very important area for the country."

His smile was as wide as ever when Tsui spoke. "You are very informative. You should be tour guides. Problem is, I made a deal for this prison."

Linden agreed. "Yeah. We know. It's got a beautiful view. You can see the California coastline right out your cell, I bet."

"It is calming."

"I'm sure it is. All those rocks out there that used to be the western part of the state, used to be buildings and houses," Linden said. "Remind me, was that a natural disaster, or did the Circle of Liberated Territories have something to do with it?"

Tsui didn't blink or hesitate. "I guess it was a natural disaster."

"Right in the middle of the war?" Linden asked. He took a deep breath. He wasn't here to debate the points of the war, it was over. "Back to Umatilla. It was also considered a high-value target during the war," Linden said. "The coastal defenses repelled about a dozen attacks over the course of open conflict."

"I wouldn't know. I only worked on the science of war, not the execution."

Linden laughed and stood up. "Right. Well, we'll have you on a transport within the hour and you'll be in Umatilla by the afternoon."

Lou and Linden headed for the door and the guards started toward Tsui.

"Oh…" Linden said, turning slightly. "I forgot why I was here in the first place. We found the *Cudgel A-9*. It's a combat machine that went missing during the war near Alliance territory."

Tsui's smile faded but he didn't speak.

Lou stepped back. "We also found something else. They described it as…" Lou looked to Linden with a questioning expression. "Black, with some sort of tusks and tentacles, and huge."

"Massive." Lou decided to add. "And it seems to be moving in a relatively straight line toward… Oh, where did they say?"

"Oregon," Tsui whispered.

Linden and Lou walked back and stood by the table again, towering over Tsui. "So, you've heard of it?"

The prisoner nodded.

"Would you rather talk here?" Lou pulled his own chair back out and sat down.

The prisoner nodded again.

"A representative of the Justice Department is right outside to discuss a new deal with you in exchange for your information, but we need to know everything about this beast and we need to know now," Linden said. "This thing has destroyed a number of ships and military vehicles already."

"And it will continue to, until it reaches that base."

"What do you mean?"

Tsui swallowed noisily. "May I have a glass of water?"

Lou nodded to a guard, who spoke to another through the bars.

"We code named it the Lusca. The generals loved their code names," Tsui said. "Do you have code names?"

The agents both shook their heads no. Though Linden had a number of them for different projects, he didn't feel the war criminal needed to know that.

"Ah, well. We called it Lusca. It was the product of experimentations we'd been assigned to do. We used an old Russian submarine pen as our laboratory. It had been decommissioned and left off the maps in the last century, and I have to say they were horrible conditions. They cleaned up the storage closets and control rooms for us to sleep in, so we wouldn't be detected entering and leaving the facility. Filthy, just…"

"What kind of experiments? Where is the old sub pen?" Lou asked.

The prisoner ignored him. "We spliced the genes of several creatures until we got something that survived. Once one lived, we spliced its gene with something else. We just kept going. We were able to genetically enhance this experiment with the Circle's technology, to get it to follow our commands... simple commands..."

"Like where to attack," Linden said.

"Yes. Very simple, basic stuff."

Lou shook his head. "I don't understand how this worked. Just splicing genes and you..."

"I don't CARE how it worked. I want to know how to kill it." Linden looked into Tsui's eyes, and found the man was not nearly as calm as he'd been earlier.

"And we were not so concerned how to kill it, as we were making sure it did NOT get killed," Tsui said. "The tech that our people put into it is amazing. You know how you can lay your electronics on a certain charging pads and it just charges? How there are buildings with that tech built in, so your tablet or phone automatically charges, even if you're not trying to charge it? The Circle's electronics people implanted a device in the center of the Lusca that does the reverse, and pulls in stored energy from a radius of five miles. It uses that energy to move, to grow, and to power a sort of disrupter in its body that cloaks the beast and anything around it."

"That's impossible." Linden looked at Lou. As crazy as it was, it explained much of what they'd seen so far. The radar and sonar's difficulty in picking the thing up, the size, and the frequent reported outages from anything that gets near it. "So what was the endgame for this thing in the war? Was it supposed to destroy the military base, and the power facility to disrupt the conflict? It certainly wouldn't have stopped the United States completely."

"No. The end was not so simple. Once the Lusca absorbed so much energy, these electronics would have overloaded its heart, its command center. We installed a nuclear device in the center of all of the command parts. Once the heart overloaded, it would trigger the bomb." He looked to the side at the walls. "It would have destroyed the area for miles, including the base, the power storage, the town, the ocean front. Everything. We were more concerned with the toll it would take on the people of the country, on their resolve to fight. The destruction of military targets was a bonus for us."

One of the guards gasped on the other side of the room.

"And this thing is loose again. It's on its way to Oregon now; will it try to fulfill that mission?"

"It knows nothing else. When it failed all those years ago, we assumed your missing machine had triggered the monster prematurely and it wasn't yet powerful enough to trigger the bomb."

"And you don't know how to stop it? All that equipment you say the tech people put in its core and it can't be shut down?"

"No. It was shielded so the cloaking wouldn't disrupt any functions. Eventually, the creature grew larger around it. It has to be buried pretty deep within by now," Tsui said.

Lou and Linden stood again and walked to the other corner. They weren't concerned with anyone overhearing them, but Linden had to walk around-his legs were suddenly tight and he felt a little nauseous with the news they'd just received. "We'll call command and let them know the end plan. They were setting up defenses on the Oregon coast, expecting the thing to make landfall, but this changes all that."

"Ideas on how much time we have?" Lou asked. "Can they evacuate the area?"

"It was moving pretty quickly, and nothing was slowing it down for more than a few minutes," Linden said.

"If they're attacking it, they're probably just feeding it energy," Tsui said. "Making it stronger, larger and faster."

"You know a lot about this monster, don't you?" Linden asked.

"I was a student, learning the applications they were using. I know what I saw, I know what I heard. That's it."

The agent moved to the guards, making sure to stand near the one who was openly shocked a few moments ago. "Look, you know the transfer was a rouse a few minutes ago. We don't have the authorization to do that. But this guy knows everything about this threat. He might be useful."

"What are you asking?"

"We need to take him with us."

The captain of the guards shook his head vehemently. "No. I can't authorize that. You can't just take a prisoner out of here."

"We might be able to avert a nuclear explosion on American soil with his help."

"No," the captain said. His men looked at each other in concern.

"I promise that if you let me take him now, we'll take full responsibility. And if he can't help us, I assure you, I will make sure that he is in the blast radius when that thing explodes."

The other guards stared at the captain, and Linden was afraid that maybe he'd incited a mutiny, which wasn't his intention. A mutiny could lead to more difficulties, possibly even he and his partner's arrest and inability to get out of the prison facility. All of which would certainly slow down their progress and doom their efforts to help stop the creature.

"Gather the prisoner," the captain said.

"What? No!" Tsui said. "I thought if I told you what I knew, you'd leave me. You lied. We had a deal."

"The government had a deal with you, and you lied to them." Lou helped unchain Tsui. "We're even now."

"Help me," Tsui said as the doors opened. He saw guards outside the door and he tried to grab them, only to be stopped by the ones from inside. "They're going to kill me."

The captain looked at the outside guards and Linden saw the man roll his eyes. The other men nodded and allowed them to continue, despite Tsui's continuing cries.

They all proceeded to the stairs and walked up to the prison's upper deck where the VTOL was waiting. The captain stopped Linden as the others proceeded. He raised his finger and pointed it in the agent's face, just an inch away.

"I know," Linden said before the captain spoke. "I will do whatever it takes." He couldn't think of anything more meaningful to tell the man who had just committed several felonies to help chase a slight possibility.

"See that you do," the captain turned and started back down the stairs.

32

The keypad lit up and showed that the hatch was starting its cycle to open. "It's working," Cass said to the others. "Now to see if it can open after all this time." She watched the hatch, and checked their airtime out of the corner of her eye. It was dwindling past the seven minute mark.

The keypad lit up, and flashed a warning that the hatch was opening. Just a few yards away, it creaked and hissed until it finally flew open violently as it expelled trapped oxygen from the airlock beyond it. "It's open. I'm headed in."

"I'll join you," Ozzie said. "These two can handle the rest out here."

"Fine, but I'm not waiting. We're closing in on the five-minute mark to start our ascent." Cass entered the open supply portal easily and moved to the next keypad, where she'd have to enter the code and the room would drain so they could move about freely. She began the sequence just as Ozzie entered the portal. "Seal that hatch behind you."

"Got it," Ozzie said. He cranked the lock shut by hand and gave a thumbs up.

Cass hit the last key in the sequence and the water began to drain.

Slowly.

"Keep your helmet on, we don't know what the air quality is like in here."

Ozzie nodded.

Both of them pulled off their swim fins as they waited. "We need to get out quick. This hatch is taking too long." Cass checked her gauge. "We'll have maybe a couple of minutes to get this stuff and get out."

"It'll take us that long to find the medical bay, let alone grab the supplies and get back," Ozzie said.

"No, I picked this particular hatch because it opens practically next to the infirmary. We should be able to get to it in seconds." Cass pointed to the right. "That way."

When the green light flickered on, Cass opened the door manually, not waiting to see if the automatic functions would work, or if there was enough power to make them do their jobs. Cass and Ozzie moved into the corridor and stopped to take in the sight. The inside of the *Cudgel* was clean, sterile, and white. It was as if it were brand new and untouched. Cass understood that it was true to a point, it had been untouched for a decade, but this surprised her. She wished she could take her helmet off to see if the air smelled of antiseptic and bleach.

Ozzie moved on the medical bay to the right and they quickly found that not everything was as polished as the halls. They both looked through the clear doors to see the inside. On one of the four beds, a skeleton rested with a tight layer of wrinkled skin wrapped tight around the skull and hands. It was wearing shorts and a t-shirt with a United States Navy logo over the chest. The bed, floor and shirt were covered in large rust-colored spots, blood faded from time and the dry air of the ship.

They didn't have time to mourn the man, not at that moment, but Cass knew the government would give them a proper burial when they recovered the *Cudgel*. Or else she'd find a way to remind them.

"Cass, over here." Ozzie was already opening cabinets and lockers, looking for the supplies. She joined him, pulling a large bag to put things in as they went. She tossed in rolls of gauze and bandages from one container, and pain killers from another. She gently set a box of injectors and medicine on top of her haul. Ozzie did much the same. He seemed to grab whatever looked important to him, and she decided to let him, since his background was in medicine, not hers.

"Here it is," Ozzie said. He turned so he could see her through his helmet and held up three small, gray, boxes. "Even better..." He held up another, longer gray box. "This is everything we need to apply InstaSkin wraps. We stitch Martin up, apply these, and they start intermingling with his skin. It'll keep him closed up and start him healing quicker."

Her watch beeped. "It's time to go," Cass said. "We need to hit that airlock."

"I can't find the reaction agent for the blood. This stuff is useless without it."

Cass sealed up her bag of supplies and came over to help.

"I've checked all of the upper cabinets, check the lower ones and I'll check this locker." Ozzie pried open the locker and started rummaging around noisily within, and Cass went to the lowest shelves, looking for the material. "Did you check this clear plastic cabinet?" Her back was to him, but she didn't turn to ask again.

"I've got it, let's go," Ozzie said. When Cass turned around, he was already at the doorway, looking back, with his bag sealed. "Come on."

As Cass ran after him, she bumped a small cover that was hanging open next to a terminal on the panel next to the wall. She didn't remember it being open when they came in, but she didn't have time to think about it, she had to get to the antechamber and wait for it to fill with water.

"The rest of you should go. We're going to be cutting it close," Cass said as the door slowly closed.

"We'll leave you the drone. *Mister Punchy* should get you moving a little faster and save some time," Takis said. "Everything okay, little brother?"

Everyone could hear Ozzie's sigh of relief through their headsets. "We're good. I'm just thrilled to be out of there right now. We got everything we should need, though."

Cass didn't say anything. She just wanted to get the supplies topside to stabilize Martin and get him somewhere safe. She watched as the water got up to her helmet and stood with her hand on the manual release to the outside.

33

"Approaching the *USS Montenegro*. Should be on the deck in two minutes," the pilot's voice came through the headphones.

"What's the *Montenegro*? I haven't heard of it," Holli said.

Linden nodded out the window at the massive structure that was moving just ahead of them. "It's a mobile battle platform, designed to be a base for naval operations far out to sea where support ships aren't enough. Normally anchored a few miles off the Canadian coast, south of the Queen Charlotte Islands—been there for eight or so years now. It's pretty slow, but it's like its own fleet in some respects." He'd seen it used toward the end of the war, and again in the search and rescue efforts to find the *Cudgel*. It was heavily fortified and, like the *Cudgel,* designed to withstand heavy winds and high seas for rescue ops. "It has landing pads for drones, aircraft, boats, submarines and just about anything else you can think of. Its armament includes traditional projectile weapons and more advanced laser and sound-based weapons. They have a good-sized infirmary onboard."

"That's impressive, it's like a small city down there," Holli said.

"Close. The *Montenegro* is about as wide as four aircraft carriers set end-to-end. Under normal combat conditions, it was about as heavily populated as a small city, too. But now, I'm guessing it'll be at about a quarter of that compliment." Lou had to shout to be heard over the massive rotors of the VTOL. "Given the short notice of deployment."

As promised, they were on the ground in just under two minutes and met by the *Montenegro*'s executive officer, Lieutenant Ornn. "Gentlemen... Ma'am." Ornn shook everyone's hands in turn. Then he stopped to stare at Tsui, a man still wearing prison orange, with full shackles that extended from his palm, up to just below the elbows.

"He's a prisoner with some knowledge of the creature we're fighting," Linden said. "I'm responsible for him."

Ornn didn't look convinced, but seemed in a hurry to get back, so they all talked while they walked away from the VTOL. "My commanding officer sends his regrets that he couldn't meet you himself. He's pretty overwhelmed by the information coming in. The first response from our forces was scattered and uncoordinated. We sent a squad of fighter jets in, and we lost contact with all of them. Just disappeared off the radar."

Linden pointed to Tsui. "Our special friend here has some insight on that. He's told us that the creature we're fighting has the capability to drain the power from sources and use that energy to cloak itself and everything around it."

"Seriously? A creature? They were right about that? It's a giant of some sort?" The XO asked. They entered the XO's small office, with a large window that looked down on a much larger control room, where sailors ran back and forth to different stations carrying tablets. It was a hive of activity, and Linden wondered whether his estimate about a small crew was correct.

Holli pulled her laptop out of her bag and set it on a nearby table. "What, you think those jets just disappeared on their own?"

"No ma'am, just hard to grip that it could be some kind of creature. They kind-of stopped teaching about sea monsters at the naval academy around General Washington's time, I think," Ornn said. "Whatever is out there, we can more than handle it. The *Montenegro* is moving ahead at top speed." He pointed out the window to the left at a massive warship cutting through the water. "And that's the USS Powell over there. One of the most modern warships the navy has to offer, hover capabilities, pulse cannons, max speed of thirty-one knots for short bursts—that kicks ass for a ship that size— and a full battery of missiles, both surface to air and ship to ship."

There was another ship off to the left and Holli pointed it out. "What's that one?"

"The *Reynolds*. Sub killer. Drops mines and depth charges to blow up anything that might be sneaking up from below."

Linden looked around. "That's it?"

The XO was taken aback. "You're crazy if you think we need more. This platform is equipped with four armed VTOLs, and the Powell has an attack copter that…"

"It won't be enough. Launch your gunships now, or they won't get out of here in time. You should evacuate." It was Tsui. He'd found an empty chair at a console in the corner and was sitting perfectly still with his hands still bound in front of him.

"Don't touch anything," Linden said. He stared off toward the horizon, looking for any reason that Tsui might have said what he did. "How long until contact?"

Ornn looked at the window that looked out at the control room. He reached up and tapped it, bringing a number of feeds to life. He expanded one that became a countdown clock. "Looks like another hour. Maybe forty-five minutes, judging loosely on the time between incidents out to sea."

"You want to ask me, don't you? How I know this battleship is in trouble?" Tsui leaned back confidently.

Linden, Holli, the XO, and Lou turned to look at Tsui. Linden nodded, trying not to be too sarcastic. "Yes, I would very much like to know."

Alarms went off in the *Montenegro* and lights began to flash. In a moment the *Reynolds* rose from the water and was broken in half by the Lusca, then, both sections were dragged down by thick, winding black tentacles. There was barely enough time for the group in the conn to see the beast before the whole thing disappeared beneath the waves.

"Jesus," Lou yelled.

"I know the Lusca has been sleeping. It was tired. It's only waking up and getting faster as it does. Stronger. It's recharging thanks to all the ships you're sending that are just ripe with juicy power," Tsui said. Though this time it wasn't nearly as cocky.

The XO turned and grabbed a mic just as the lights flickered all around the room. "This is XO Ornn. Launch all craft and engage." He clicked the mic again and again. "It's dead." To their right, the lights went out in the *Powell*, and below them, on the control room floor, the consoles and monitors blinked erratically until they went out.

Emergency lighting clicked on in the control room, and the klaxon began to sound again. Ornn turned to a junior officer. "We can't raise anyone on the com. Run down to the deck and tell everyone to get in the air."

"Aye, sir." The officer left the room in haste.

"I told you," Tsui said. "You didn't listen. Those vehicles aren't going anywhere."

The *Montenegro* lurched as the front of the massive station rose. The Lusca came up in front of it, giving everyone a fair view of its fat, grotesque body, the huge head was smooth, with long tentacles that twitched and writhed as the sea water dripped off of it. Though most of its body was black and grey, its mouth was a bright pink and flanked on either side by light grey tusks. Long tentacles rose from the sea before it and began to slither onto the foredeck of the *Montenegro*. The eyes caught Linden's attention—gigantic shiny black orbs on either side of the head that seemed to take in everything. There wasn't a pupil that Linden saw, but the more he stared at the eyes, he felt he could see light within or a glint from the sun. He was brought from his trance when Holli spoke.

"You believe us now, don't you Mister Ornn?" she asked.

The ship's XO didn't take his eyes off of the beast rising before them. It was two hundred yards in front of the ship. "What the hell are those things falling of it?" Ornn pointed toward the deck and Linden came forward to see.

Rocks or coral the size of medicine balls dropped off the Lusca and onto the *Montenegro*. "I have no idea what those are."

"Slags." Tsui was standing right behind the others, looking over their shoulders at the red-black rocks landing on the deck, falling into the water. "It's too late. Can we get to our craft and get out of here?"

Linden took Tsui by the collar and slammed him into the bulkhead. "We brought you here to help. So start talking."

There was an explosion on the launch pad and everyone turned to see one of the VTOLs slam into the deck as it tried to take off.

"Slags are the byproduct of trying to create the Lusca. They were the early model, so to speak. In their creation, they bonded with the Lusca and they have somewhat of a symbiosis. They are terribly hard to kill; their shells solid like lava rock. "Look." Tsui pointed to a group of the slags as they began to rock and shiver. In seconds, long crab-like legs spread out from beneath, and fins appeared on their backs which slowly split until at least four stalk-like tentacles appeared on top of each of the craggy shells. Approaching soldiers opened fire with side arms and automatic weapons, to no avail. The creatures began skittering across the deck with a speed that no one had expected. The lead sailor was impaled through the neck by one of the slag's lumpy legs; the next man lost an arm to a swipe of one of the tentacles.

"It's too late. You see? I said it was too late, it is too late," Tsui said. Out on the deck of the massive mobile platform, a dozen or more of the slags were rushing about, attacking the crew and shaking off everything that the sailors attacked them with. "We have to go."

"You said they drain power. Do you think our VTOL has any energy? It runs on battery power as well." Holli looked around at all of the dead controls in exasperation. "Even my laptop is fucked. We're dead in the water here."

There was nothing Linden could say. He stared at the Lusca and traced the paths of the so-called slags as they zig-zagged around, attacking crewmembers and slashing at the structure of the ship itself. "We... we need to get to life boats or something, right? Those wouldn't have power in them and wouldn't be a target for the big beast, right?" Where are the inflatable rafts?"

"Brilliant, Agent Kemp. Brilliant." Tsui started for the hatch and turned left before Lou grabbed him.

They grabbed their things, and Holli folded up her laptop as they left the room.

"This way," the XO said as he pointed to the right. "Get everyone to head for the escape route. Rear boat launches. Sections one and two." He passed the words on to each sailor he passed, and so did everyone else, though the words really meant nothing to them; they were just aping the things the XO said. They dodged debris that had come loose with the Lusca's initial upending of the *Montenegro*. In a few moments, Linden saw a hatch ahead that pointed to the Section one launch. They slid to a halt when Linden heard a rhythmic tapping on the deck. He turned to see a slag charging toward them.

"This shit had better work," Jakob said. He stood at the side of Martin's bed and helped assemble the IV stand. The remark seemed pointed at Cass, but the rest of the room got tense as well.

"Or what?" Ozzie asked. "We all went in for this; it's on all of our heads."

Cass didn't respond to either of them, she just continued to prep the mixture on Martin's bar, using his sink to wash everything up with the hottest water the tap could muster. The powder went into the glass bottle, and then the catalyst went in: a watery, pasty substance that the label identified as XR20. The expiration label suggested a date nearly three years ago. Cass thought hard on that. Something that far past the date could do more damage than good. They could try to look up the whole thing using the internet, if they could connect to it, but that would waste more time.

With all of the equipment working and hooked up, the silence of the room was broken by the slow, steady beep of the heart and pulse monitor. It was alarmingly low.

"Okay, we'll give him the blood and see if we can stabilize him, then we'll properly seal the wound with skin glue and watch the results closely. We'll need at least two more bags of the blood ready for after that, then apply InstaSkin wraps if we can," Ozzie said. Cass watched him move in medical role with just as much confidence and skill as he did underwater. He obviously knew much more than she did, but Cass felt like she was holding her own with him when it came to trying to care for Martin. She handed Ozzie the old-fashioned glass drip container and stood by while he shook it, and attached the tube to the end. He tapped on Martin's hand, looking for a vein.

"Are you sure this is the best course of action?" Martin mumbled. "I feel just fine."

"You're not fooling anyone. You'll be stone dead in a moment," Jakob said.

Martin laughed and started coughing. "I think I'll go for a walk."

Cass stared at the two of them, slightly appalled by Jakob's comments.

Jakob realized Cass was staring and looked at her with a smile. "What? You've never seen Monty Python and the Holy Grail before? You need to come to movie night in the communications room more often. It's a classic."

"I feel happy," Martin said, with a few coughs thrown in. "He's right. It's a classic."

Ozzie stopped tapping on Martin's wrist. "Just a little pinch and we're done." Ozzie slid the needle in and covered it in cotton and tape. "We're halfway there."

"Feels warm," Martin said as the processed blood began to flow into his body. He smiled.

Cass and Ozzie both folded their arms across their chests at nearly the same time as they waited to see if Martin's body accepted the mixture or not. They'd know pretty quickly.

34

Martin felt the warmth spread up his arm, into his shoulder and across his chest. He didn't remember closing his eyes, but they were shut nonetheless. He felt light, like he was floating.

He opened his eyes and found himself on his old ship, the *Marionette*. There, on the other end of the deck, he saw Ben standing at the railing, watching dolphins breaking the waves off the bow of the ship. It was Papua New Guinea, after the war and drones were cleaning the city of Lae, on the land and in the harbor. Another crew member, Dana, came and stood beside him. They laughed. They always laughed at everything, at least that was how Martin remembered them together.

In the distance, the sun faded into the water, and everything was light and orange and yellow. He was in the wheelhouse then, his hand on the controls, his speed steady.

He could feel the explosion beginning at the bow, like a careless man tripping over his untied shoelace. This dream, or hallucination, or rewind – Martin couldn't be sure what it was, but it suddenly went into slow motion around him. He moved as he always did, but the world ticked on, just at a minute pace. Martin turned from the wheel and walked toward the stairs, but found himself suddenly at the bottom of all the flights of stairs, some three sets. He walked quickly toward the bow, until he saw the start of the explosion which was little more than a flash, with pieces of ship flying away from it. He reached down and pulled long strips of the hull away, just so he could see below, just to witness the mine below doing its job before becoming a mass of shrapnel.

He saw it, a mass of explosives surrounded by a metal casing and spikes that triggered the device. Just like the after reports said. A remnant of the war in an area that supposedly was cleared in the months before. He marveled at how the design of a mine hadn't changed in more than a century—a weight, a chain, a buoyant ball with tripwires. Navies had used them in both world wars previous, and variations had made appearances in conflict after conflict before that.

He watched the ball of flame spread and then turned back to the steps, remembering Ben and Dana on the deck. He ran to the staircase, thinking this time he could change something. But there was no magically skipping from the bottom to the top, on the way up he had to plod each and every painful step. Looking behind him, he could see the fireball expanding up the steps behind him.

By the time he touched the top of the stairs, a wave of fire and debris had caught up with him and enveloped him. He felt the heat pass him by, without harming him, and he followed it out onto the deck. Martin turned quickly to see where Ben and Dana were.

35

The *Montenegro* listed to port and knocked the whole group into the railing, including the slag that had come up on them. Still, it flailed with its head stalks, slicing Holli's coat with one. The XO forced the emergency hatch in, and led Lou inside. Linden turned in time to see the beast rear back and strike at Tsui with one of its bumpy legs, bringing it down on the metal cuffs that held Tsui's hands in place, getting stuck in the process.

The monster panicked and started swinging all of its other legs, trying to get loose. "Help me," Tsui said. He did his best to pull away, but the slag's leg was stuck firm.

He didn't think about it, but the key card to the cuffs was already in Linden's hand and searching for the proper place to swipe. Despite her injury, Holli jumped in as well, pounding at the head tentacles with a fire extinguisher. The cuffs fell off Tsui and with them, the beast dropped to the deck.

"Go," Holli shouted, and Linden didn't wait for her to repeat. He pulled Tsui into the corridor just as Holli doused the slag in flame retardant foam from the extinguisher. As the monster slipped around and shook to get the white material off, Holli joined the others and they slammed the portal and locked it.

Ornn moved down the stairs, sliding on the rails from one level to the next. The rest followed using the steps, not quite desperate enough to launch themselves so forcibly at the next deck.

"Are you all right?" Linden looked at Holli's arm as they waited to get on the stairs.

"I'm fine, it just grazed me." She showed him what amounted to a paper cut. A thin cut that probably hurt like hell, but looked like it would stop bleeding any time. "I'm starting to believe your crazy theory about the monster, if that's any consolation."

"Should have trusted me and joined my team." Linden's steps echoed in the confined area of the ship.

"I'm probably going to be looking for a job soon," Holli said. Linden watched her cover the cut with her hand and wince.

At the landing, sailors were prepping several small submersibles. They turned at the sight of the XO and saluted smartly. Ornn returned the salute and kept moving.

"You can take this first one. I'm setting a course to the north, there's a civilian pier just south of Seattle where you can land." He looked inside. "And there's survival gear, rations. I'd send you to the nearest base, but if that's where this Lusca is headed, then you'd pop up right in the thick of things where you started."

"Aren't these just going to lose their energy like everything else?" Lou asked.

The XO shook his head. "These run entirely on Magneto Hydrodynamic Propulsion. They use the water to pull themselves along. These are specially built to eliminate the need for power storage; they rely on the sea and the earth. The *Montenegro* uses similar methods, but unfortunately our energy is still stored in batteries. You'll be fine, I assure you."

The platform rocked again. "Good enough for me. Thanks," Linden said. "Good luck to you." He shook the XO's hand and climbed aboard, followed by the others. The sailors closed the door and the mini sub immediately began to sink, the propellers whirred to life and the vehicle jerked forward.

As they dove beneath the waves, the *Montenegro* was still visible in the sub's rear portal. There was room to move around, but barely. They all watched the underside of the giant platform as even their emergency running lights dimmed and flickered out.

"Holli?" Linden asked.

"Yes?" She kept her gaze fixed on the *Montenegro* and the black mass visible beyond it.

"Any chance you saw how they set up the auto pilot, and if so, can you change the heading?" He said it as casually as possible, but if they were travelling toward Seattle, they wouldn't arrive until after the creature hit landfall, and after that, it was pretty much all over if a plan wasn't formulated.

Holli looked around the cabin of the small craft. "I'm a sound analyst, not a hacker."

"That wasn't a no," Linden said.

Tsui seemed to be stifling a scream from deep inside. His face was red and his chest puffed out. "For the love of fuck, I'll do it. I was watching, in case I got a chance to beat all of you to death and steal this thing and take it home." He stood and moved to the one-man control area and began flipping switches.

"Wait," Lou moved toward the prisoner.

"I suggest you sit down and tell me where you want to go." Tsui typed at the keys and adjusted several levers and the sub suddenly jerked downward. "Whoa. Touchy controls."

"Look..." Linden got up closer to Tsui's seat.

"I know. If I even attempt to escape or fuck you over, you'll pound my face with a wrench and flush me out the latrine." Tsui looked back quickly with a smile. "I'll be good."

Holli quickly smacked the back of Tsui's head. "You DID just say you were thinking of killing us and taking this vehicle home, right?"

"Joking," Tsui said. "Just a joke."

Holli pulled her hand back and smacked him again, this time on his cheek.

"Oww." Tsui put his hand on his cheek. "What the hell?"

Linden pulled Holli to the back of the sub. "Holy crap, what was that?" he whispered.

"I'm sorry, I'm not a field agent. I got nervous. Just trying to look tough."

"It's okay."

"I'm locked in a sub with a war criminal and there's a giant monster following us which will eventually explode in an atomic fireball." She held up a shaking hand. "I'm a little on edge, you know?"

"I know." Linden nodded.

"I have it under control now."

Linden nodded again and forced a smile. "Great."

"Hey. So where are we going?" Tsui asked.

"You'll find out when we tell you," Holli said.

"Holli? Enough." Linden walked back to the front and stood next to Tsui at the controls. "Set a course for Cape Meares base off the coast of Oregon. We need to get ahead of this thing and help with preparation on the coast."

"Cape Meares, aye-aye sir." It sounded like Tsui said it with the maximum amount of sarcasm he could muster.

"Best speed."

"You could get out and push, that might speed us up a little," Tsui said.

"We could also go faster by throwing out extra weight," Holli said. She'd turned back to watch the *Montenegro* fade in the distance.

"After we've put some distance between us and that creature, I need you to surface. I have to make a few quick calls," Linden said. He needed to get a report and a warning to the rest of the fleet and the mainland defenses to let them know some serious shit was coming their way. He hoped that someone from the *Montenegro* would have managed a distress call, but he couldn't be sure. Surely the sudden lack of communications from the battle platform would be an indicator of trouble.

And he had to call Cass. He needed to know what happened on the *Cudgel*, both today and ten years ago.

36

Ozzie was asleep in a chair by Martin's bedside. He'd been monitoring Martin's condition since the injection. Before that, he dove the *Cudgel*, before that he'd helped fight on the ship. Cass couldn't fault him for drifting off. She looked at the monitors, and was happy with what she saw. Everything seemed stable, and would hopefully remain that way. The blood substitute was working.

She turned and nearly ran into Jakob. "Sorry."

"How is he?" Jakob asked. "Is it working?"

"Seems like it," Cass said. "His blood pressure is steady, his pulse is good. I think he just needs some time."

"I hope so."

"We just need to decide what to do now. Do we move? Can he handle that?" Cass wasn't a doctor and didn't want to venture a guess. It might take some time for everything to stabilize. Travel on the high seas might be too rocky, but conversely, if they stayed here, a storm could pop up and make life difficult for everyone.

"We'll have to talk with the others, but I think staying here is the way to go right now," Jakob said.

Cass patted him on the shoulder and walked down the hall. She walked into her room, shut the door and locked it. She sat herself down on her bed and ran her hands through her hair. She looked on her dresser and noticed that Rina had returned the sat phone and plugged it in to charge again. The light was blinking green for a full charge, so she slipped it in her pocket-no need to hide it-and walked to the mirror. She was a bigger mess than she felt. Her eyes had dark circles under them and her clothes were the same she'd been wearing for days. She washed her face in the sink, pulled her red hair back into a ponytail and wrapped it with a band, before finding some relatively clean jeans and a t-shirt. Just as she was beginning to feel less like a street urchin, her phone rang in the other room. She hurried back to where she'd dropped her dirty clothes and fished it out.

"Cass?" It was Linden. And he'd apparently dispensed with all the cloak-and-dagger business of code names. "Cass, we just left the platform *Montenegro* as it was being torn apart by your creature."

"What? That thing is the biggest and best we have," Cass asked. "How can that be? The creature was big, but..."

"I don't know, it took out the *Montenegro*'s escort ships as well," Linden said. "It neutralized their energy sources and then just started ripping shit apart. The ships barely got off any shots of their own. The Lusca was dropping what Tsui called slags. These little balls of rock or something that had legs. They were tearing through the crew like nothing."

"Those are what killed our science team, and put Martin in the condition he's in now."

"How is Martin?" Linden asked.

Cass was still sorry about how that conversation went down, and fully expected to hold him to accepting her resignation. "He's better. I just came from checking on him. Seems to be accepting the medication and blood we pulled from the *Cudgel*. So far, at least."

"Good." The line crackled for a few seconds before Linden continued. "What was it like? Inside the *Cudgel*?"

"Amazing. It was still perfectly preserved down there. The inside was pretty pristine. The whole thing was just like it was in the pictures in the office," Cass said. "I wish you could have seen it."

"Hopefully, I will."

It was quiet for a few seconds as Cass thought about the tone of Linden's words. "They're calling it the Lusca now?"

"The R.L.T.'s science team code-named it that," Linden said. "We didn't want to strain ourselves coming up with something original."

"So what's next? Where are you now?"

"We're getting ahead of the creature to rally the troops and advise them how to fight this thing—or how NOT to fight it, at least. I hope someone listens," Linden said. "Odds are good, they'll send drones by land, sea, and air."

"But those will just get their energy supply sucked out and strengthen this beast even more."

"And after *that*, maybe they'll listen to me," Linden said. "I'll check in later."

The line went dead and Cass put her phone away. She walked to the kitchen for some water and found the rest of the crew sitting around the dining table, except for Martin. Cass grabbed a bottle of water, noted how low the supplies were getting, and then stepped toward the table with all eyes on her.

They stood just as Cass started to sit down, and they walked for the door.

"We need to have a discussion in the comms room," Ben said. He wheeled himself out behind the others.

Cass sat for a moment, unsure if that meant they needed to talk without her, or if she was actually invited. Ben turned his chair and looked at her, then nodded toward the other room.

Once in with everyone else, Cass immediately could see not just the normal movie-viewing screen, but several other large monitors that had

130

been brought in from other areas, mostly Rina's room or the drone control area. All of them had images or schematics of the *Cudgel* on them. Some of the images had to be in real time, there were fish drifting in front of the camera. "Wow. This is impressive." She looked at the dozen or so screens and tried to analyze what each of them represented. She also glanced at the crew when she could to try to gauge their intent.

"Look," Rina said. She was holding her phone, controlling the screens. "We get that you lied to us because you were doing your job. We get that. It sucks, but there it is."

"Okay."

"So, to help ourselves get over it, we deceived you too."

The room full of people did not look smug or happy with themselves, so it took Cass a minute to respond. "How?"

"When the *Cudgel* was built, people still thought it was okay to use various disk and mini-disks to store their data, mostly in the construction phase. I cooked up a disk that could exploit their diagnostics programs." A tiny disk appeared on the largest screen to bring home her point. "I had Ozzie put it into a port while the two of you were gathering supplies."

"You didn't have time, we went on the spur of the moment."

"I've had it ever since we started looking for the *Cudgel*. We planned to turn it over to the government, but we wanted inside, and we wanted to get souvenirs. I created it with some info that *Subtle Bagpipe* gave us. She wanted a souvenir, too." Rina looked over at Cass. "All we needed was someone to put in the codes to open it up."

It wasn't something that Cass could figure out how to respond to. They didn't want to steal the weapon, just look? That was still against the law. All of the governments involved in the treaty had made separate provisions for that in order to keep the *Cudgel* from falling into the wrong hands. "So, what did that little disk get you?"

Ozzie stood and pointed at the side screen. "We have real stats on how the *Cudgel* is doing. With that creature gone, it seems like this giant is getting power levels back." He pointed again, this time to a series of bars that indicated power consumption and collection. "Only at three percent right now, but it was nearly zero when we got control."

"We raise that thing, and its solar receptors could start collecting and help load up the cells. Hell, nearly everything is in working order so far. Diagnostics show a breach near one of the feet, but that was sealed off by the crew way back when." Takis was excited about the ship in a way Cass wasn't aware he could be. He was a joker, self-deprecating, occasionally sullen, but here he was-talking fast and breathy.

"Wait. Those lift bags. That's what this is all about? You just want to raise the *Cudgel* so you can go inside and loot it?"

"No. We want to make it work again," Jakob said. "So we can go kill that thing that we released."

Cass scanned the room to see if they were making fun of her. If maybe they were pulling a prank to get her back for lying and deceiving them.

They were not.

37

Six miles out from the coast, the tiny escape pod began to receive radio challenges from the coastal defenses. Linden explained their situation and gave them whatever information he could to verify his story. Luckily, there were a number of other craft washing up on Oregon shores from the *Montenegro* that matched their pod's profile, and they weren't hassled too much. Still, the Navy sent two drones to escort them to a dock set aside from the main port.

When they finally opened the hatch and Linden stepped out, there was a small, armed contingent waiting for them. "Agent Linden Kemp?" A woman in a dark flight suit, different from the other soldiers held up a piece of paper to read Linden's name off.

"Yes? That's me."

"My name is Sergeant Dana Johnson. I have been ordered to escort you to my C.O. immediately for a quick word," the soldier said.

Linden nodded and turned to help Holli out of the pod. Tsui had wisely stayed back out of sight for the moment. Linden was also glad Tsui was no longer wearing his prison clothes, and that he had lost his cuffs earlier.

"No sir, I'm to bring just you. The rest of your crew can use the facilities and then get some chow in our mess, if they'd like." She nodded to the four soldiers with her. "These men will help them find their way to whatever they need."

Linden wondered if coming here was such a good idea after all. If they split up, who knew what would happen? Would they throw Tsui back in prison, ship Holli back to her cubicle? He decided not to think about it for now. First things first; he needed to explain everything he knew to whoever was in charge onsite.

"Scuttlebutt has it that your team found the old *Cudgel*. That true?"

Linden looked at his escort as they left the docks and began climbing a short set of stairs to a small building.

"I have clearance," Dana said.

"I'm sure you do. I'm just not sure what I can say for sure." He couldn't really confirm anything technically until he saw the thing himself. Technically. But the little kid in him, heck, the Linden in him that started this job, wide-eyed and expecting to find the thing immediately, wanted to tell someone about the impossible find. "I've seen pictures and video, but that's as far as I can say."

The woman smiled and nodded her head. "I just won fifty bucks." She opened a door with her key card and waved Linden in. She then stepped forward and opened another door with a card and ushered him ahead. She led Linden down a hall, past sailors and soldiers who were gathering in a wardroom, before taking him up a flight of stairs. "The Fleet Admiral is getting ready to sit in on a briefing, so we need to be quick."

Though his head had begun to spin with the notion of distilling the events of the last few days into a short summary, Linden nodded. He knew how the military liked quick and simple bursts of information.

They left the stairs at the third floor and walked down one of a number of hallways to a man at a desk.

"The Fleet Admiral wanted to see Agent Kemp for a moment before the briefing?" Dana nodded toward Linden.

"Go ahead; he's going over his notes." The man pushed a button under his desk and the door began to buzz.

Dana pushed the door open and held it for Linden. Inside, there was a fairly sparse office with two metal framed chairs in front of a metal framed desk. There were some pictures on the wall, but not many. The desk held a thin computer, and a standard issue coffee mug.

There was no Fleet Admiral.

On the far side of the office was a door with a small frosted window, and a shadow appeared there. Dana walked over and pulled the door open. "Sir?" The sounds of the ocean and the smell of the salt air blew in causing Linden to miss what was said next, but she waved him over. Through the door was a small balcony that overlooked the harbor and all of the ships in it.

A wiry man in a khaki navy uniform stood with a handful of sunflower seeds. "You're Agent Kemp?" he asked. He chewed on a seed and spit the outside of it over the railing. Linden watched the pieces fly down toward a grassy area below.

"Yes sir," Linden said. He started to stick his hand out to shake, but realized that the man had seeds in one hand, and that the other was shoving those seeds into his mouth. "Pleased to meet you."

The Fleet Admiral nodded. "Tell me." He leaned over and spat more over the side.

Assuming that meant he should explain what he knew, Linden started recounting the events of the find, up to the *Montenegro*'s demise. "My agent was embedded with a salvage crew, the crew found an item of ours, and in securing it, they released this beast."

"The item was the *Cudgel A-9*." Dana chimed in. The Fleet Admiral's expression didn't change.

"The monster destroyed several ships in travelling on a course for this location. Research found that it may be a remnant of the Lusca, a biological weapon trapped by the *Cudgel* all this time. It somehow sucks in stored energy from enemies, rendering them inactive and defenseless. According to a scientist that worked on several projects, the thing is headed for the power storage inland, where it will absorb energy until it explodes in a blast akin to a nuclear explosion."

"Okay," the Fleet Admiral said.

Linden took it as a sign to continue. "After an interview with the prisoner revealed this information, we flew to the *Montenegro*…"

The admiral held up his now free hand to stop Linden. "Okay. I have reports on what happened there." He dumped some shells over the side and rubbed his hands together to get the rest off. "Thanks for your help." He turned and walked inside.

Linden looked at Dana. "That's it? He doesn't want any more information?"

"He has what he needs, I guess."

"Well, my team and I could use an office or even just a couple of desks to communicate with the salvage unit. We may have a way to help, if we can get the resources," Linden said. He looked around at the nearby buildings and other structures. "I mean, this place is huge. Give us a charging station and point us to the coffee, you won't even know we're here."

The look on Dana's face was a pitiful attempt at a smile. "I'm sorry. We can't do that. You don't have clearance with us, not right now, and with a live threat out there, we can't keep you on the base."

"Seriously?"

"Sorry." She opened the door, and Linden found two armed soldiers standing by the desk. "These men will escort you to your friends. You can grab a coffee or a sandwich in the mess if you'd like."

That did not exactly go as planned. Linden sighed.

38

Cass stayed on the *Adamant* with Rina, Ben and Martin. They stared out at the sea and waited for the others to finish securing the outer buoyancy devices. The balloons would work in conjunction with the *Cudgel*'s own flotation devices to slowly bring the craft up to the surface. The disk that Rina had devised gave her control over a very limited number of functions on the *Cudgel*, mainly water drainage areas, and the buoyancy compensators. At least that was all she'd been told about. After the whole deception that got that disk placed in the first place, she wasn't sure who to trust. She wasn't exactly a prisoner, they hadn't locked her away, but she'd been put at arm's length from the act of raising the *Cudgel*. "This isn't going to work. We're talking about a machine that normally takes up to two dozen crew members, a ground team, command and logistics, navigation…"

"Don't worry about it. We'll figure it out." Rina shoved one of her ear buds in and fumbled for the other. "We are a pretty resourceful crew."

"What the hell does that matter? You can be resourceful, but still come up short. This isn't looking for ancient lamps off the Amalfi coast, this is piloting a war machine the size of an ocean liner," Cass said. "You mess up; you might land on a highly-populated area. You could kill us all and take a huge number of civilians with us."

"Sounds like we need a chaperone. Know any?" Rina stuck the other earbud in and some loud metal/pop/rap hybrid of a song bled out, just loud enough for Cass to hear.

The sun drifted across the afternoon sky, shimmering on the ocean, another beautiful day on the water. There was a point that Cass considered going inside to talk to Martin, but she wasn't sure how coherent he was, and certainly Ben wouldn't be much help, as he made occasional appearances on the upper deck, looking out much like Cass was, before straightening the red blanket on his lap and heading back inside the top deck. It looked like there wasn't anyone on the ship that had a problem with raising this battle vehicle and doing the most foolish thing possible with it. As they'd revealed their plan, they suggested that Ben could be their radar/sonar man, relaying information from the *Adamant* to the *Cudgel* so the crew wouldn't have to bother, but Cass saw it as another distraction, one more thing to listen to, one more piece of information to verify and act on. It was an added step in a situation where they needed as few steps as possible.

The top of the first giant grey balloon broke the surface nearly a quarter mile away, sending waves out to raise some of the *Adamant*'s red marker buoys. Rina lifted her phone and her fingers began their dance with the interface. Another balloon appeared and rose until it was as far out as it could go once Rina adjusted the inflation rate.

Cass was taken aback by the appearance of any of the balloons, let alone two of them. "How the hell did you do it? How did you get those balloons to raise that ship? It shouldn't be possible."

Jakob stood at the railing and watched. "Once we had control of some of the functions of the *Cudgel*, we activated half of the ship's own buoyancy regulators. We basically took a chance that the emergency flotation devices were going to work on the ship itself."

"Coupled with ours, it was enough to bring it up." Rina flipped to another screen and started adjusting another balloon and then another, until all six had appeared; half were near the *Adamant*, the other half were well out of sight, nearly nine hundred feet away, supporting the *Cudgel*'s feet. The ship itself, however, was nowhere to be seen.

"Well?" Cass asked. "Where is this behemoth?"

"Just below the surface," Rina said. "The internal tanks aren't inflating all the way for some reason."

Ozzie appeared with a thinscreen in his hand. "It looks like the internal floatation devices are leaking. Maybe they decayed after all this time?"

"No." Jakob looked over Ozzie's shoulder and pointed at the screen. "It doesn't look like it's leaking, looks like maybe it just can't inflate anymore. Maybe the readout that shows how far to inflate the bags isn't calibrated?"

They all looked up at the nearby balloons bobbing on the surface of the sea.

"So, it's just below the water, then?" Cass asked. So far, her crewmate's plan was going about as well as could be hoped.

Rina's brow furrowed and she started swiping screens on her phone again. She stopped at the controls of each of their floatation devices, inflating them just a bit more, driving the balloons closer to exploding and ruining the balance, sending the *Cudgel* slowly back to the bottom of the sea.

Her tinkering paid off, if only just a bit. Somewhere in the distance, a large gleaming white chunk of metal broke the waves slowly. Off the starboard side of the *Adamant*, *Champ* raced off toward the visible chunk of the *Cudgel*. Takis was in the con room handling the controls, and he brought it about quickly, training the video camera down at the outline of the *Cudgel*. Soon, all of the screens around Cass showed what the visible part was: the chest plate. It was a wide rack that held a great variety of defensive and offensive ordinance. According to the manuals Cass had read, this early model was equipped with anti-radar flares, mini-missiles, and advanced torpedoes housed in cases as small as footballs.

"I'm taking the drone down closer," Takis said. "I'll secure the hatch up here."

"I'll get the *Adamant* hooked in and start assisting with our solar panels," Jakob said. He turned and made his way down the stairs and out toward the diving equipment. The plan involved using the collectors from the *Cudgel* and the *Adamant* to charge up the battle vehicle and get it up to acceptable levels.

Rina's lips pushed together tightly and she tinkered further with the inflation controls. "Hang on," she said. As she did, the *Cudgel* rose just a bit more, until more of it was above water. The whole body of the ship was lying flat on the surface of the ocean nearby, it wasn't much, just a thin layer, with the bulk of it still underwater, but the whole outline of the metal vehicle could be seen. "There were some buoyancy compensators in the *Cudgel*'s back. I wanted to wait before we deployed them, just in case we needed this extra push."

"Shit," Cass said. She'd seen the plans and schematics, she knew the dimensions, and all the other specs, even sat in a simulator, but she'd never seen it for real. Underwater it was like some lost statue from an ancient civilization, moss-covered and hidden in the depths of the ocean. But here, it was in the open air, the ocean washing it clean. It was magnificent, and frightening.

"Just because I'm not behind this plan, doesn't mean I can't help set up," Cass said.

"And what, then you'd find some way to sabotage us? Keep us from doing what we want to do?"

They both looked over to see Jakob climb onto the partially-surfaced metal body with a long line of cable wrapped around his shoulder a number of times. He let it out as he went, laying the line from the *Adamant*.

"No, Rina. Believe it or not, I'd rather not see the crew get injured or killed." Cass moved away, headed back to her cabin. She wasn't sure if she'd call Linden, or take a nap. She knew that she couldn't stand helplessly and watch what was happening around her.

As she reached the doorway inside, she heard a loud explosion behind her. She turned to see parts of one of the nearest balloons flying through the air. It had popped and now that part of the *Cudgel* was sinking. On the water, she could see Jakob fall into the sea, wrapped in cables.

39

They stared at the sign for Kay-Tee's Ocean View Motel for a moment, taking in the amenities touted on the giant sign. "They have free Wi-Fi," Tsui said. "And a continental breakfast. That's something."

Linden and the rest had walked from one hotel to the next near the military base, but most were boarded up already in anticipation of the monster making shore. Those that weren't had staff hastily making those preparations. The navy had kindly driven Linden, Holli and Tsui off the base and dropped them at the edge of Oceanside, Oregon.

An older woman came out of the front door to the Ocean View, carrying two suitcases, which she put in the trunk of a waiting car. A man came out a minute later with three kids. They all piled in the car and thanked the woman, who waved as they drove off.

"Are you Katie?" Linden asked.

The woman looked at him. "Pardon?"

This time he pointed to the sign. "Kay-tee's Ocean View Motel. Are you Katie?"

"Oh. No. We named the hotel after my daughter. I'm a little old to be a Katie. No, I'm Ellen. My husband and I own the motel. Something I can do for you?"

"We need a couple of rooms. Maybe for a few days."

Ellen nodded. "You must be from out of town. Or you haven't watched the news or something. The military has an evacuation order in place. Everyone has to leave. All up and down the coast for miles."

"Aren't you leaving?" Holli asked.

"I don't care much for the military telling me what to do." Ellen laughed.

After fishing in his jacket, Linden produced his badge and identification. "I'm with the government, but I don't much listen to what the military says either," he said. "If you're staying and the motel is going to be available, we'd gladly pay for some rooms."

"What's going on, Ellen?" A man stood in the glass doorway to the motel.

"Just some people looking for a room, Ted. I think we have a few available, don't we?" Ted looked puzzled, and walked inside.

After fishing out a few keys, Ellen led them to the second floor and gave them three adjoining rooms in the middle of the motel. She dramatically pulled the blinds apart in the middle one, showing the sunny view of the ocean. "Don't know what you're here for, but you have to admit the ocean is just gorgeous."

From the sliding glass door, Linden could see the bay and the military complex, and the ships floating and flying in preparation of what was to come. Drones loaded ships with supplies just a couple of miles away. "It's perfect." The rest of the room was a little… dated. Old wood paneling, wallpaper with sea shells and waves, and conch lamps placed the motel somewhere in the last century by Linden's estimate. But the room was large, had a kitchenette and a couple of tables. It would have to do.

"Well, other than me and Ted, you have the place to yourself, sent the last guests packing already." Ellen looked away from the view to talk to Holli and Linden. Tsui had hung back to look through the kitchen. "I know you're government folks, but you should really think about leaving too. I don't know exactly what's coming, but it could be pretty bad."

"Thanks," Holli said. "We know what's coming. That's why we need to stay."

Their host departed with a nod and disappeared down the hallway.

"Well, since there's a bed for each of us, I think I'll take a nap and we can get started fresh in an hour or so," Tsui said.

"Grab the other end of that table," Linden replied.

"What?" Tsui looked confused. "I need a break."

"From what? We haven't really done anything yet. Help me move this table."

"You pulled me out of prison, flew me to a combat zone, pulled me off of a sinking battle platform, had me hack a submersible, walked me through a naval base, and then we had to walk through town looking for a place to stay. I need some sleep." Tsui folded his arms and stood defiantly.

"Help me move the table, and you can sleep while we set up." It wasn't a compromise that really benefitted Linden, but he hated to give in to their prisoner. He needed it to appear he was in charge and called the shots. He needed a victory for once in this weird string of events.

Tsui walked over and lifted his end of the table, and went on to move tables from the other rooms, and configure them. It was more than Linden asked for and he didn't bitch when Tsui dropped himself into the bed and fell asleep soon after.

Holli opened her laptop case and pulled out not one, but two nearly paper thin workstations. She wired them next to each other and started connecting to her servers back at home. "Once we get logged in through all the security protocols, we should be able to communicate with the *Cudgel* and hopefully find a way to help control it."

"I can't believe they're even attempting this," Linden said.

"And yet you're willing to help them try." Holli typed smoothly on the keyboard while she talked.

It was a lapse in judgement, maybe. Or it could be a genuine belief that the crew could handle it. Or desperation. There was always desperation.

40

Cass dove into the water, barely taking the time to slip off her shoes before she did. She swam for a couple of minutes underwater, propelled by her dive from the high deck. She could see the huge outline of the *Cudgel* to her left, but during that initial dive, she didn't see Jakob. She surfaced, caught her breath, and looked around. She found the place on the robot where she'd seen Jakob fall off, and headed that way, underwater. As she moved, she could see part of the cable that Jakob was spooling out, hanging from the *Cudgel*. She followed it with her eyes until she found the other end of the cable, wrapped around Jakob. He was struggling, and she counted it lucky that the man was in good shape and an experienced swimmer or panic might have set in and caused him to run out of air more quickly.

When she reached him, she grabbed for the knife on Jakob's belt, but he stopped her and shook his head no—He didn't want the cable cut. Cass marveled that he was so intent on making this happen that he would sacrifice himself to save a charging cable. Whatever motives she questioned about what the crew was doing, she certainly couldn't fault their commitment.

Cass felt her lungs start to ache with the need for air. She got below Jakob, and started to kick as hard as she could; shoving the cable and her crewmate with all the strength she had left. Jakob joined in-his arms were pinned, but he kicked with her, toward the sunlight. They surfaced and moved quickly to the *Cudgel*, where Cass held on with one hand, while trying to help untangle Jakob with the other. Luckily, the movement had loosened the coils around him and he could slip out with her help.

They held on and caught their breath, Jakob coughing as he thanked her.

"No problem," Cass said. "What the hell do we do now?"

Once he looked around and got his bearings, Jakob replied, "Well, unless I guess wrong, this end of the *Cudgel* is still sinking slowly because of that balloon, so we'd best plug this in at the ship's mid-section and then find a way back to the boat."

"Sounds right."

They helped each other up to the part of the leg that was still above water, and began to head all the way up toward the chest. The *Cudgel* shifted occasionally with the waves, but it was steady going other than the slight incline due to the sinking. They reached the midsection easily and began looking for the correct place to install the line. Neither had a phone or an earpiece in to ask anyone a question; Cass had taken hers out, and Jakob lost his in the sea. They kept looking until Jakob literally tripped over it.

"Christ," Jakob said, tumbling onto the shell of the *Cudgel*. He laughed as he got to his feet, realizing what he'd done. "That's it. That's the damn junction we need." He leaned down and Cass helped him pry open the sealed input. They took the other end of the cable, fed it in, and sealed it off to keep water from getting in. A green light came on and flickered to indicate it was properly attached. Now they just needed to know if the power was coming through.

From back the way they came, Cass heard a sound that made her knees buckle: another balloon broke. Then another. The *Cudgel*'s legs began to sink faster, taking the midsection down as well.

"Head upward, Takis was talking about a hatch. Maybe we can make it there, before this ship takes us down with it." There was no way they could jump clear of the ship and into the water, they'd moved too far into the center for that. She was certain their only hope was to make it to a hatch or up to the head section.

The angle got steep, but they could still run without much trouble. Ahead-the chest plate loomed and the hatch that Cass had seen through the drone's camera had to be just before it. It came into view just as it was getting tough to move upward. They had to actually climb the last few feet on their hands and knees, but eventually managed to pull themselves in.

"Crank the hatch shut," Cass said.

Jakob leaned out to see they were nearly straight up and down, and they were sinking down toward the sea with an open door. He turned and did as she said. The *Cudgel* was low enough that the waves were splashing salty water into the compartment they were in. Cass jumped up to help him crank the door shut faster.

A little more water managed to make it in, but the door sealed with a hiss after Cass locked it. The compartment was nearly empty, an airlock for divers to enter when needed, like the one they came through to get Martin's medicine. Only three deep dive suits hung on the wall nearby and one had fallen on the floor below the others.

It was hard for Cass to fathom the fact that she was standing *in* the *Cudgel*. She'd gone through training before joining Linden's team, she'd watched videos of the construction, the crew training, the dedication at the Naval College. She did a few of the modules that students used to prepare for actual flight on more than a few occasions. And now, here she was—ten years, millions of dollars in search efforts, after briefings and meetings and undercover assignments, *she* was the operative that found it.

In the corner of the air lock, an orange light flashed slowly and dimly. Everything outside was blocked out—Cass heard no sounds, and they couldn't see a thing. With both of their headsets gone, they couldn't hear any chatter from the rest of their crew.

"What should we do?" Jakob asked.

Cass wasn't totally sure herself. "Well, I guess we aren't going out that door, the *Cudgel* is still sinking, then that door is certainly underwater by now."

Almost to emphasize her point, the *Cudgel* lurched to the side. Cass and Jakob ended up on the floor and slid into the wall. The dive suit on the floor slid along with them and thudded next to Jakob.

"Shit. Let's see if we can get higher up in the ship. Maybe we can get out before this thing sinks completely." Cass held out her hand to help Jakob up, only he wasn't looking at her, he was staring at the suit next to him.

"I don't think this thing is empty," Jakob said. He got to his knees and pushed at the rigid tan suit next to him. "It's heavy, there's definitely something in it."

Cass looked in the clear visor of the helmet. "Nothing there." She grabbed the releases on each side and twisted the helmet off. Immediately, she stepped back as a pungent smell hit her nostrils.

Jakob stepped back and covered his face. "What the hell is that smell?"

It seemed fairly obvious to Cass, but she didn't want to make any assumptions before she checked. It didn't exactly smell like a dead body, but it didn't smell good. She moved the helmet away and looked down into the neck hole of the suit. The light was too dim to be sure, but it looked like a skeleton, or a partial one. "I think we found our first crew member."

"Are you serious?"

"Did you think they wouldn't be here?" Cass stood up and wiped her hands off on her pants. When she removed the helmet, a small amount of dust came out onto her. "There were only a few scenarios where we wouldn't find their bodies if we found the ship, right?"

"Hadn't thought about it," Jakob said. He wiped his hands too, though he hadn't come in contact with the inside of the suit.

"Really? You and the others said you were all excited to get in here and get a souvenir when you found the *Cudgel*, you didn't think you would have dead crewmen to step over?" Cass went over to the airlock that would let them into the body of the giant machine. "You didn't think you'd be pulling jewelry off of the bones of dead people like this?" She tapped the keypad, but it didn't light up.

"It wasn't like that. We just wanted to get some pictures, some proof that we bagged the big one, we didn't mean any disrespect."

Cass tapped harder this time before responding to Jakob. "Well, there's your picture." She pointed to the suit on the floor.

The *Cudgel* shook and Jakob pried a panel off the wall. "Obviously, the power hasn't begun circulating to the power systems yet." With some effort, he pulled a lever that had been concealed by the panel, and the door started to open. He followed Cass as she walked out. "Look, we feel like shit already, that's part of why we want to make this right," Jakob said.

Something about what her companion said suddenly resonated with Cass and she stopped just outside the door. "We are sinking."

"Thanks for the recap. Are you listening to me? I'm trying to apologize for..."

Cass held up her hand. "Listen to me. This giant robot is sinking. You and I attached the power line to it very securely." She paused, hoping he would catch on. "Where is the other end of that cable, Jakob?"

"The *Adamant*."

"Is that cable going to release at either end, or are we going to drag that boat down with us?"

"It would snap, right?" Jakob stared at Cass with widening eyes.

"I'm asking you. You had the cable."

Jakob shrugged.

They had to assume that the cable wouldn't break, just to go with the worst case scenario. Cass thought about their options. "We could go back out the portal we came in, swim back and unplug the cable."

Jakob looked around the hallway they were in, and Cass joined him. There wasn't much there: a narrow corridor, ladder rungs up the opposite wall and doors that led to places neither of them could guess. Without their tablets they had no maps or schematics of the *Cudgel* at hand.

"Up?" Jakob asked.

Cass looked up the rungs and couldn't see the top of the ladder in the soft fuzz of the emergency lights. She put her foot on the first step and the whole ship began to shake violently. A loud roar seemed to make it shake even more. "The fuck?" Cass held on to the rungs and Jakob braced himself against the wall.

After a minute, the shaking seemed to stabilize, though the sound was still horrendous. Cass grabbed the rungs and started up as fast as she could, checking to be sure Jakob was just below her as she rose. A nearby light suggested there might be another landing up ahead. They stepped off the rungs and followed a small corridor to another airlock, somewhat smaller than the other. Here, there were no suits, no stench, and there was no dust, but there was a monitor that worked. It blinked in and out of a picture, and showed snowy lines across it.

"Want to try opening this hatch? Maybe we can get out," Jakob suggested.

It was a good play, but there were too many variables. They had no idea how deep they were, no clue if the airlock would work correctly. "I think we keep going up."

The monitor changed, and cleared, and Rina's face appeared. "Guys? Are you okay?"

Jakob waved his hands at the monitor and shouted, "We're here."

"I don't think she can see us."

The audio on the monitor buzzed and crackled. "I'm detecting you're near the mid-level airlock on the forward side. Open the hatch. Trust me."

Jakob and Cass looked at each other and shook their heads. "Trust her, she says." Cass was getting dizzy trying to figure out whom to trust at this point.

The two of them put their hands on the manual crank and turned until the indicator showed they could open the hatch. Jakob turned the last lever and pulled the door open.

There was no rush of water. They were not undersea. They were level with the upper deck of the *Adamant*. Ozzie and Takis were waving from the railing, and Ben smiled from his perch at the top of the ship.

"Hi," Rina said from the television. "I started screwing with all of the controls that sounded like they might control liftoff or flying, and I managed to make it hover." She sounded pleased with herself, even through the speakers. "Cool, huh?"

Cass nodded. It was all she could do. She was standing on the very ship she was supposed to protect, and all because someone had hijacked it with their tablet.

41

A coughing fit woke Martin from his drug-induced sleep. Coughing led to his chest and stomach muscles contracting, which led to his wounds shaking, which led to pain. He leaned over, grabbed his water glass.

He'd been sleeping so much that he had no real idea what time it was. It was dark out the window, so he was loathed to bother anyone in the middle of the night. When he turned to the entry to his room, though, it was bright as daytime. Light was streaming in through open doors and portals.

He turned back to his windows and realized that it was daytime, but something was blocking out the sun. It appeared to be a huge building, but that wasn't it. He looked again.

The *Cudgel* was upright and just outside his room.

He tried to get up, but couldn't, so he slouched down to try to see the top, and eventually managed it. The robot was up to its chest in the ocean, and holding steady as the waves hit the hull. The head unit was wider than the *Adamant*, much wider.

"It's pretty amazing, isn't it?" Ozzie leaned in and walked to the window. "It took a lot to get it up and stable, but we're good for now. They're using solar and hydro power to get it charged."

"Beautiful."

"We'll load it up and take off. Then we can still use solar and harvest the wind as we go," Ozzie said.

Martin was marveling at the giant war machine when Ozzie's words registered. "Go? As you go where?"

"No one told you?" Ozzie looked back at the door for help, as if someone would suddenly come through with a perfect response. He turned back when nobody came. "With Caroline and Lewis dead and that giant thing on the loose out there, we feel responsible. We're going to take the *Cudgel* and try to fight the monster ourselves. This machine beat it once, it can beat it again. Or maybe someone else will know how to use it."

Water cascaded off of the machine not five hundred feet from Martin's window. Sunshine glared off the hull, showing off occasional patches of mossy green. It was everything Martin had heard it was, everything he'd dreamed. He took in all of the *Cudgel* that was visible. Normally, a treasure hunt would end with him holding a doubloon, or a necklace in his hands—he could feel the weight of it, touch it, and determine how it was manufactured. Here, this chase ended with him in a bed staring out the window at something he'd never see again. Even if the crew took it and found a way to stop the monster, the government would immediately reclaim it, and tuck it away in a warehouse or dismantle it altogether.

"Martin?" Ben had entered the room while Martin was staring. "Don't you have something to say to these people? They're your crew. Don't you want to tell them how stupid this sounds?"

Martin nodded slowly, and leaned back on his bed. He was already tired again. "Ozzie, can you close those blinds? I need my sleep."

The crewman did as he was asked. "Sure. You need anything else?"

"I'm okay." Martin looked at Ben and thought about what he said. "I maybe need some pain medication."

Ozzie lingered at the door for a moment. "Sure."

"Hey," Martin said. "You guys…" He thought about it. They were all grownups and could think for themselves. He'd known Ozzie and his brother Takis for years. They'd joined after their military stint was up and they were looking for something constructive to do with their lives. They both worked with the Hellenic Navy as divers and demolitions experts. Takis took to blowing things up like it was a calling, and Ozzie took time to become a medic to help his fellow soldiers on the battlefield, or wherever he was needed. They were an important part of his crew, but they made their own decisions, much to Martin's chagrin sometimes. "You dent that machine, it'll have to come out of your share of the reward."

Ozzie smiled and gave a slight wave as he left.

"You should've just stayed asleep." Ben left the room shaking his head.

Martin looked at the now-closed blinds and thought about the prize just beyond it. Just outside his reach.

42

Cass walked around in a circle in her room. Her satellite phone was on the bed, fully charged. She'd called Linden as soon as she got back, but he didn't answer, didn't respond. She didn't want to pull her gun on the crew and they were better armed than she was. The inside of the *Cudgel* beckoned her. Once she'd put a foot on the first rung, she was hooked. But this mission? She could see flying the war machine to the naval yard and letting someone take over, but doing it themselves?

The crew didn't waste a lot of time on reunions. By the time Jakob and Cass got back on the *Adamant*, everything was packed into nice duffle bags and ready to roll. By the time Cass came back from her room, the crew was already loaded up with the bags.

She stood in front of them on the deck. Her own gun felt heavier than usual strapped to her belt behind her back. The crew looked at her expectantly.

"Well?" Rina asked. "What now?"

The decision came down to whether she was willing to fight these people over something they obviously believed in. She thought of the two crew members on the *Adamant* killed by the slags, thought of the *Cudgel* crewman dead in the airlock. "If anyone wants to leave, leave now. There's no pressure." She looked at everyone and they looked back. "My only request is that we try to find someone who can help us fly this thing and fight. If they have a crew that can fly this, we hand it over to them."

The rest of the crew looked around at each other and nodded. "Agreed," Jakob said.

Cass's hands shook as she picked up a duffle bag. "You guys know we'll probably crash on take-off, right?"

"That's why we wanted you to come with us; your sunny disposition," Takis said.

They walked into the *Cudgel* with whatever weapons they could carry. Jakob had the heaviest one-the double shotgun with the feeder drum on the bottom, from there, most carried pistols, though Ozzie insisted on the assault rifle that had somehow made it into the pile on the *Adamant*. Martin claimed it had been liberated from a thief on one of the group's treasure hunts, but everyone remained skeptical. Cass still had her pistol, checked more than once to be sure it hadn't been tampered with.

The air in the machine remained as fresh and antiseptic as the first time they'd come aboard for the supplies to help Martin. They swept the hall with their flashlights in the darkness, looking for a control panel, listening to Rina behind them, reading off directions from her tablet. They made their way to the small panel where Ozzie had attached a drive on that first visit that allowed them to take it over.

Takis and Ozzie both held their lights on the panel while Rina plugged in her tablet. "Jesus," Rina said. "This hulking mass of tech, and my little hand-held has better software."

"It's kind of been stuck in the past, Rina. It may need a few updates," Cass said as she and Jakob walked ahead toward the medical bay, where they'd seen the crewman in the sickbay. She stopped, not liking the darkness ahead, even though she'd been there before. "Let's just wake this thing up and see what we're dealing with. Any luck and the flight controls won't start."

"Who has the keys?" Takis asked.

"I meant, if it doesn't initialize, this little plan of yours is over before it begins." The fact that Rina got the thing to hover on just the lowest power, probably proved her wrong, but it would make things much easier if they couldn't fly. As Cass spoke, the lights overhead and along the corridor flickered silently to life and bathed the group in soft white light. Nearby, the clicking sounds of computers booting up filled the air. Stale air softly blew against Cass's face from a vent somewhere above her.

"There's at least enough power for lights, ventilation and computer functions. That's a good sign." Jakob had his hands on his hips and looked around like he had an idea of what he was looking at. "Now, let's hope it can nuke that fucking thing."

"There are no nuclear missiles." Rina looked at her tablet like she was navigating the high seas with a compass and sextant. "And if there were, I'd be the one that gets to push the button to launch them."

"That hardly seems fair," Takis whispered. "We should have a vote, or we should each get to shoot one or something."

"Why are you whispering?" Ozzie asked.

Takis shrugged.

Now that the passage was illuminated, Cass stepped forward again, moving toward the medical bay. "I need to have a closer look at that crewmember that we saw."

"He was a skeleton in a uniform," Takis said. "What's he going to tell us?"

It was tough to say exactly what Cass was hoping to find, other than a clue to the whereabouts of the rest of the crew and possibly more of the creatures. "Don't know. But remember there was one of those slag's shells at his feet. Maybe there were more."

"You don't think they'd be alive after this much time?" Rina asked.

There was no way Cass could answer that. It was an unknown species of what she could only assume was sea life. There wasn't much of a precedent for their behavior and no way to research them. "Don't know. But we'd better find out quick." She led the group to the infirmary around the corner. The soldier was still on the bed, the husk of the thing was on the floor at the base of the table that held the man's body.

"Ozzie? We have a little time. Very little. Can you dig around in here to see what you can find out?" She looked around at the half shut drawers and supplies strewn about the floor from when they desperately dug around for supplies to save Martin, and realized Ozzie was staring at it all as well.

"A computer would be more helpful," he said.

Cass held up her hands. "As soon as they're up and running completely, you have full access. But I don't know how long that'll be."

Ozzie nodded and moved off silently, stepping carefully around the debris and Rina followed him.

The rest of their heavily armed party followed Cass as she continued along the curved hall. To the left she could see sealed doors with yellow and red signs prominently warning of the dangers presented by the power supply that evidently was housed in the center of the robot. To the left, they quickly came upon the elevator for the crew to quickly move from floor to floor and section to section. Buttons to the right of the door were dark, but Takis pushed them anyway. When nothing happened, he pushed them again repeatedly.

"Seriously?" Cass asked him as she started moving further down the curving hall. It would lead them back to the area where they entered, then to the medical bay. It was quiet and clean. Nothing out of the ordinary and, other than doors that led to the core of the vehicle, there was nothing that stood out to any of them. A hum filled the air as more lights came on and the whole ship began to come to life. Indicators for the core lit up, screens that were invisible on the walls suddenly made their presence known with identical rebooting messages.

The medical bay also came to life, with lights, vital sign monitors, and screens of their own, all showing the *Cudgel* symbol and the same boot message as everything else.

They'd all stepped gingerly around the shell of the slag when they entered the medical bay, but this time when Cass returned from the quick tour of the level, she went directly to it. She knelt and looked as close as she dared without touching it. It appeared just to be a dried shell. She was looking at it so intently that she startled when Ozzie touched her shoulder. He held out a long-handled medical instrument that she didn't recognize and she took it. As she turned back toward the shell, she noticed everyone had stopped what they were doing to watch her. All of them had a weapon in hand, or their hand on a weapon.

With the instrument, Cass pushed the slag shell away from her a little, then pulled back. When nothing happened, she decided to push it again. Nothing. "Feels pretty light."

She took a second to find a nook along the edge of the shell that the tool could fit under and wedged it in. She looked at the others, who nodded or otherwise expressed their approval for her to flip the thing over. She got on her knees, ready to back up when she turned it, just in case something came her way.

"Come on, already." Takis rocked back and forth, putting his weight on one foot and then another. "Jeezus."

Cass flipped the shell and moved back, but nothing came for her. Instead she and the others found an empty shell, and a sizable hole in the deck below where the shell had been. Inspecting closer, Cass found the edges around the hole looked familiar. "This looks similar to the way the pegs that kept the *Cudgel* secured to the rock were eroded."

"Is it from some kind of acid?" Ozzie knelt down to look at it too. He reached out and touched a jagged edge. "Feels rough, I suppose it could be acid or a saw of some kind."

Against her better judgement, Cass reached out and touched it as well. "It's fine, like it was sanded away."

"Or worn down by rows of teeth chewing on the floor for years?" Everyone turned to look at Rina, who'd taken her headphones off and placed her tablet on the counter. She had a pistol in her belt, but didn't look like she planned on using it anymore. "What? Just a thought."

"Scary-ass thought," Takis said.

They leaned over and found the hole led to a duct lined with several cables of varying colors. There was a narrow empty space next to the cables.

"My fat ass isn't going to fit in there," Takis said from a safe distance. "I'm not going in. Not even trying."

Ozzie and Cass looked at each other, just above the hole. "Not a chance," Ozzie said.

"I think we can *all* skip that for now, don't you?" Cass asked. Even if she wanted to, she knew there was no way she could get in and maneuver.

"So are we just going to ignore this?" Rina was looking down the hole.

Jakob shrugged. "The thing's dead, right? It's been a decade."

"Sure, but where are the other crew members?" Rina looked around at everyone for an answer.

"Good goddam question," Takis said. "Hey. Maybe this was a bad idea. Right? We should just go…"

There was a hum from down the hall and everyone turned to see the lights flicker on around the elevator. "Hey. The lift looks like it's got power. Should we explore the rest of the place while we wait for the computers to get going?" Jakob was already on his way.

"Just because it has a light doesn't mean it's working," Cass said. She'd been happy to keep going a floor at a time, and not split the team up. If Rina and Ozzie kept working on the computers from here, they would have to do just that. "Hey…" she started to yell over to the medical bay.

"Just go. It could take a minute to get this thing going, or it could take an hour. I'd rather we were here when it happens. We can tell that much faster if this monstrosity will even move," Rina said. She stuck one shell of her headphones over an ear and turned her back on Cass.

An insistent clicking told Cass that Takis had found the elevator button again. "Grow up. We're not here to play around."

There was a low tone, and then the door opened. Instead of a big boxy elevator car like they were used to, there were only cables with small straps for hand rests and flat platforms for the feet. Cass stepped onto the foot placements and interlaced her right hand in the strap. From there, she could click a switch to indicate up or down. "Start at the bottom?" She didn't wait, and with a click, she was on her way down the dimly lit shaft toward the blue light at the bottom.

"What the fuck is this?" Takis asked.

Jakob put his hand in place and got on the mini platform. "It's a personnel elevator. They used them on some of the construction sites I worked as a kid. They let one person go up, and another go down, without much fuss. They're usually temporary while a building is being built. More efficient than making your crew wait for a big ass elevator if they don't need to." Jakob showed Takis how to wrap his hand into the strap and how to work the unit's solitary control for up and down.

"What happens if I fall?" He looked down at Cass and the long fall beyond her.

"Don't fall," Cass said as she waited for the other two. "There's also a way you can use one of the other straps to secure yourself to the cable by attaching yourself with your belt."

Patting himself frantically, Takis panicked. "I don't have a belt."

"You'll be fine." As Jakob began to descend, Cass did the same, only occasionally looking back up at Takis as he put his hands in the strap and hugged the cable.

43

True to his word, Tsui fell asleep almost immediately after he helped rearrange one of the rooms. Holli pulled out her laptop, opened the top, then folded it out so that she had three screens to look at.

"That's a great workstation. We get crappy equipment that's ten years too old most of the time. The government must really treat you right," Linden said. He looked over her shoulder to watch it boot up, but it was online and ready before he even got there.

"Well, they give us good equipment, and it's usually only five years behind the current technology, but, this one is actually mine." Holli shrugged. "I don't have a car and I live in the smallest apartment I could find, just so I could afford this thing. It was worth it, I think. Except my bosses occasionally need me to use it for work, considering it's better than theirs."

"You like working for Gary Matthews?"

Holli clacked away at the keys while she considered it. "Yeah. I mean, he's a boss. Nothing notable about him. He's kind of dull. Vanilla. You know? Not one of those leaders you can have a fun conversation with. It's work. No mysteries. What you see is what you get."

"I've had those."

"Really? When?" Holli asked.

"Let's leave that a mystery for now," Linden said. "How's the hook-up coming?"

A rustling behind them stopped her from answering. "Do you two need the bed?" Tsui asked.

"What?" Linden felt his face grow warm at the accusation. He'd just been talking to Holli with no intentions beyond passing time. The insinuation that he'd been romancing her somehow made him uncomfortable. "Funny. Did you have a good nap?"

"Little uncomfortable with these on." Tsui held up his wrists, chained together by handcuffs. Ornn had borrowed them from an MP, remembering that Tsui's cuffs were broken on the *Montenegro.*

"You're still a prisoner," Linden said. "Can't have you walking off on us, can we?"

"I fucking helped you get away from the sinking naval thing. I..." He pointed over at the computers. "...Moved stuff." He clanked the mugs on the kitchenette, and poured some water. "Anything to eat? It's been a while."

It occurred to Linden that none of them had eaten since the visit to the command center much earlier in the day, and it was nearly nightfall. "I don't have anything. I can check downstairs with the owners. I doubt anything is open around here, everyone took off to stay away from the Lusca."

Holli produced some packets of crackers from her laptop bag. "Snatched these from the mess over in the HQ. Not much, but enough for each of us to have some."

"Water and crackers?" Tsui scooped up his allotment and tore the plastic open. "I was better fed in prison."

A beep brought Holli's attention back to her computer. "Looks like we're into the network back at the office, and connected to the satellite."

The idea was to get into the archives and find any way for them to get into the *Cudgel*'s control mechanisms so Linden and Holli could help control the machine from their location.

"You know these files better than I do, why don't you sit down and start looking through all of this and I'll set up the other laptop in the meantime. I think we'll need it eventually."

"You have a second laptop?" Linden asked.

"Yeah, it's not as nice. Just one screen and more of a phone/tablet combo, but I have the programs to hook it up to a television monitor." Holli turned to look at Tsui. "Any chance you can move a TV from another room and put it on this table?"

Tsui held up his arms to show off his cuffs again.

He'd helped before, so Linden shrugged. "Fine." He threw the key to Holli and turned back to the files he was combing. "If you escape, or try to escape..."

"Pain, death, punching, whatever." Tsui's voice faded into the other room.

"This computer will take a sec to get ready, I'll help him," Holli said.

She pulled a headset from her bag and put it on her ear. "Hello?" She got back to work for a moment. "There."

She handed the headset to Linden. "You should be able to talk to the crew on the *Cudgel*, if they're listening."

He had to think a second to remember her code name. It had been a crazy few days for him and everyone else. "Blind Date Citadel calling Chaperone Delta-One. Come in Chaperone Delta-One." He'd already given up the secret shit when things got hairy, but he figured saying her call sign might cut through all of Cass's radio chatter and everything else she might be monitoring right now.

"Ummm. This is Rina. Cass can't come to the phone right now."

44

They landed at the base of the elevator like they were floating on air. The touchdown was light and easy. Cass looked around in the dim lighting, with such a small space, nothing could possibly be hiding in a corner to maim or dismember them. Hopefully. She unhooked herself, moved to the door, and waited for her two companions to disengage themselves. Jakob had no problems, and Takis looked embarrassed to have made a big deal about descending into the lift. "Easy enough, right?" She looked to the other two.

"No problems," Jakob said.

Takis nodded and stood by the door. The elevator shaft may have been clear and easy to see, but it was hard to say what was behind any given door.

She took a deep breath, then Cass hit the button. It opened to a short hallway, barely long enough to hold the three of them, and ended in another doorway.

"Jesus. I'm going to have a coronary by the time we get through opening all these doors," Takis said. It was getting warm in this part of the *Cudgel*, basically near its crotch, slightly above where the actuators and tendons for the leg's movements were housed. Ahead, beyond the next door, a light clanking sounded in some random pattern. It was the sound of metal meeting metal.

"There can't be any of the crew still alive in there, right?" Jakob asked.

Cass thought about it for a moment. "Nah. That can't be possible. They would have run out of food or oxygen. We already know the *Cudgel* was shut down when we got here."

Ever the optimist, Takis guessed next. "Those things? Do you think they could have lived? Fuck. They might have, right?"

"No idea." Cass listened at the door. The pattern could easily be from one of the slags walking around slowly in the next room, the thin legs tapping on the metal deck. "But we need to find out." She reached for the button and ducked down in the narrow corridor. Both of the others aimed their weapons over her head. She held up three fingers and counted down with them… three… two…one… She hit the button with her other hand and then skittered backward from the suddenly open door. Inside was a relatively round chamber, with a white floor and a panel of lights directly opposite Cass and her party.

She stood and walked toward the door, slowly peeking around the right corner, then the left. She saw nothing but the rungs of metallic ladders on both sides and doors or hatches at regular intervals.

"Great. More fucking doors," Takis moaned.

In another second, the tapping sound rang again. Louder in this room, and it originated above them. Cass raised her weapon and pointed it upward toward a mass of equipment that jutted down at them. She took them to be more of the mechanics that moved the *Cudgel* in one way or another. Everything was static, so it took time for her to notice movement between a long needle-like protrusion, and a boxy grey metal device. "There." She pointed for the others, who'd been scanning as she had.

They all flicked their lights over to see what was causing it and were shocked to see legs – boots and a flight suit, at least - swaying in the metal jungle of machinery.

"The hell?" said Jakob.

Cass climbed one of the nearby metal ladders, and put her flashlight in her pocket. "Keep the light over there," she said. The rungs were icy to the touch and it kept her moving quickly upward. Somewhere around forty feet over her crewmates below, the ladder cut into the various equipment in the ceiling and she was in a tight maintenance shaft as she ascended. She found a hatch that led back toward the flight suit, opened it and shined her light down what turned out to be a narrow beam that connected all of the devices she'd seen below. The top of the corridor was overwhelmed by fiber optics and other cables that Cass had no expertise in. She made her way out, careful to watch her step, and careful to notice that the machine was still clean and dust-free, possibly a side effect of the *Cudgel* being sealed up after things went bad.

She got to the end and slid an access panel open, and came face-to-face with a man in a flight suit. What was left of the man. His skin had turned mostly to flakey dust, most of which had fallen off, though some dropped even as he swayed back and forth lightly from the cable around his neck. What little Cass could see was badly decomposed, dry and flimsy. Cass let out an involuntary yelp and stepped back.

"You okay up there?" Jakob shouted. "Need me to come up?"

Cass heard the shotgun being racked and the whine of a Taser powering up. "Cass? What the hell?" Her yelp sounded like it had done nothing for Takis's nerves.

"I'm fine," Cass said. "It's a crew member. He's got a cable around his neck and he's hanging from the rafters."

"Dead?" Takis asked.

"He has a cable around his neck and he's hanging from the rafters."
She didn't mean for her reply to come off so terse, but she also had never
seen a man dead like this. She moved close to see if she could find a way
to untangle the cable and lower the body to the deck, but the cable had
been tied so it would deliberately keep him from falling. "Should I try to
get him down?"

Through holes between the equipment, Cass could see the men look
at each other. "I don't know. I suppose if someone found my body
somewhere, I'd want them to cut it down," Jakob said.

"What the hell are you talking about? Where would someone find
you in that situation where you'd want them to do that?"

"I'm just saying."

"Look," Takis said. "If we're seriously going to be trying to fly this
thing and fight that monster, I don't want to know a dead guy is rattling
around somewhere in the ship. That's all I'm going to think about. Dead
man."

On one hand, Cass liked that the men were joking to cope with the
situation. It made things feel slightly less dire than they actually were.
On the other hand, she constantly wanted to slap them for those same
poor attempts at humor. As she untied the cable, laughter was the
furthest thing from her mind. She thought about what the rest of the crew
had done to hijack the *Cudgel* and wondered if there was a point where
she should have stopped it. There was. There were many, but she didn't
take them. Maybe she still would have to take one in the future.
Somewhere deep down she really hadn't wanted to end this. The hunt for
the legend that was the *Cudgel* was over and it felt hollow.

She shouted down to her crewmates. "Hey, a little help? I'm going
to lower him down to you guys and would rather not drop him on your
heads." The men looked up and raised their arms as Cass slowly let the
cable slip through her hands bit by bit. She could feel Jakob and Takis
take up the slack. She looked down after one of them yelled they had
him. It was obvious that Jakob was shouldering the bulk of the weight, as
Takis looked as though he might vomit and run any second.

Cass looked around from her vantage point at that height but
couldn't see much beyond the electronics, bundles, casings, and
everything else. She took a breath, just to steady herself, but as she did,
she saw her companions holding the body of the long-dead crewman,
and she felt anything but steady.

She climbed down the rungs and joined her companions who'd put
the body on the deck. "You think he did this to himself?" Jakob asked.

"I do," Cass said. "I don't see any other way. Unless his fellow crew members killed him for some reason. I guess being trapped down there could've driven them mad after a while."

"Shit," Takis said. He backed away toward the door a few steps.

"What?"

"It moved." Takis pointed at the suit. "The damn suit moved."

She found it troublesome that she'd just been talking about someone going crazy in the *Cudgel* right before Takis made another strange comment. "Just air blowing out of the suit, I'm sure."

"Or the bones and whatever else is left of the poor guy settling in there," Jakob said. It made Cass happy that one of her party had a level head at least.

"I'm telling you."

Jakob walked up to Cass, looked at her, then looked at the body in the flight suit. After a few seconds, Jakob looked at Cass, then back to the body.

"Keep watching."

They did. And nothing happened.

"Damn it," Takis said. He left the doorway and pushed the others aside. "It fucking moved." He pulled his leg back and kicked the body as hard as he could. The flight suit broke in two, brittle as leaves, pieces flying into the air and the parts sliding toward the middle of the room.

They were silent as they looked from Takis to the suit.

"Jesus," Jakob finally said. "What did you do?"

As Takis stepped toward the top half of the suit, the skull fell off the top and cracked in two, half turning to dust and falling away. Several bits and pieces fell from the torso portion as the dust settled. They were parts of bones, ribs and spine, and four prickly orbs the size of apples. They looked just like the slags that had attacked the crew onboard the *Adamant*, but they were a quarter of the size or less, wrinkled, and grey. Their shells were dented and caved-in. They sat among the small pile of bones- each part gnawed on and half-gone.

"Shit," Takis said. "Shit. I told you."

"Did they live off the crew for a while?" Jakob asked.

Cass was just as curious as Jakob, but probably as nauseous as Takis was about the past crew of the *Cudgel*. "Looks like it." She reached out with her gun and poked one of the slags with the barrel. It gave way slowly, like a balloon, and then expanded when she removed her gun.

"Disgusting," Takis said. He backed away, waving his hand in front of his nose. "Like rotting fruit."

He was right, Cass could smell the awful stench clearly emanating from the slags now that she was closer. Backing away from the smell, she noticed movement out of the corner of her eye. One of the slags moved slightly, she was sure of it. Then another one extended a leg. "Guys?" The others turned to look just as the two creatures began to pull themselves forward slowly.

"Oh shit." Takis encapsulated what Cass was thinking perfectly. She watched the slags crawl at a snail's pace, leaving a trail of black sticky mucus behind them. They were not the fearsome monsters. Two others wobbled slightly, then rolled, but didn't advance.

"They've been alive this long?" Jakob asked.

"Barely," Cass said. She looked to Takis, who was barely containing his reaction.

"See? I told you it was moving." He seemed thrilled and horrified to be right. He smiled slightly. He unslung his rifle and stepped forward. "We're not saving these to study this time, right? Not after what happened the last time."

"They don't really seem to pose a threat right now, so…"

"We're not saving these. Right?" Takis asked. He raised his weapon and brought the butt down on one of the slags that were crawling toward the group. The impact cracked the surprisingly brittle shell, and smashed the body of the creature that was inside. It was quickly just a black mass with thin slivers of white shell sticking out of it. Takis lifted his rifle and stepped closer to the next one.

Cass and Jakob did nothing to stop him as he repeated the act again with each of the four emaciated slags. As he did, Cass looked around the room, looking in nooks and between equipment for more of them. Had they been the larger size, they would be easy to spot, but at this size, they could hide or nest nearly anywhere. Her search turned up nothing, and when Takis was done with his smashing, she keyed on her mic. "Guys? Rina? Ozzie?"

"This is Ozzie. How is the exploration going?"

She took a breath, mainly to get over the ammonia-like smell of the creatures. "Not well. We haven't gone far, and we've run into more of the slags."

"Shit." It sounded like Rina in the earphones.

"The good news is they are small, slow and seem to be starving. They're easy to kill."

"Bad news?"

"No idea how many of them there are. Could be one, could be one thousand."

"You're a real ray of sunshine."

"I said it was bad news, didn't I?"

Takis turned his mic on as well. "Ozzie? Hey! I killed four of them. It was gross and awesome and..."

"Slow down," his brother said. "You okay, you sound pretty freaked out."

Takis looked at Cass and Jakob, and must've noted the concern on their faces. He shook his head. "Hey. I'm fine. I'll be fine."

"Okay. Drink some water. Deep breaths," Ozzie said. "You must chill."

Takis laughed. "You must chill." He pulled the plastic straw connected to his backpack and took a long drink. He seemed more relaxed almost immediately.

"We have good news and bad news of our own. We're into the system and just about everything is coming online. We ran a systems check and most of the reports are good," Ozzie said.

"The bad news is, not everything is good. We have errors coming up in a control junction on the left side. It controls the right arm and some of the connections to flight control in the main cockpit. We aren't going anywhere until that is fixed," Rina said. "We can't. We're fucked."

"Did someone call me a ray of sunshine?" Cass nodded to the door and the others followed, though Takis lingered to look at the shredded flight suit, and the bones.

"Shouldn't we do something for him?" Takis asked.

Jakob turned. "Like bury him?"

"Yes."

"We're on a giant robot," Jakob said.

"Right now, we need to clear this thing and see if we can get it going. I wasn't the one that suggested this. If you want to stop and take care of all of the victims here, I'm all for it," Cass said. She wasn't angry with him, but she felt herself being more forceful than she intended. She pushed him, but it was meant to get him moving, not give up. As much as she hated feeling it, she wanted to get the *Cudgel* moving and get it to fight. It was a thrill that seemed just within reach.

"We aren't fucking backing out," Rina's voice erupted in the earpiece. "Get your shit together Takis, we can take care of other stuff later."

"You mean we aren't backing out, unless that junction you mentioned is beyond repair, right?" Ozzie seemed to want to qualify Rina's statement.

In the background of Ozzie talking a familiar buzzing started. "Cass, I think you left your phone up here with us," Rina said. Her voice getting more distant. "Hello?"

45

"They should stop. There's no reason for this." Martin flipped around the news channels and mumbled to himself. His eyes drooped as he fought sleep and his head spun, probably from the lack of blood he'd experienced.

A news drone showed footage taken a mile away from the creature as it attacked a naval station in the Pacific. It had been made from a group of three abandoned oil derricks that were made into a rally point during the war. It was still used for weather and for fueling drones and other ships as they made their way across the ocean. The water was relatively shallow, all things considered.

The Lusca had torn apart one of them, sunk some smaller ships, and, according to the announcer, drained the power from all of the derricks before disappearing under the ocean and off radar.

"They could use that to land if they needed to. There's room," Martin said. He reached over and grabbed a cup and threw it toward the hall. "Hey." The cup fell just past Martin's bed. "I have an idea. Depending on the condition of the *Cudgel*'s storage cells, they may need to recharge before they reached the Lusca. Assuming the base got back up to speed quickly, they should have power to help." Martin yelled again, but he was quieter than planned. The wires in his arms and chest seemed to go everywhere, strapping him into his bed.

"Hello?"

46

"Are you concerned at all about losing the signal if the Lusca gets between us?" Cass asked. "I'd hate for you to have flight control and suddenly have the signal blocked and we have to go into emergency mode." She was thrilled to have more people involved in running the *Cudgel*, even if they couldn't be in the machine itself. The plan was to let Holli control the flight, while everyone took the time during the six hour journey to try using training modules and simulations to learn their prospective jobs and positions.

"It's a possibility, but we're bouncing our signal off the same satellite as the sat phone, so as long as we don't lose power, we should be fine. The signal will go directly over the interference," Holli said. "We'll do our best to stay out of its range, but I'm setting the autopilot to kick in if you lose touch with us."

"Great, I'm going to check in with everyone and get them settled," Cass said. Leaving the control room., she looked around at all of the banks of controls and lights, switches and panels, and felt overwhelmed. The area was bigger than she expected, a tall ceiling, wide view screens and two rows of work stations for the crew. She was hardly a substitute for so many people. In the early days of the search she'd read their bios carefully, gotten to know their families, their talents. She barely had the skills of one of them, yet she and Rina would be alone on the bridge, covering all their jobs, with Holli's help of course.

Cass stepped onto the lift that took her down toward where the repairs were happening. She grabbed the handle and held on, the ride was silent and slightly dangerous, as the lift was only one square coupled magnetically to the walls of the maintenance shaft. As she swiftly descended, she could already hear shouting below. She stepped off and walked up behind her crewmates.

"This..." Jakob held up a tangle of wires. "...needs to be removed completely. We don't need it."

Rina was having none of it. "We don't even know what it is. We can't just fucking remove it." She looked to Takis, who was standing beside her with an armload of tools, for confirmation.

"How in the hell should I know?"

Cass keyed her mic. "Holli? If you can find our position, we're running into a problem fixing the damage. Can you key in on our location and bring up a schematic for us?"

"Oh, thank God you're here," Rina mumbled. "We're saved." She turned and shined her light on a wall panel and opened it. Jakob walked up and leaned close to her and started looking over her shoulder. "Get back." Rina was clearly annoyed at having her ideas challenged.

Jakob kept on. "Look. This blackened wire leads to the junction marked 'Override' up there. We..." He reached around Rina and grabbed at the wire. The compartment suddenly shook and Cass threw herself backward from the wires. A loud rumble of sound trailed off into the distance.

"What the hell was that?" Linden's voice came through the headphones. "What in the *hell* was that?"

Cass, Jakob and Rina all stared at each other.

"Hello? What the hell just happened out there?" This time it was Holli. "I can't see anything on my monitor."

There was a second or two of silence before static broke in and Ozzie's voice came through from up in the control room. "Uhhh. That was a finger."

It was silent in the maintenance shaft as the three looked at each other and thought over those words. "What?" Cass asked.

"A finger. We just shot off a finger. One of the fingers of the *Cudgel*'s right hand just launched like a missile," Ozzie said. "What did you guys do?"

Rina pointed to Jakob. "I don't know what the hell any of this stuff does. Do *not* look at me. It was him." Jakob was speechless.

"Which finger?" Linden asked.

"Pinky finger. Right hand." The crackling voice came back.

Cass lifted up her pad and started cycling through the camera inputs until she found the channels with outside feeds. The one set up closest to the right hand showed nothing but smoke, so she switched again and again, until she found one that showed the trail of that smoke leading off into the sky. And once it crackled into focus, they could see the flare of a rocket booster propelling the finger skyward. It was faint but they managed to watch as the booster became a tiny red dot in the feed, then, as it got about two miles out, it exploded in a bright burst that rained down pieces the camera couldn't follow.

"Cass," Linden said, his tone suddenly grave. "Uhhh... Let's be a little more cautious." It was clear he was upset about the mistake from his tone, but they had come this far, he couldn't really make them stop now.

"We've got four more, boss," Cass said.

"Next one we lose comes out of your paycheck. Fingers are expensive." The line went quiet.

"We still have the middle finger," Rina whispered into the mic. Cass watched as Rina began carefully untangling the wires Jakob pulled.

"That's true," Holli laughed. "Linden left. He has to coordinate with the ground troops here. He suggested we take *Mister Punchy* along in one of the bays just in case we need a drone."

"Already working on it. Securing it in the main bay," Rina said. "We'll leave *Champ* with the *Adamant*."

"Okay, how does everything look?" Ozzie asked.

There was a break and everyone else on the ship checked in, ready to go.

"Other than that one junction, I see no problems, nothing stopping us," Holli said. "Solar collectors have your power at about fifty-seven percent, guessing it'll be at seventy percent by the time you're ready to get in the air."

"I can live with that," Rina said.

I hope we all can live with that, Cass thought.

Once Holli walked Rina and Jakob through the repair, they all met back in the control area.

"We need to hand out jobs, and then we need to get in the air."

The radio squelched again with an update from Holli. "Okay, the brothers have the arms and weapons, Cass has the *Cudgel*'s brains and other weapons, Rina navigation and more weapons, and that just leaves you Jakob."

"Finally," Jakob said. "What's my job? Missiles? Lasers?"

There was a buzz on the radio and Holli responded. "Legs."

"Legs?" Jakob looked at Cass and Rina. "Did she say legs?"

"Don't look at me, I'm the brains," Cass said. She'd tried to make things lighter since she revealed her employer. It didn't always work. "Look."

"Head down to the lower section—level two. Take the yellow ladder on your left, leading out of the control room, go down four levels. Let me know when you're there," Holli said.

"This is Cass; I'll accompany him down and help get him in position." She could tell he wasn't excited about any of this. His face was frozen with his eyebrows furrowed. She keyed off her microphone. "Come on. It should be pretty easy on you, if I recall. You don't have too much to do." Jakob stepped onto level two and hand-cranked the door open.

They stepped into a mostly bare room in the bottom of the machine's mid-section. In the center was a harness for Jakob to put his legs in, a set of gloves for him to control other aspects of motion and what angles he could see on the screens that surrounded him. "Let's get you strapped in," Cass told him. He stood on the leg stirrups and let Cass work on fitting the braces properly on him. "Should feel a little snug, but not overly so. We wanted you to do this because you probably have the best leg strength, and you're about as tall as Ellis, he was the guy that had the job originally."

It was obvious Jakob wanted a lot more instruction. "So, I just walk?"

Cass nodded. "Yep. Fairly simple. You walk, the control keeps you hanging in place without actually moving anywhere." She pointed to the controls at his waist. "This changes the camera angles that are featured on the screen in front of you. If you look down on the floor in front of you, you'll see what's below you, including the *Cudgel*'s feet."

"Okay. But what if something goes wrong? What...?"

Cass took Jakob's hand and guided it to the red emergency release lever. "Pull this and the leg restraints release you." She took his hand and raised it over his head. "If that doesn't work, there's a release up here to pull yourself free of the mechanism. You may end up walking around with the leg restraints on, but at least you won't be trapped in the machine."

"All right."

It wasn't real training, but it was all she remembered from the notes. "Look. We're going to test working together soon, but there's a training program to get you up to speed a little more, okay?" She stepped away from him for a second to raise their small support team in Oregon. "Holli?"

"I heard. Jakob? There will be a flashing light on your console. Push it once Cass leaves."

Cass lingered at the door. "Look, if you need anything, just call one of us. We'll do whatever we can."

Jakob nodded, looking around his position nervously. "Yeah. Sure." Cass watched him feel above himself for the second release, then below for the other.

A mini-lift took Cass back up toward her level, she considered stopping to talk to Rina, but couldn't decide what to say. When she got to the command level, she saw Takis and Ozzie testing their respective arms. Their controls were less confining and restrictive than what Jakob had to deal with. Each arm unit consisted of a glove wired to a wrist band, then to another band on the bicep. The bands allowed the *Cudgel*'s arms to mimic what was happening with Takis or Ozzie's own appendages. The brothers even got to sit down on thin-backed seats that gave them better range of motion when swinging or reaching back, but still allowed them to strap in safely. She'd found them giggling and laughing in the right hand command pod. This was Ozzie's and was housed in the right shoulder joint of the *Cudgel*.

"Let's go." Cass leaned into the relatively small room. "Takis, get into your position."

She turned and sat at the huge command station. The Pilot's chair was large and had a thick harness that Cass started securing right away.

Her earphones came to life again. "Cass?"

"Yes?"

"It's Holli. I've isolated your headset, so it's just you and I in on this conversation."

"Okay."

"What do you think so far?" Holli asked. "How is everyone doing?"

"Considering it was all their idea, they're surprisingly freaked out," Cass said. "Not sure what I expected, or what they were envisioning, but this thing is pretty intimidating. Maybe once they can actually move it and try things out, they'll get a little looser." She tightened her harness a little more. "Or they'll decide to back out."

"Well, by us handling the flight controls and general altitude, it should take a lot of pressure off, but we can't control anything else from here right now. We're locked out of the other functions."

"Understood." Cass translated that as one less thing to worry about. "Where's Linden?" Cass asked.

"Off to plead with the military not to be dumbasses."

"So... he's picking up lunch?"

"Yep," Holli said. "Once they get through their little tutorials, we need to get them to try everything for real. The fleet is on its way out of the harbor to intercept the Lusca now."

"Understood."

It was a few moments before Holli replied. "Good luck and whatnot."

Cass nodded her head in agreement. *We certainly need it.*

47

Once everyone was strapped in and ready, Rina and Cass started to run through a preflight checklist. They'd learned some from their own tutorials and Holli had some things taken care of on her end.

"Deploying the hydro generators certainly helped get us up to an acceptable energy level," Cass said. "Good thinking. That saved us some time."

Rina grunted in reply, still watching a screen on the far end of the console. Cass hoped Rina would get past the fact that she'd been deceived, and hoped time would help that.

"Guys? I don't see any reason why we shouldn't launch," Holli said. "What do you think?"

It was quiet for a moment. Nothing but the sounds of the ship itself filled the control room.

"I'm ready." Jakob answered first.

"I'm go. Go time," Takis said. "Let's go."

His brother didn't sound nervous in the least. "Right arm, checking in. I'm ready," Ozzie said.

Cass looked down the long control board to Rina.

"This was mostly my idea, you know?" Rina said. "Of course I'm ready."

The three booster controls were flashing in front of Cass—one for each of the leg or foot boosters, and one switch for the waist and back rockets. Cass thought about what was next, what would happen once she clicked those controls.

"If you want, I can push the buttons. I have the same set up for now," Rina said.

"No. I got it." Cass flipped the switches and pushed the power up to full. The whole robot shook and swayed, and the roar of the engines blotted out everything else. Alarms and buzzers went off immediately.

"Looks good. I've got the vectors and all that good stuff programmed in, should be a smooth lift-off," Holli said. "Five seconds to go."

With that, the noise got worse and Cass was shoved back in her chair. The *Cudgel* spun slightly and righted itself. In the screen nearby, Cass could see the ocean get further away, and the *Adamant* got smaller and smaller.

"Oh shit," Takis's voice came into everyone's headphones. "I think this is a bad idea. I want to be on the ground."

"Little late, brother." Ozzie sounded just as shaky.

"Hold it together, guys," Holli said. "Things will get better in a few."

Ten minutes in, the pressure lessened and Cass could move. She couldn't stand up, yet, but that would come. The auto-orienting cabins made sure that everyone in the ship would stay upright no matter what way the *Cudgel* faced or how level its body unit was.

To fill the time until she was able to move around or take control, Cass started looking into the ship's onboard war records. The list was shorter than she expected, but it looked like the *Cudgel* hadn't entered the fight until well after it had started.

It was technically world war three, though no one called it that. The leaders were too embarrassed to admit a handful of minor and breakaway Russian, Korean, and Chinese factions had managed to create so much chaos with novel and deadly use of technology. Their hackers had made a mess of an already crumbling infrastructure and power grid, not to mention the damage that their internet interruptions had done to the U.S. and European countries alike. It seemed like it would be easy to roll in with the usual armaments and troops, but the Circle of Liberated Territories was far from the usual enemy. They weren't a giant country with obvious targets like nuclear facilities or missile launchers; they didn't have ports to cut off from supplies or airstrips from which to launch strikes. They hid deep in the cities of their former countries and led their fights online.

It wasn't until two years into the 'hostilities' that the allies even managed to discover the Circle had actual bases and research facilities hidden in innocent-looking factories in the United Koreas, Western China and Central Siberia. One base, near Palana on the Kamchatka Peninsula in Russia became a focal point. The main research and development sector was there, a large contingent of their army's ground soldiers was housed there, as well as their contingent of weapons. Once that was found, the war began in earnest. The allies, mainly a recon team from Great Britain, discovered that a small solar farm and wave harvesting facility that was supposed to be providing energy to the whole island and part of the mainland Soviet Union was supplying far less than it should have been.

Once the team landed, the Circle unexpectedly deployed a huge contingent of weapons, missile launchers, anti-aircraft, electronic disruptors and more. It was a surprising arsenal from a group that the allies were classifying as a cyber terrorist organization the longest time. As the group further revealed itself, intel surfaced that they'd built a huge base underwater, with connections to the island.

More bases were discovered, not in the small territories that made up the Circle of Liberated Territories, rather in neighboring countries, deep in the mountains, off shore, even in the sewers of the large Ally powers. It made it tough to pin them down and eradicate the threats they posed. The *Cudgel* was seen as a way to help do that.

Cass flipped over to the crew's video logs, though the computer showed there were few for this mission. The first she decided to watch was from the day of the disappearance, an entry by the commanding officer, Captain Lenning.

> *"Still stuck in here. Not sure how to handle it. We can't let this thing go, but we really haven't a choice. We get a few surges of power, as the Cudgel collects some light for power, or it converts the current to a tiny bit of power for us,"* Lenning said. *"At first we were trying to power up any weapons we could, but nothing would come online. Then we tried to cycle on the engines to see what we could do, but the power always went out before we got far."* The grainy video showed the shadows of a couple of crew members moving back and forth in the background. *"We decided to start leaving messages like this and archive them immediately, in the hopes they'd survive if we didn't. We're using the lowest resolution, and quality to make the files small, hoping that would help in some way. Who knows?"* Another crew member tapped him on the shoulder and Lenning nodded. *"Need to go. It looks like time to cycle down."* He put on a mask and began to breathe through it before clicking off the video.

It was a video from after they'd become stuck in with the Lusca in the cave. There weren't many, and they got less frequent as Cass checked the dates. She clicked on another a few days later.

> *"We're still good on oxygen. Using the backup tanks has helped, as has the recycler."* Lenning picked up the camera and moved it, causing the video to shake wildly. *"I've kicked up the rez on this recording to show you something."* The video finally settled on another

screen. "Sorry I can't get an angle on this through a portal. We've only been here a few days, and..." He adjusted the camera again. "...can you see that?" The camera focused and Cass could see the shape of one of the slags that had attacked the crew of the Adamant. "We've only been here a few days and these weird black coral-like formations have begun to appear on the legs and other parts of the Cudgel. No idea what they are." The screen came into focus a little more crisply. "We're not sure what to do about them."

Cass clicked over to the monitors to see how the others were doing. She noticed Rina's head bobbing with the motion of the ship and heard loud snoring sounds coming from her vicinity. The feed from Takis showed he and his brother playing a training game together and laughing their asses off. Jakob was watching a video about the construction of the *Cudgel* and, nodding off as best he could. Cass didn't mind them sleeping, she hoped they would all nod off at some point. The last few days was nerve-wracking and she couldn't imagine anyone had managed more than a couple of hours a night.

A new face appeared on the next video. It was a younger man, red-faced and anxious.

"This is Corporal William Clay. Uh... Lenning started these messages and felt they were important, so I think someone should take over for him now..." Clay looked off to the right for a moment, then leaned in and turned the video off.

A voice in her ear startled Cass and she stopped the videos.

"Cass, it's Linden. How are you holding up?" A soft line of static settled in after he spoke.

"Good. Not great," Cass said. "I think everyone will do what they can."

"Sleep?"

She knew he could monitor everything about her at the moment and could see she wasn't or hadn't slept. "Some of the crew, but I haven't managed any myself."

"Try. You've got a few hours ahead of you. You will pass right over a naval base that got hit by the Lusca earlier, but it looks like you are good on energy thanks to the solar and wind collectors, so there won't be any need to stop."

"Okay. Thanks for the updates."

The line went quiet again and sleep sounded like a good idea again, but she wanted to try a couple more videos.

> *"Staff Sergeant Joann Leeds. I've reviewed the previous videos. I'll fill in the gaps from the last week or so."* She was very matter of fact in her tone, her voice even and professional. *"We investigated the lifeforms on the hull by launching a small tethered drone to observe them. No response from them to light or to a light collision by the drone. As unnatural as they seemed, we had to assume it was some form of reef life."* Here she actually paused and swallowed. *"We have supplies, but the air is so dry."* Leeds started coughing. *"Every morning, my throat is like I've been gargling a mouthful of sand."* She started to talk again but couldn't. She held up a finger for the viewer to wait. But then shook her head and switched off the camera.

> Leeds came back for the next video, recorded nearly two days later.

> *"We decided that some of us should suit up and swim for the surface, in the hopes that we could get a signal off, light a beacon without the creature's interference, or something. We sent out a team of four. They were set upon by these... things that are clinging to the Cudgel's hull. They attacked so suddenly that we weren't able to seal all of the hatches fast enough. Lenning was on his way back, and at least one of these coral things managed to get into the airlock. Lenning didn't make it.*

Cass cycled back and listened to the first recorded message from the day. It turned out to be something she'd already heard.

"Strike Base, this is A-9. Listen, we're seeing some kind of object on radar. No idea what it is. Running identifiers now."

"*A-9*, this is Strike Base. Can you get a visual?"

"Negative Strike Base. Not exactly. All we can make out visually is some sort of shadow beneath the waves that seems to be approaching us from the opposite direction."

"*A-9*, you are authorized to take any evasive or defensive moves you deem necessary.

"Affirmative Strike Base"

48

The combined military forces decided that the best way to handle the situation was to throw more high-tech weaponry at the monster. The Navy launched the aircraft carrier *Genero* from the Gulf of Fresno with two destroyers as an escort. The *Genero* was a low altitude hovercraft that floated nearly one hundred feet above the ocean. It used the latest technology in its forward guns, using liquid metal munitions in concert with magnetic propulsion, while firing laser-guided mini-missiles from its belly cannon. Though still stuck moving through the water, both of the destroyers were equipped with advanced designs to cut through the sea at higher speeds than past models. In addition, they had fast attack boats prepared to do whatever they could.

The Air Force sent in a drone bomber squadron, coordinated to attack just as the fleet was set to arrive. All were unmanned craft originally meant for airstrikes during the war in the Circle's home territory and the mountains and hills nearby. The ordinance was meant to drill down past bunker defenses and explode deep in the ground, destroying any assets hidden there.

Linden asked if they had more. He asked if the group leaders would keep a mile or so away from the target. He asked if they had a plan based on what they learned from the *Montenegro* and from the *Adamant's* crew.

He was brushed aside by pretty much everyone, in the case of the Air Force; they wouldn't take the time to hear him out, not even a little bit. He stopped trying. He got on his borrowed motorcycle, and dashed down the road to the hotel he'd rented as a base of operations in the town of Oceanside.

He keyed into his room and found Holli there, alternately staring at the laptop she'd brought with her, and then at the television, tuned to the news channels. The door between their rooms was open, and extension cords snaked from one side to the other.

"Anything?" Linden asked. He tossed a bag with sandwiches in it onto the table near the ice bucket.

"The damn TV hasn't said shit. Nothing about ships sinking, nothing about a giant monster, and certainly nothing about a giant robot." Holli unwrapped a sandwich and bit into it.

"What? It's what you wanted, right?" He pulled a note out of his pocket and read it. "Tuna salad, lettuce, tomato, no onion, on lightly toasted Italian bread."

"You got it right."

It took a second but Linden was sure he understood. "You're starting to think I'm not such an ass, aren't you? You may even be thinking I'm kind of cool."

"Cool? You got a sandwich order right. Let's not get carried away," Holli said.

Linden held his hands up in surrender. "What about the *Cudgel*?"

"They have been practicing for a half hour or so."

"How's it going?"

"Kind of early to say," Holli said.

"What do you mean?"

"They're doing simulations." Holli reached over and unplugged her headphones, and the sound feed from the *Cudgel* came flooding out of the speakers.

"Jesus, Jakob. Plant your damn feet, we nearly stumbled into that cliff," Ozzie shouted.

"Come down here and I'll plant my foot up your ass." Jakob sounded frustrated and serious.

"Guys, we're huge. Fuck the cliff. What's it going to do to us?" Takis was anything if not tactful.

The feed began to melt into one big voice—a huge cussing hiss of acidic aggression. "Turn it down," Linden said. He walked over to the window and pulled the curtain. The good thing about the small hotel was that they had windows that overlooked the bay. He could see every ship that left the nearby base, and everything that came in.

"Hey, maybe you should wake up Tsui?"

"He's asleep again?"

"Yeah. He really didn't bitch much after you left," Holli said. "Just that he was hungry." Holli focused on the bag that Linden had brought back. "You did bring him food, right?"

He hadn't. The turmoil with the military had made him forget the other reason he'd left the hotel. "Of course." He scowled at Holli and held up the sandwich in his hand. "This one. This is his. I ate mine on the way back from the base."

"I think I was very helpful getting us here and you could use my help with the Lusca when the time comes," Tsui yelled from the other room. "May I eat with the handcuffs off?"

Linden looked at Holli and she nodded affirmative. She also showed him she had a pistol strapped to her ankle, then put it back.

"Fine." Linden cautiously unlocked the cuffs. After he was free, Tsui rushed into the other room and grabbed the sandwich. He smelled it. Unwrapped it slowly and smelled some more. "Do you know what kind of stuff we get in that prison?"

Linden thought about it and he really wasn't sure what they got in a maximum security prison for sensitive war criminals. "No?"

"I don't either. It was based on color. *What's for lunch today? Green. Green is for lunch. Tomorrow's orange.*" He took a tiny bite and chewed it slowly, and with a smile.

Linden was afraid the man might hug the sandwich if things went much further. "The modern American navy is about to clash with your beast. What do you think is going to happen?"

Another tiny morsel dangled in front of Tsui's mouth, just on the verge of being devoured. "I told you, it's not my monster. I was just sort of there." He bit the sandwich piece and slowly chewed it up. "But... from what I've overheard? My money would be on the Lusca."

"Is there anything you can tell us that might even things up? You said you have no stake in this. Help us out," Linden said. "I'll make sure you get a sandwich every week."

Tsui held up his food. "One of these? One of these exact sandwiches?"

"I didn't mean that. We're not having food catered in from hundreds of miles away, but I'll get another sandwich for you from somewhere around the prison."

"So you need my help, but you don't need it that much?" Tsui popped an onion slice in his mouth. "Hmmm."

There was a loud sigh from Holli. "You're good at painting yourself into a corner, aren't you, Linden?" She turned to Tsui. "Here's the deal. He will order a sandwich for you from the Kay-tee Inn, or wherever we are, in Oregon for you, once a month. The other weeks, you get whatever is closest." She stuck out her hand to Tsui. "Deal?"

The prisoner stared at her hand suspiciously. "Two Oregon sandwiches a month."

"One Oregon sandwich and a side of onion rings. I can smell your breath from here. You obviously like onions." Holli extended her hand even further.

"I want..." Tsui began.

"In five seconds the deal disappears. Don't push it." Holli began withdrawing her hand. "Five..."

Tsui shook her hand immediately. "The Lusca is really fucking you guys over with the energy drain. Knock out the electronic nerve center, and you're in business."

"Wouldn't that end the threat of the atomic explosion as well?"

"Theoretically."

"You initially said it collected energy until it overloaded and triggered the nuclear reaction," Linden said. "If it can't collect energy, then it shouldn't explode, right?"

"True, but I don't know if has any failsafe connected to it. It shouldn't explode because of the lack of a catalyst."

"But?"

"But it's not my project. I can't be sure."

Linden looked down at the monitor and saw the *Cudgel* stumbling around in the simulation. Additional feeds showed the crew squabbling with each other over their comms. "I gotta say, if we all get killed by a nuclear explosion, I'm less likely to buy food for you."

49

Within a couple of hours, a small crew from the *Alba Varden* arrived at the *Adamant*. They dropped everything at the *Swansea* treasure site as soon as they got Rina's call about what had happened to Martin. By the time they'd arrived, Martin was sitting up, just a little. Ozzie had suggested against it before he'd taken off, but Martin wasn't having it, and Ben didn't want to fight with him.

Angela, Hakim, and Theo arrived in time to stop Martin getting up to make a martini, though in truth Martin couldn't get up if he tried. He just said he was going to do so in order to calm their concerns. "Jesus, I'm fine. Ozzie did a great job; I'll still be able to play the violin."

Hakim changed Martin's wraps and took a close look at the wound. "It looks like maybe he went a little heavy on the glue, but otherwise, you're doing okay." He put the temp strip on Martin's head. "Close to normal, no real fever. We brought some supplies from the *Varden*, just in case."

"How's the site? Any new discoveries? What did you find?" Martin asked. He figured that the site would be a wealth of items, but he couldn't be sure what might have been destroyed over time, or lost when the *Swansea* sank.

"Seriously?" Theo asked. "You were on death's door less than a day ago, and now you're getting back to business?"

Angela laughed. "You've met Martin, right? That's how he works."

"Can I get a monitor in here to see the dive site, and see what's happening with the *Cudgel*?" Martin was worried more about everyone else than himself. It was a stupid move to take the machine like that. He hoped they wouldn't make it in time, hoped they lost power and didn't wade into a stupid fight and get themselves killed.

Theo tapped Martin on the leg lightly. "I'm on my way to get hooked up with communications here, I'll see what's up, and see what I can do about giving you a feed in here. Just take it easy."

"I'm not an old man; you don't have to talk to me like I'm your grandpa or something," Martin said to Theo as the man left.

Hakim waved the others out, too. "Okay, they're gone. Are you going to tell me how you actually feel, or are you going to stick with the thumbs up?"

Martin looked at him, thinking about that very thing. He looked toward the door, thinking about the new arrivals.

"They're all gone. They have more important shit to do than wring their hands by your bedside," Hakim said. "Now come on. I need to know how you feel so I can take care of you." He looked over at the tablet clamped onto the wall that was serving as a monitor.

Of the whole team, Martin knew Hakim the least. He'd been on the team for years, but had always asked to be on the second team, the one that came and catalogued the finds, rather than the team that came in first and made the discoveries. They'd talked, but not much, Hakim was closer to Ben than anyone. He'd volunteered for crap jobs to make a little extra money once in a while—he'd wash down gear, fill air tanks, and paint the boats when they needed it, whatever. In fact, he'd screwed up a very important task when he painted the ship this time out. "How long have you been in America?"

"Excuse me?" Hakim stopped what he was doing, but had a smile on his face. "Why are you asking?"

"Just… how long?"

"I came a few years before the war, maybe fourteen years now." He stared at Martin for whatever was forthcoming.

"And you don't know who Adam Ant was?" Martin was baffled, sure he was long dead, but his music was still played. Occasionally. "A singer? British? He sang a bunch of hits. You have to know him."

At that moment, Martin saw Ben wheeling up to the door. "Ben, you know Adam Ant, right?"

Ben rolled himself on down the hall, not stopping to answer.

"Come on. He sang 'Goody Two Shoes' and 'Strip'… 'Dog Eat Dog?" Martin was nearly pleading.

"Nope."

"My grandmother was a big fan. She'd sing me to sleep with Adam Ant songs when I was a kid."

"Your grandma sang you songs about stripping? That seems awkward," Hakim said. "I've been in America long enough to know that doesn't sound right."

In spite of himself, Martin laughed until he was suddenly coughing and holding his wound.

"Now, how bad is that pain?" Hakim asked.

"Honestly?" Martin asked. When he saw that Hakim might punch him, he answered. "It's mainly when I take deep breaths. As long as I'm lying down or sitting up a little like this, it's not bad. But sudden movements are a terrible idea."

"Okay. We're taking the ship back to the nearest port that has a real hospital. We'll take our time. We'll keep an eye on you the whole time. If something starts to go poorly, we'll… I don't know… we won't take our time," Hakim said. He was smiling. "We'll get you to help, I promise."

"I don't want to leave them on their own."

"Them?"

"The crew. The crew on the *Cudgel*, they aren't ready, they aren't trained for that shit. They're just a bunch of god damn swimmers." Martin turned to look out the portal over Hakim's shoulder. Martin had lost all sense of time, and was surprised to see the sun rising in the distance.

"Look. They decided that themselves and there's nothing we can do."

Martin didn't want to look back at Hakim. He suddenly felt weak for talking about how bad he was hurt. "Just get me a monitor and a feed, so I can see what is going on."

Bag in hand, Hakim walked to the door. "Your vitals are good, you've got clean bandages." Hakim held up another tablet, identical to the first. "I'll keep an eye on you while I get settled and talk to Ben about my suggestion to get the hell out of here."

"Don't forget my…"

"Monitor and feed. Got it," Hakim said. He left and stomped down the hall.

The pain in his chest and stomach subsided a little, Martin assumed due to the pain medicine that he'd been given. He couldn't shake the feeling that he should be with the crew aboard the *Cudgel*. They were in the predicament mainly because of him. He looked around, but no one had left him a wheelchair or crutches. Probably because they knew he'd try to use it.

50

The pounding on their hotel room door came as a surprise to Linden and the others. It had been so quiet in the little mom and pop joint, that they'd assumed no one else had even checked into it.

"Linden? Open the door," a voice came from the hall.

Lou and Linden looked at each other. The voice was more than familiar to the both of them.

Holli grabbed the door, the same look of puzzlement on her face. When she opened it, they all saw Commander Braun standing in the hall with a number of armed soldiers in black uniforms on either side of him.

"Hello, Linden. Probably time we talked."

"You probably didn't bring lunch with you this time, did you?" Linden was suddenly longing for the thick peanut butter sandwiches that he wasn't at all allergic to.

"No."

Linden nodded for Holli to step aside and let the Commander in.

"You kind of forgot to follow up on your report about possibly finding the *Cudgel*, Linden. And now, I have people telling me that there's an object in the air, flying this way, with the same flight profile as our missing machine." Braun sounded as friendly as he always had over their meetings, but his words held a note of anger in them. "I thought we had an agreement."

"Things got out of hand."

"Out of hand? That's…" A woman walked into the room and found a chair to plant herself in. She was much younger than Braun, in her late thirties, Linden figured, and wore civilian clothes. "That's a good one. Out of hand. You not only found the *Cudgel*, you let people get into it. They released a huge monster, and then they flew the classified weapon. Let's see, what was your only directive? *Don't let people take the Cudgel.*" She nodded. "Out of hand, I like that."

"This is Sergeant Johnson. She was with the last class that trained to operate the *Cudgel*. She's here to make sure you bring it back in one piece," Braun said.

"We met. She escorted us to see the base commander earlier." Linden nodded to Johnson. "Look, we really thought it made sense to bring the *Cudgel* into this, since it had trapped the Lusca before," Linden said. He had expected to be called on the carpet for this whole thing, but really didn't think it would be so soon. He thought maybe it would be after a giant robot crashed into something important. "They're doing their best to right this situation."

"We get that. But you need to call them off. Have them land at the coordinates on this paper." Braun passed the note to Holli and she handed it to Linden.

Without looking at the writing, Linden spoke again. "But, are they wrong? After what we've seen, after that thing has easily destroyed everything that's been thrown at it so far, isn't it possible that the *Cudgel* could do some good here?"

"An untrained skeleton crew in a ship that's been dormant for a decade?" Johnson asked. "They'll only do harm here."

"Do you have a real crew for it? Where are the rest of your pilots? Bring them in, and we'll gladly turn it over to someone who knows what they're doing." Holli leaned against the table they were using as their makeshift command center.

"Wouldn't matter." Johnson crossed her arms and sat back in her chair.

The commander sighed and picked some lint off of his uniform sleeve. "Look. You're all cleared to hear this, I think. I know Lou and Linden are. Miss?"

Holli nodded. "Edson. I'm with Gary Matthews' team. TS/SCI clearance."

Braun nodded and turned to see Tsui sitting on a bed in the corner. "Is that…" His eyes narrowed to slits. "Is that a war criminal?"

"Not really…" Lou started. "Well, yes. He was captured during the war, and he has been in prison ever since, if you want to be technical."

"Technical? Sounds pretty non-technical to me," Johnson said.

Braun returned his attention to Linden. "Look, we… I admire what you're doing. I really do. We made your division to recover the *Cudgel* and by God, you did it. With no staff, few resources, and no support, you did it," Braun said. "But that's the thing. You weren't really supposed to find it."

51

Martin stared at the screen and tossed his small, empty paper cup at it. He couldn't believe his team was dumb enough to be there, putting themselves in harm's way. The beast had survived hits from missiles, lasers, and more, and had still come out without a scratch.

"Officials say that the military have given the okay to attack the creature by any reasonable means," the news anchor said. "Currently all of the branches of the military are working together, including possible airstrikes, land-based strikes and more support from the Navy, though the spokesperson admits the Navy has taken a hard hit today from this incredible threat."

"Jackasses." Martin sat up straight in his bed and immediately regretted it. Pain shot from his abdomen for a brief, but not brief enough, moment. When it passed, he swung his legs around to touch the floor. He swallowed hard as he got up the courage to stand, and his legs wobbled slightly once he got up. He clutched his right arm to his belly and dragged his IV stand along in the other. Such a dumb idea, he thought. He moved toward the dresser by the big window, when a noise began to register with him, one that was increasing with each second. It was like someone was shushing him, but louder. He stepped to the window just as two large ballistic missiles roared past them nearly overhead.

"What are you doing out of your bed?" Hakim asked from the doorway. "You're going to kill yourself."

"Did you see that?" Martin pointed out the window to the missiles that were streaking across the sky. "What the hell was that?"

"Sit down. Please." Hakim motioned to the bed. "You don't have to lay down, you big baby. Just sit."

Martin tottered over, fairly sure it was some kind of trap to get him in a position to be sedated again. He sat anyway, because standing hurt.

"We're idiots, but we're taking you toward Oregon. You were out for a while and we decided to take you there. No idea why." Hakim shrugged. "We're idiots, like I said."

It took a moment for his head to clear, he felt like he was underwater all of the sudden. "That's... I appreciate that."

"Now, please. We'll be there in a few hours. I don't know what you think we'll do there. But we'll go."

"The news." Martin pointed at the screen, still hazy and having trouble breathing suddenly. "They said they might launch missiles at the creature. Is that what just passed us? Is that thing on its way to them?"

"Martin, move your arm." Hakim suddenly looked concerned.

"What?" Hakim's voice suddenly seemed very far away. Martin felt the man gently pull away the arm. "What?" He looked down at his shirt to find it covered in blood. "Shit. Whose blood is that?"

"You tore something. It looks like that patch job your friends did is coming apart."

Martin could see Hakim scrounging for something on his belt, could hear him call the others on the ship for help, but that was the last thing he remembered comprehending at that moment.

He awoke many times, but it was difficult for Martin to stay conscious. He tried. He didn't know if it was his body healing, the blood loss, or if Hakim had slipped a sedative into the fluid drip. But he tried to keep his eyes open. He wasn't sure how much time passed before he realized someone was in the room with him.

"I don't know what you expect to do when we get there," Ben said. "Hell, you know if we stayed put we would've likely missed any of the effects if this monster explodes. By chasing after your crew, you've doomed the rest of us to die if they fail."

"We're moving?" He really thought he'd had a fever dream where he begged them to let him help the crew on the *Cudgel*, but it wasn't, or at least not all of it was. That was a thing that weighed heavily on Martin about the crew when he could think straight. They would be lucky to make it in time for the battle, and there was nothing that anyone on the *Adamant* could do to help the *Cudgel* once they got there.

"We can still turn around." Ben rolled himself around the bed toward the door. "Just say the word." He left Martin alone in the silence of the otherwise empty room, with waves and the hum of the engine cutting the silence.

Martin thought about what he'd lost already on this journey, this job. Two people had lost their lives from his own crew, maybe more; he didn't know what had occurred while he'd been out. And civilians? Military personnel? All because he had to find the unfindable? Because he couldn't leave well enough alone? There was a find of possible historic significance that he'd dragged his team from for this, all for his own vanity. And now he was risking more lives because of his own inflated sense of self-importance. He turned to see if there was a way to call Ben back when the boat jostled hard and Martin heard the frightening sounds of metal scraping against metal.

Shouts came down the hall, each of the current crew's voices yelling from one to the other, but Martin couldn't understand a word. The *Adamant* made a series of quick maneuvers as it slowed and finally stopped, turning slowly back the way it came.

"Hello?" Martin shouted. "Hey. Ben?" The voices continued down the corridor, just far enough away to be indiscernible. Out the nearby portholes, Martin could see nothing but sky. He heard footsteps coming his way and saw one of the crew headed his way. "Hakim. What's going on?"

The tall man stopped in the doorway. "We hit some debris and circled around to check it out. Looks like some kind of craft went down."

"Craft?"

"Probably a large private boat, doesn't look huge. We're doing a visual search for survivors, but it doesn't look good," Hakim said. He came over to Martin's bed side and checked the monitors. "How are you? Feeling okay?"

"You tell me, you know what all that gibberish means on the screen."

"Well, I can see your heartrate is slightly low, but not terrible. BP is up. But I want to know how you feel."

There was a lump in Martin's throat that hadn't been there when he started speaking, he felt terrible, physically and emotionally. "This downed boat? Did the creature do it?"

"Man, I don't know. If that thing was really doing a straight line for Oregon... It probably came through here." Hakim lifted Martin's hand and checked the needle that fed fluids into Martin's arm. Satisfied, he put it back on the soft sheet and patted Martin's forearm. "I'll let you know if we figure anything out." With that he left Martin alone again.

52

Linden was sure he'd heard wrong. "Excuse me? We weren't supposed to find it?"

"We were pretty gung-ho about finding it early on, because we worried about the *Cudgel* falling into enemy hands, secrets getting out, shit like that. But after the war, we were less concerned. And as the years dragged on, we just didn't care. Who was going to find it? We assumed it was buried in an avalanche or something. Or crashed and broke apart over miles of ocean. Anything. That's why we took so many people away from you. We couldn't close it completely, not just yet. Maybe at the twelve-year mark?" Braun said. "Anything much sooner and we'd look like we didn't care about the missing crew."

Holli pushed back her crappy chair and stood up by Linden. "Don't you?"

"Of course we do. Look, we genuinely, you genuinely looked for that ship for years, Linden. You know we went out of our way to try to find it. But we had to stop. Hell, once *we* officially called off the search, we'd announce a good reward, or we'd hire private search firms to keep looking."

"Maybe it would've even been these assholes that are in the *Cudgel* now. They could've been handed a nice fat check if they'd kept their noses out of the goddam ship. Now there is all kinds of shit going to rain down on them for illegally entering a vessel against a federal order," Johnson said. "Shit, it's too bad your agent couldn't do her job and keep them out."

As the argument continued, Linden noticed Tsui slide from his own seat to the one behind the laptop controlling *Mister Punchy*. The prisoner slyly looked down at every opportunity at the screen in front of him.

"That agent made a judgement call. She thought the weapon could do some good now, seeing as all the news she was receiving was about your troops back here getting their asses handed to them by this monster." Holli crossed the room and pointed at the map they'd tacked to the hotel wall. "First here, then here and now it's right on top of us here. There isn't much to stop it after this, is there?"

It was a mystery to Linden then, whether Holli was in on it. Whether she'd noticed Tsui moving to the computer or if she'd somehow sent a message to him on that laptop's screen. But she had everyone in the room looking in the opposite direction.

"If it gets past us here, there's only mile stretch to the plant and the possibility of a nuclear-level explosion."

The men turned then, and looked back at Tsui, who had leaned back in his chair to act casual. "Right, the nuclear explosion that this man told you about. Tsui, is it?" Braun said. "Weren't you in prison yesterday? I only ask because a lot of our investigators went to your cell to ask you questions about this monster, and were shocked to find you weren't there. Once we determined Agent Linden here had visited before us, it took almost no deduction to figure out you were here."

Tsui looked at them in all seriousness. "Was there a question I was actually supposed to answer in there? There were a bunch, but they seemed rhetorical."

It didn't matter, the general turned back to Holli and Linden. "This is all insane. You've illegally moved a war criminal, stolen government property..."

"More insane than an eight or nine-hundred-foot monster destroying the fleet?" Holli asked.

Time wasn't something that the team had too much of, and it was being wasted arguing and sniping at each other. "You were about to tell us something about why you didn't want the *Cudgel* found? What does clearance matter now? We are running out of time."

Johnson and Braun looked at each other and the man nodded.

"It doesn't work," Johnson said. "It never really did."

"What are you saying?"

"The *Cudgel* was an experiment we never got right." Braun opened his jacket and pulled his phone out of his pocket and held it flat in his palm. A six-inch 3-D image of the *Cudgel* appeared slightly above the device. "Look at the thing. It's huge, it's complicated, it's bulky, it's impractical."

"The machine was so large; we had trouble powering it efficiently. That's why it's equipped with those solar collectors around the shoulders and cowl. That way it could draw energy as it was moving, if it had to. Same with the intakes around the waist and legs. If it was flying, it could draw in energy from the wind, underwater, the current charged the machine. Problem was, if it were in the dark and stationary for a long time... it was screwed."

"That's it? So it could still put up a fight now. It's flying. It's charging," Holli said. "It's powering up."

There was a rumble in the distance, first a single whistle that disappeared soundlessly in the distance. Then another and another. The ships at sea were firing. In the hallway, some of the soldiers left, their boots thumping on the stairs. Linden looked out the window and saw them getting in their vehicles. They all tore off toward the nearby base.

"The *Cudgel* had simulation programs to train us in how to use the weapons. We got pretty good at those trials. Trouble was, they never got around to installing the actual weapons."

"What?" Holli asked.

The look on Johnson's face seemed pretty serious to Linden. "But, we saw the *Cudgel* in battle in all those news feeds from early on in the war. It was at the Battle of Timons Square, the uprising in Anders Forest. Those are all iconic images."

"They never happened. Not the way they were reported. The *Cudgel* was there to help in the clean-up and assist with the medical team."

"Clean-up?" Holli asked.

"It has a ton of things that were active for search and rescue; medical supplies, the arms were strong for lifting debris, it could hold a lot of water for fighting forest fires, the shovel was good for a variety of things." Johnson pointed at the hologram as she mentioned the features.

"But no weapons?" Linden asked.

With a shrug, Johnson pointed to the right hand. "The fingers were low-payload missiles. The left hand had a rail gun that shot ammunition the size of my car."

"That was it?" The sounds of gunfire got more prominent outside.

"By the time we got that far, the power problems were evident and impossible to ignore," Braun said. "We had to go back to the drawing board to figure the scalability troubles out, but the military was breathing down our necks to deliver something to turn the tide. The whole conflict was going south quickly."

"So they delivered an inferior product, to buy time to work out the problems with future units?" Linden asked.

"Why not just work with your allies? They all had working mechs and war machines. Surely they would've given you the solution to your problem." It was Tsui. He was standing now at the computer he'd been using.

"We were the leader in this tech," Johnson said.

Braun fiddled with his phone and an image of an imposing machine appeared where the image of the *Cudgel* had been. The new thing was wider, squatter and stood on four legs. Gun barrels jutted out at various angles.

"The Italian Parenti mech model," Linden said. He'd studied the machines of other countries, thinking that they might have stolen the *Cudgel* to make improvements to their own weapons, but allies wouldn't have done it, and no Triad power ever made a mech. "That one was active in Italy, Poland and Germany."

An image of the Parenti Mech replaced the first, showing the robot standing, smoking from battle, with prisoners of war marching in front of it, guided by allied soldiers. "This is what you mean?"

"Yes. I heard firsthand that the Parenti routed our forces in Genoa," Tsui said.

"Well, your source was a liar." Braun enlarged part of the image. "Do you see where this picture was taken?"

"Looks like a rail yard. So?" Holli asked.

"The Parenti was brought in by mag-train because the mech couldn't fly. It was broken up into three pieces, put on the train, brought in AFTER the battle, and reassembled next to the rail yard. See that smoke?" The image shifted again and focused closer on the smoke pouring out of the back of the mech. "That's not from combat. It was on fire because they tried to make the thing walk and one of the six engines burned out. They had to march the prisoners past the mech to get this shot, because they couldn't get it to move to *them*. It was all an effort to boost morale."

"Same story with everyone else you'd see with a machine like that; they couldn't get it to move, couldn't get it to shoot right, wouldn't fly, caught on fire, crashed, sucked power to an incredible degree, or was just plain worthless." Johnson stared at the hologram of the mech on Braun's phone. "We were the best out there, and ours barely functioned. Isn't that sad?"

"But the *Cudgel* wasn't worthless. It attacked the Lusca and stopped it," Lou spoke up. "That's not a failure."

"It was a fluke." Braun shut his phone and the image disappeared. "It shouldn't have happened, and there isn't a way of repeating whatever the hell they did. So let's get back to the matter at hand. We need to land the *Cudgel*, so a team can recover it."

A siren started howling in the distance and the soldiers in the doorway grew nervous and looked at each other. The sound of boots resounded on the stairs again, though this time they were coming up. A gruff voice spoke to the men and they disappeared down the hall and down the stairs.

"Where are you going?" Braun stood up and moved for the door to see what exactly his men were doing. As he got close, another man entered: Lieutenant Ornn of the *Montenegro*. "Who are you?"

Ornn ignored the question and looked at Linden. "I got your message."

Everyone looked at Tsui and he waved back. "I noticed he was listed as alive and on the base. I just said hello."

"We're thrilled to see you alive. We didn't know if you went down with the *Montenegro* or not. It was looking rough," Linden said.

"And I am surprised to see you all here as well. I sent you three up north to keep you out of this thing's path."

Braun got up close to Ornn and shouted. "I outrank you, sailor. I don't know what you think you're doing, sending my men away like that, but I'll have you arrested for…"

Ornn didn't touch the superior officer, he just held up his index finger to quiet the man. "I just saw a lot of people die because of that creature, and it's headed this way. I need you to be part of the solution right now."

Linden agreed, but it wasn't so simple as saying it had to be done. They had to figure it out and work together. He looked over at Braun and then at Johnson. "We need to stop this monster, and we need the *Cudgel* to do it."

Johnson looked willing to help, but her brow furrowed as she turned to her superior.

Braun laughed and walked for the door. "Do what you want, I'm leaving. I sure as hell don't want to be here for the big boom. Even if you manage to stop it, you'll all be in the brig soon. This is a mistake."

An alarm beeped frantically on one of the computers. Tsui looked at his screen. "There are multiple contacts on the beach."

Linden turned and looked out the window. He could see a bunch of dots surfacing on the shore and knew immediately what they were. "Shit. Those slags are here. They're all up and down the god damn beach."

"They're even headed this way, toward the town, not just the military targets," Ornn said. "Those things could finish off anyone left along the coast that didn't evacuate."

Tsui sat down at a computer and typed furiously. "They don't exactly have a plan. They just fall off of the Lusca and destroy whatever they find." Linden watched as the prisoner started typing away. He walked closer and looked over Tsui's shoulder.

"What are you doing?" Linden could see camera feeds from a drone similar to *Mister Punchy* lifting off down by the docks. "That thing isn't ours."

Lou crowded behind Tsui's computer to watch, while Holli and Johnson sat down at the other work station. They commandeered another similar drone. The video feed from Tsui's showed the drone's point of view as it swooped over the trees near the shoreline and closed on slags as they made their way out of the water on their spiny legs. There seemed to be more this time, a horde that skittered ashore.

His jaw set firmly, Tsui took the drone in and started using it to smash slags with the machine's fists, punch them with the metal hands, and tear them apart whenever possible. Linden watched the bloody spectacle on the monitor. It was helping, but there were so many of the slags coming in with the tide, it was hard to say how much it helped.

With nimble fingers, Linden punched in the numbers to reach Cass off the headsets that everyone else used. "Cass? Bad news."

"New bad news, or the same old bad news?"

He jumped right in, not having time to mess around. "That weapon is fairly useless. It was never finished. Those training programs are just training programs. It doesn't have most of those weapons, just survival and disaster assistance equipment."

Cass laughed.

"I'm serious," Linden said. "You have to abort."

"We can't. The destination is locked in."

"We can unlock it," Linden said. "Holli?"

The conversation ended abruptly when the line went dead. Linden looked around for another way to contact her, only to find the computers had frozen up and lost contact. "I'm sorry, we're out. Something's blocking us." Holli started another screen. "I'm afraid we're being blocked deliberately."

"Your friend Braun seems intent on fucking us over," Tsui said.

Linden turned to the window at the sound of the alarms. Further out to sea, the dark form of the Lusca breached the surface.

53

Martin opened his eyes to find Angela and Hakim staring at him. "What the hell? Why are you always staring at me when I wake up?"

"Makin' sure you aren't dead." Hakim shrugged.

"Sorry," Angela said. "We heard you mumbling and thought you'd be coming around. Wanted to wait a little to see if we could talk."

Over on a tablet, Hakim tapped away. "How are you feeling?"

He was still too sleepy to know how his injuries were actually doing, but could tell they still hurt. "Really? Look at me."

"We're using some of the tech we took off the *Cudgel* to accelerate the tissue growth around your wounds. It's going to hurt like a bitch for a while, but it looks like your body is already responding well," Hakim said. "That's good news. We need to get you to a hospital, but it doesn't look quite as desperate as we'd feared."

"Dandy." It was hard to believe that he was in good shape, when every breath hurt his chest, but he'd take their word for it.

"You're welcome," Angela said. She turned down the sheets to look at the dressing across the wound.

"Look, we got a message from Cass's boss, Linden. He says there's a possibility there's a control module over on this sinking ship that might help stop the Lusca." Hakim put the tablet on a nearby table and looked at Martin seriously. "We're thinking of sending someone over to look for it."

He wasn't thinking clearly quite yet, but Martin was disappointed they hadn't caught up with the *Cudgel* yet. A delay would make it worse. "Who's still on the *Adamant* with us?"

"Just the three of us in the room, plus Ben and Theo. Theo can go. He can handle it."

"You really need two divers, just in case something goes wrong."

"I know, buddy system, but we don't want to..."

"Leave me alone here? Christ, what if there's still pirates over there?"

"Rebels."

"Whatever the fuck we're calling them now. If there's anyone still alive, they'll certainly attack Theo. So he can't go alone." Martin looked out at the ocean again. "Don't worry about me. Ben will watch out for me. Besides, you said I was getting better." He stared at Hakim as defiantly as he could. "Right?"

"Right." Hakim got up and headed for the door.

"I'll go with Theo." Angela stopped him at the door. "You know better what's going on with Martin. You should stay with him." The pair walked down the hall and their voices faded.

Once they'd grown silent altogether, Martin looked down at the bandages. "No, that's okay. I'll be fine here alone while you work things out on your end." The remote was within reach, so he clicked on the large screen across from his bed. It was on the same news channel he'd left it on the last time he'd fallen asleep. The news was suddenly all over the giant monster headed for mainland America before, but now it was zeroing in on the fast-moving object headed for the scene.

"Satellite images haven't brought back a positive identification, but visual imaging from automated weather stations and oceanic outposts are claiming to have matched their photos with images online of a wartime vehicle, shown here." The newscaster paused as combat video began to roll on the screen. "Called the *Cudgel*. Reports have that vehicle missing since near the end of the war."

"Of course it hasn't been seen. It was buried under the god damn ocean," Martin said. He sipped his water through a plastic straw. "I found the thing. Not you. I did."

"If, indeed this is the *Cudgel*, it is moving this way fast." The camera cut away to a wide shot of the sky, with a yellow streak headed for the coastline and the Lusca. Another camera caught soldiers who were behind cover, shooting at the beast, suddenly stop and stare at the flash of light.

It closed to within half a mile of the giant beast, righted itself and then landed perfectly on its feet, knee-deep in the ocean. Steam rose from the water and huge waves rippled out from the massive robot.

On the camera, soldiers cheered, albeit cautiously and from behind trucks and tanks, but they couldn't contain their elation.

"It looks as if those initial reports were correct; this is positively coming up from our automated research system as the *Cudgel*. Where has this thing been for the last decade or so?" The anchor had a slight smile himself, as if, from his studio in New York, he had been in real danger at some point. "Has the military brought this project out of mothballs to aid in the effort to stop this chaos? Let's see how the legendary *Cudgel* even begins to figure out how to tackle this beast."

The room echoed with the slurping sound as Martin finished the last of his water. He was thirsty, as if he'd slept for days. He wasn't sure he hadn't. "Damn right they'll tackle it. Better not damage it, though," he mumbled, realizing how that sounded—that he put the value of the treasure above his own people.

The screen showed the *Cudgel* standing where it landed. "They may be powering up some weapon here for a decisive strike against the creature." The announcer puzzled.

After a minute, the robot tottered and then fell forward into the Pacific.

Martin dropped his plastic cup on the floor as he watched the monster on the screen turn to look toward the *Cudgel* for the first time since it landed.

"Christ, get up." Martin stared out at the debris of the sunken ship that floated in the Pacific just a bit off the *Adamant*'s starboard.

"Theo and Angela know there's a time factor involved here. They're doing their best," Ben said. He wheeled easily around the bed to Martin's side. "You just need to take it easy before you tear your stitches, or that wound cement, or whatever the hell it is keeping your guts in place right now."

"I'm fine."

"The hell you are. You were at death's fucking door nearly twenty-four hours ago. Nobody—not even the great and powerful Martin Taylor—just shakes something like that off. You're going to kill yourself."

"I'm fine, Ben."

"I'm not going to let you kill yourself because you think you can help that crew somehow." Ben nodded to the black screen.

Martin had turned the television off, thinking somehow if he didn't see something bad happen, it wouldn't actually happen. "For now, can we just agree to wring our hands while we wait for those two to find that briefcase over there?"

It took a moment for Ben to nod, but eventually he agreed. "Good luck with that needle in a haystack. What did they say? A red case with a laptop in it? Could they have been a little more vague?"

"It looks something like this."

Behind Ben and Martin, a soaking wet man held up a red brief case in one hand and a Russian-made MP82 machine pistol in the other. Martin recognized the gun as one used by the Circle immediately, as he'd been commissioned to find a similar weapon for a client, and the gun's history had become ingrained in Martin's mind. The man's face was matted with blood from a recent slash across his face. His plain white dress shirt and blue jeans were ripped in places.

"Who the hell are you?" Ben asked.

"I don't think it matters, but my name is Guillermo Vinoit. *Doctor* Guillermo Vinoit." He paused, looking for an acknowledgement, but got none. He waved the gun from Ben to Martin. "Now I'm going to guess that neither of you can operate this vessel. So, we'll just have to wait until one of your companions comes back from our ship," Dr. Vinoit said. Martin guessed the man hadn't found the other crew member that was supposed to be loose on the ship. Unless they'd decided at the last minute to send everyone to search the wreck.

"I'm the captain of this ship." Ben turned his chair around to face Vinoit.

The doctor looked Ben over. "From that chair? I hardly believe you."

"Check the wheelhouse. All of the consoles are built to adjust to a height that I can reach, and see out the forward viewports."

"That would be something, wouldn't it? I'll go look and you can put some plan to kill me, or warn the others, into motion? No, I think not. I'll just wait right here for your colleagues." He leaned himself on the far side of the room and looked up at the screen. He gazed at the creature shown in the news feeds. "Looks like they didn't need me, the Lusca will fulfill its mission after all." He swallowed loudly and then noticed the pitcher of water next to Martin. He walked over and took it, then shambled back to lean against the wall. He waved his gun quickly at the men to warn them off, and then drank in giant gulps straight from the pitcher, spilling some down his face, and neck, then onto the floor.

As he watched the man, Martin considered what he'd been through. The monster had to destroy their ship not too long after leaving the crevice. "If you want more, we can get you more. I mean, you've been through an ordeal, after all."

"You don't know what happened to me." The doctor let the empty pitcher fall to the deck.

"I'm pretty sure you've been either sitting on top of that wreckage in the sun for two days..." Martin had to think about it. Had he been passed out for two days, or three? He'd faded in and out; maybe he missed a sunset or two. "Or you were treading water under some cover, watching for sharks, or whatever else might come for you. No food, no drinkable water. If you got any sleep, it probably wasn't much."

"You know nothing."

It was just a wild guess on Martin's part, but he was pretty sure one of those scenarios was close. "Look at you now. You're almost too tired to stand. I'm pretty sure the only thing keeping you moving is the adrenaline of pointing that gun at us."

"Shut up," Doctor Vinoit said as he straightened himself up.

By the time he turned back, Ben had pulled a pistol from under his blanket and fired the Taser. The loud zap startled the hell out of Martin, not to mention Vinoit, who twitched, dropped the case and gun, and fell to the deck.

"Jesus, Christ." Martin flopped himself backward on his pillows. "You could have gotten us killed."

"Oh, don't be a baby. I'm an excellent shot." Ben's wheelchair bumped the bed before he managed to get it around to where Vinoit lay. "I got the job done, right?" He picked up the case and weapon from the floor and moved them out of the doctor's reach. "Besides, no one ever expects to get Tasered by the guy in the wheelchair, do they?"

"Is that supposed to make me feel better?"

Martin sat up and leaned over his bed, careful not to hurt himself, or reopen his injury. Together, he and Ben stared down at the motionless doctor. "I wonder if there's some sort of reward for him?"

Shouts came down the hall-the rest of the crew were hollering for Martin and Ben.

"If there is, I'm the one that shot him. So I'd be the one that gets the money," Ben laughed.

His side hurt when he laughed, so Martin tried not to. But he looked at the briefcase proudly. It was the only thing he could help with. The battle on the west coast was already underway and the *Adamant* was a day away at top speed, and that was only if nothing else went wrong. This case could be his contribution to saving his crew. He turned and looked up at the dark television screen and then felt around for the remote. The TV sprung to life, showing the announcer again.

"We've lost contact with the crew on the west coast. Just as the *Cudgel* fell into the ocean, our feed went out and we lost communications with everyone out there. Land lines seem to be out, cellular communications, everything. We'll join that scene as soon as possible. Meanwhile..." The announcer looked offscreen for a moment. "Let's take a look at the images we received. Here is the *Cudgel* landing to confront the creature... and here is where the power goes out. If everyone else lost their energy at the same time, it stands to reason that the *Cudgel* did too." The video showed the *Cudgel*, knee deep in the ocean around the small island defense station suddenly falter and fall into the water again, and again in slow motion replay.

54

The crew of the *Cudgel* moved about in the cockpit, in the darkness. "Rina?" Cass called. "Are you okay?" The cabin had reoriented itself as the *Cudgel* fell so they weren't stuck at an odd angle, falling on their faces, slipping out of their chairs. The whole cabin had simply rolled until it was oriented at the proper angle, even as the machine was falling.

"I'm fine. Check on everyone else."

"Anyone hear me? Is this working?" Cass tapped her headset and tried keying it on again. "Hello?"

"Mine's out too," Rina said.

Cass unbuckled her restraints and walked for the elevator. "I'll head down to check on Jakob and work my way up."

"I'll check Ozzie, then Takis."

Cass opened the elevator doors and realized quickly that there was no way for the shaft to change orientation, so she'd have to walk down the wall, which was now the floor. Also, the emergency lighting hadn't kicked in. She stood there, letting her eyes adjust as much as she could, before hurrying on as fast as she could, dodging the various structural pieces that got in her way. She came to the leg control area and cranked open the door.

"This sucks." Jakob's voice called out to her from the darkness.

"I'll help you out. Then we may need to hand-crank the solar collector open together."

"This is embarrassing. That thing just zapped us like we were some giant punk. We went down like nothing, never even swung on him."

"Hey, it was our first flight. At least we didn't crash," Cass said. "And we're alive."

"Everyone's okay?"

"Rina is checking on the brothers." Cass found her way over to Jakob and felt the straps above him, but could barely see them. "Hold still."

"Okay. Not going anywhere."

"If I remember right, we unclamp this, and pull..."

"Whoa, wait. You're tightening it. You're tightening it right in a really sensitive area."

"I'm sorry."

"Stop. Jeez, let me get it."

"You can't do it by yourself."

"I'm going to try. Please take your hands off for a second."

Cass raised her hands in the darkness and took a step back. "Sorry."

After loosening the strap himself, Jakob then clearly indicated what Cass should move and what not to, they unbuckled the clasps together.

"Let's never speak of that."

"Sure," Cass said. "Not a word."

"You're going to speak of that, aren't you?"

"Every chance I get." Cass led the way into the elevator shaft and moved back up to the control area. The pair climbed in and called for Rina.

"We're good." A bright phosphorescent light emerged from Takis's chamber held by Ozzie.

"There were emergency lights in the arm units, portable bio lights. No batteries needed." His bother emerged with Rina next.

"Can we use one? We're headed up into the attic of this thing, so we can start the solar panels."

"I don't think it's called an attic, Jakob." Takis laughed. "If it's further up in the head, it would be the brain."

"Great, we're heading up into the brain to kick start this bitch," Cass said.

"Hey, did we sweep that area when we came in?" Ozzie asked. "I know we didn't look in there, did you guys?"

Cass looked at the others. "No. We handled all the lower parts. I forgot the head."

Takis and Jakob looked at each other and shrugged.

"Shit."

They gathered and picked up their weapons again-those that hadn't kept them strapped to their side or tucked close. Jakob led the way, holding one blue light high, and Rina brought up the rear of the group with the other light and a mini shotgun. They climbed through the elevator shaft-easier this time, Cass noted, with some light to guide the way.

They came to what would have been the top of the elevator, and carefully opened an access hatch. Ozzie held the light as Jakob popped his head through the opening with his pistol. He crawled through and motioned the others on. "Watch your step," Jakob said. He stayed and helped everyone inside. Each gasped just a little as they entered.

On the opposite side of the room, actually the ceiling of the room since it apparently didn't reorient like the main chambers, was a pile of broken, jagged bones and dust. Scattered around the pile were a dozen or so tiny white slags, writhing in the dust.

"Everything must have shifted when we crashed or when we raised the *Cudgel* the first time," Ozzie said. "Is this the rest of the crew?"

Cass knelt down and guided one of the lights around. "I count parts of maybe six skulls."

"I see eight." Rina pointed to a paper-thin section of a jawbone stuck in a section of chords on the wall.

"Jesus," Takis said.

"Ozzie? Can you take your brother back down to the control room and see if you can get the emergency lighting started? We'll all stay up here and dispose of these and crank open the collectors."

Takis wasn't thrilled at the proposition. "I can help. I can kill those things just as well as anyone else."

Apparently sensing Cass's reasoning, Ozzie guided his brother out into the corridor. "We all have a role to play here."

"I'm not helpless for Christ's sake."

Cass watched him go, and closed the hatch behind him. "Jakob? Smash those things. Rina? Help me get to the manual controls." She moved as fast as she could in the conditions, hurrying so as to not have to hear the sickening crunch and squish the slags made as they were crushed.

Together, they deployed the solar collector and the *Cudgel* came back to life. The power gauge moved slowly back to the positive side, but once the tidal collectors were added, things moved a little faster.

"Launch *Mister Punchy* as soon as it has enough power. We might be able to use it to keep an eye on the monster from a distance, just try to keep it out of range of the power drain," Cass said.

"I'm doing everything I can right now." Rina sounded out of breath. "I'll get it when I come down the stairs."

Cass did her best to help everyone back into their positions as they came back. The fight ahead was going to be rough on everyone.

55

"Linden?" It was an unfamiliar voice coming across the computer's speakers.

"Hello?" Linden returned.

"My name is Ben. I'm sitting with Martin Taylor." There was a pause. "Is there something we should do with this briefcase thing?"

"You have it?" Tsui asked.

"Yes we do," Ben said. "See this guy snuck…"

"I desperately want to hear that story, but… we need you to plug it into your upload device and boot up the computer inside the case, and then you need to initialize the device as only sending to our satellite, there should be instructions that Cass left. Then, find the menu on the device inside the case, if I remember you should have nine options to choose from…"

"I'm going to stop you right there. This is Martin Taylor." The man coughed and cleared his throat. "I'm going to hand you over to our associate, Angela. She probably understood most of what you just said."

"That's a good idea," Linden said. "You do that and we can shut this thing's best weapon off like a light switch. It'll stop the monster from sucking up the *Cudgel's* energy."

56

"Let's stand up," Cass said. None of her crew responded. "Look, this sucks. We have almost no weapons. We have a fifth of the normal crew, and we're tired and hungry. But we're it, people. There's nothing after us. That thing is just a couple of miles from exploding and destroying the whole area. We're it."

"It's just going to drain our power again and leave us high and dry," Rina said. She was sitting just a few yards from Cass, but her words went out to everyone.

"You people wanted to try. You wanted to make up for something? This is the time to do it." Cass looked at Rina as she spoke.

A new alarm went off. "Irregular power surge from the creature. Not like anything we've seen previously."

"Come on, guys."

"I'm walking." The whole ship shook as Jakob moved them forward with purpose. He picked up the pace as he went.

An orange glow sizzled on the surface of the Lusca, like a web that enveloped it in neon. It writhed with the effort to neutralize the approaching *Cudgel*; but nothing stopped the oncoming metal giant.

Emboldened by the creature's difficulty, and their own apparent success, Cass ordered everyone to press their advantage. "Takis? Let's see if the rail gun can help."

A squealing series of thumps came from the left side of the *Cudgel*. "Holy shit. This thing is crazy." All the left monitors showed the rail gun unloading a large projectile every second or so. The monitors showed the bullets impacting on the Lusca, and making it twitch with pain, but it also began moving forward itself.

"Ozzie?" Cass took a deep breath. "Give this thing the finger."

Groans came from her earpiece. "How long have you been wanting to use that?" Takis asked.

Hisses, like deflating tires zipped away from the *Cudgel*'s right side and everyone watched the four remaining fingers impact in tiny bursts on the beast's skin. Again, there was little visible effect.

"Rina, get the chest missiles ready."

The click of a mic. "They're flares. Can we stop pretending?" Rina mumbled.

Willfully ignoring her, "Takis, when we get up close, you're going in with the... spade."

"I don't mind pretending. Can we call it my Star Sword instead of a shovel?"

"No."

The eyes of the monster became narrower and it lowered its head as best it could with no visible neck and no hint of a spine. Its long, yellow tusks pointed toward the giant robot. The light around the Lusca faded and it charged, half-swimming, half pulling itself along like a walrus, crushing anything in its path, creating twenty-foot waves as it splashed itself down into the water.

"Flares. Aim for the face," Cass said. She felt the giant machine move forward. "Jakob? Let's stay here. Let it come to us."

"That doesn't sound like a good idea. That thing will crush us if it runs us over," Jakob said.

There was a pause before several hisses fired off in quick succession. On the monitors and out the front portal, streams of flares issued red, blue, and orange from the *Cudgel*'s chest. The smoke obscured the Lusca, but Cass followed the heat of the flares all the way to the creature's face using her infrared sensors. Two of the canisters bounced off an eye, and the thing slowed, shaking its head, but still coming forward.

"Holli? How are the drones?"

"Hovering just behind the *Cudgel*. *Mister Punchy* is loaded with as much ANFO as we could. I just need somewhere to place it," Holli said.

"Great. Jakob? Forward." Cass said. "Takis? Star Sword. Just below the eyes."

Takis cheered. "Hell yeah."

The *Cudgel* leaned forward far enough that everyone looked to Cass, probably fearing the same thing that Cass was; the thing was going down again. But, just as she was going to call Jakob, one of the *Cudgel*'s legs jutted forward and planted firmly in the shoreline, followed by the other one. The whole control room shook violently with each step, but they were lunging forward at an unexpected speed for the huge vehicle. The Lusca continued to stumble forward in a fog of colored smoke.

They met somewhere in the middle with Takis stabbing with the shovel just below the creature's eyes, exactly where the schematic showed the brain center would be. The tool glanced off the thick skin without even scratching the surface of the Lusca's body.

"Shit," Takis said. "I thought we'd get it."

The impact stopped both combatants, and knocked them off balance. The Lusca, with its huge mass recovered better, as it had more contact with the ground. The *Cudgel* stumbled as Jakob tried to get the feet beneath them. The infra-red video was useless in such close quarters. The entire screen showed up red.

As they finally balanced, the monster turned and slashed with the sharp tusks, knocking them off balance again. Tentacles from beneath the beast reached out and grabbed at the *Cudgel*'s chest and stuck to the head, partially covering the forward portal. Rina started to stand, staring in awe of the huge suckers and baleen-like hairs around them. Luckily, she was strapped in and couldn't get up. The *Cudgel* braced itself in the sand, but was quickly overpowered by the limbs that wound around it. The sudden weight of the creature sent the *Cudgel* tumbling onto its back. The control cabins reoriented to the new position, so everyone within the *Cudgel* remained upright.

"Shit," Cass said. "Jakob, get this thing back up."

"We have a fucking mountain on top of us. You move the mountain and I'll get us up."

"Cass?" Holli clicked in.

An alarm blared in Cass's headset. "Not now, Holli." It took a few screens to figure out what was making the noise and why; the sheer size of the Lusca was crushing the *Cudgel*. "We have to get this thing off of us."

"Holy shit," Takis said. "Hey. It fell on the spade. The blade is piercing the skin because of the bastard's own weight."

Cass scrolled through the cameras, trying to confirm what he was saying. It was a bitch trying to do all of the work of a full crew without any training or experience. "Damn it. What camera is that?"

"External four," Takis said. "It's right on the wrist of my arm." He said it calmly, though excitement bubbled just below the surface.

She switched and immediately could see the darkness that extended around the camera, as it was covered by the thick flabby skin. "I can't see anything."

"Wait for it to turn and you'll get a glimpse."

Another alarm went off and Cass ignored it, turning it off with a click.

"Little Ozzie? Can you give me some leverage? Push off or something and maybe we can get the blade in deeper?" Takis said.

"No." Ozzie let the rib from his brother go by without comment. "These tentacles have my limb pinned," he said. "Should I try the gun? Maybe I can shred it?"

The mic got fuzzy. "This is Holli. The gun would be ineffective at that close range. Not enough velocity to do anything."

"Holli? Hey, kick in the thrusters in the ankles and waist. Maybe the heat and fire will injure it and make it drop us or loosen up," Rina said.

The warning about crush damage was still flashing on Cass's console. "Great idea."

"Giving it whatever I can." The *Cudgel* shook right after Holli's message. "Waist engines to full and—here come the ankle boosts." The giant machine rumbled and shook.

Cass checked the cameras again, and the Lusca was, indeed, reacting to the thrusters. Unfortunately, the beast's body wasn't moving away, rather, sections of skin were retreating, moving away from the areas of the waist and ankles where the painful fire was scorching it.

"My arm is close to the waist thruster. The tentacle is loosening some. I can push up some," Ozzie said.

The altitude display moved up by inches instead of feet or miles, as the right arm found leverage. In a moment, the thrusters were able to aid, lifting the giant ever so slowly.

Cass thought ahead a step and realized that this was going to drain their energy just as fast as if the monster were sucking them dry itself. "Okay. When I say 'now', I want Holli to cut all of the thrusters, and Ozzie, you need to move your arm and let us fall."

"What?" Rina looked over from her console across the room. "We just need to keep going. We've almost got this."

"Takis? Use whatever power you have to, but keep your Star Sword right where it is. Got me?"

"We were getting crushed before. The power of our sudden fall will…" Rina started.

"Shove the sword in deeper, with any luck." Takis finished.

That was the plan, the only plan she had. "Brace yourselves." Cass inhaled and scrolled through the camera angles until she was as sure as she could be that it was the right moment. "Now," Cass said. Within seconds, the roar of the thrusters in her headphones disappeared and the *Cudgel* shifted violently as the arm below them moved away. They fell a slight distance, the Lusca with them and within a handful of seconds, stopped.

Immediately, the beast let out a rumbling screech that shook the *Cudgel*. What bled through the frame of the giant machine sounded like a mix of an old jet engine taking off, and the roar of a charging elephant. Tentacles immediately released the *Cudgel* and began to push at the torso section, attempting to distance itself and dislodge the blade from its abdomen.

"Oh shit, it worked!" Takis said. "Hell yeah, right arm!"

There were some cheers through the headphones, but Cass knew it was a small victory. When the shouts died down, she made them focus again. "Jakob? Get us up on our feet and stay with it. If it tries to back up, you press the bastard. We don't want it to get it off that blade."

"Got it," Jakob said.

A new alarm began to sound and Cass started to search for whatever it was connected to on the console. There were so many flashing lights at this point that she had to look every one of them over.

"I got it." Rina pointed to a small readout on the far end of the control panels. "Flip over to screen two. Looks like the military are bringing in fresh weapons now that we did the hard part and knocked out the Lusca's energy draining capabilities."

Screen two confirmed what Rina was saying. There were tanks gliding across the beach, setting up positions less than a mile away from the fight—rocket launchers crested the nearby hills, armed with what looked like the same sort of missiles the naval convoy used in the last fight. She glanced over at the radar and satellite images. "Some contacts from the air. Can you figure out what all of those things are? Missiles? Drone ships?"

"On it." Rina turned back to her station, where she could bring everything together more easily. It only took a few seconds, and Cass had turned to try to absorb as much info as she could from her own instruments. "It looks like missiles. Closing pretty quickly."

"What kind?"

"I don't know. The computers are trying to update to recognize new technology since it last saw combat. The big kind?"

57

The wrist camera became useless once the Lusca's blood began spilling out all over the arm. It was a raspberry color that dripped out thick and slow like jelly. The camera still worked, it just sent back useless pictures. Takis confirmed that the blade was still stuck in the giant beast. Cass took that as a win.

The *Cudgel* continued to move forward, shoving the Lusca even as the monster tried to retreat. Cass swept the control board, trying to keep up with all the flashing lights, alarms and monitors. "Those missiles?"

Rina responded. "About twelve miles out and closing fast."

"Ideas on where they came from?"

"Computer is trying to identify exactly, somewhere out to sea rather than land, though."

Flashes started to dot the Lusca's skin as the old-school tanks and guns on shore began firing again. This time they were just as ineffectual as their stranded counterparts on the shoreline, but at least they were still fighting. Every few seconds the computer would warn that a stray shot glanced off the *Cudgel*, but Cass ignored them. "We have to end this before more people get killed. And we don't have much time to do it," Cass said. "Those missiles will be here in about five minutes. I don't want us stuck to this thing when they arrive."

"I think we're all in agreement there," Takis said. "What do you want me to do here?"

That was the problem. They'd tried everything under the sun and nothing worked until they got lucky with the blade. "Ozzie? According to the schematics, you have a welding torch on the hand somewhere. For underwater repairs and other bullshit emergencies. Do you see it?"

There was clicking audible on the line. "Uhhh..."

"Ozzie?"

"Yes! Yes, there is. This program originally labeled 'Laser Cannon' in the training is now renamed 'Welding' now that we're in reality. That. Sucks."

It was the only tactical option Cass could conjure as she thought about the loss of life, and the missiles approaching. "Your brother is going to rip that sword out of this bastard and I want you to go after that wound with the torch. Right now that's our only way we've hurt his thing, so let's keep at it in the same spot."

The whole *Cudgel* began to rock as the Lusca recovered and fought back. The stronger tentacles wrapped around the head, blotting out the forward windows. "I don't think it's going to let itself be surprised by the jet engines' heat again," Rina said.

Cass was getting tired of trying to run the majority of the board to control the minor bits and pieces that it took to keep the *Cudgel* moving and alert. Physically, she was exhausted of having to do the quick movements from monitor to monitor, gauge to gauge. "Takis, I need you to pull that blade out as quick as you can, then we need a second to shift our body so Ozzie can get to work on that wound with the blowtorch, or whatever else he can find."

"We're going to work on this thing with a blowtorch? You ever do any collection work for the mafia?" Jakob asked. "You sound like a natural born enforcer."

"Probably the nicest thing I've heard all day," Cass said. She started shutting off everything that she didn't understand, or didn't think they needed on her console. It cut the flashing lights by two-thirds, and, the *Cudgel* didn't shut itself off or explode. Seconds later, the whole torso shifted as Rina moved the body in support of Takis pulling.

The *Cudgel* jerked as the pilots attempted to coordinate enough to yank the blade out of the monster. As it did, it left a long swath of blood and entrails that arched across the sky and splashed down into the ocean in huge clumps. The *Cudgel*, or rather, Jakob, fought to keep the machine's balance, stepping back a step or two to keep from falling over. The Lusca roared and loosened its tentacles, retreating quickly into the water until its lower tentacles were covered with sea water.

This was their first and best chance to stop the thing and they didn't want to lose their advantage. "Ozzie, hit it with the torch."

"We are fighting this thing with fucking camping equipment," Takis said. "This is nuts."

"Missiles getting close. We should get out now," Rina said.

On the monitors, Cass saw the blowtorch on Ozzie's hand come to life. The machine moved quickly forward and the torch connected with the Lusca's still-gushing wound. Jakob's steps took them slightly further than expected, and the red-blue flame plunged deep into the opening.

The Lusca squealed in pain again, lashing out with all of its limbs with enough force to send the *Cudgel* sprawling backwards, landing on its back.

The crew gave a collective grunt as they were jolted upon landing. "Everyone okay?" Cass started checking the monitors for vital signs. Each of her team responded affirmative and they started the process of getting back on their feet.

"Wait," Rina said. "Stay down."

Before anyone could question her, the still-flailing Lusca was hit by one of the large missiles. The ordinance hit the slippery hard surface of the beast's back, and was deflected skyward by the angle, soaring upward over the fracas on the beach where it exploded with a flash and rumble.

"Shit." Cass couldn't tell if it was Takis or Ozzie, or both.

The force of the missile impact turned the Lusca sideways, turning it so the flat surface of its chest was facing the next missile that came screaming in, scoring a direct hit. The following explosion dug deep into the beast's wound and shredded the skin around it. The blast tore off a number of tentacles from under the Lusca's head and sent flames across its body.

The *Cudgel* also rattled with the explosion, the shockwave of it caused more alarms and more flashing lights.

Everyone reported back that they were fine except for Ozzie. "I think that explosion cracked the hull or something. I think I can hear a leak somewhere, but I don't see it."

"Might not be a cracked hull, could be anything. I don't know if its coolant, or whatever. I'm checking." The realization swept over Cass that maybe they didn't have any sort of fluids in the machine or if they were even needed, but she didn't want to alarm anyone. She looked over to see Rina frantically checking off alarms and gauges.

"Okay. I'm looking around to see what I can find as well," Ozzie said. His voice seemed fairly even to Cass, even in the face of everything being piled upon him.

There was so much to do to keep the machine moving and Cass could feel the situation slipping away from her.

58

"Look, guys. I know we have other problems, but this fucking leak in here is getting worse," Ozzie said. "I can hear it behind me."

"I'll check it out." Cass started scrolling through the screens and looking from monitor to monitor. Finally, she found one of the alarms she'd shut off and closed was flashing a warning about a hull breach. When she clicked the screen, it gave options on how to fix it. Options that would not happen automatically. "Shit. Ozzie, hang on. I can open an access hatch from here that will drain anything out of there while I figure out how to seal the leak itself."

"Cool." Ozzie sounded decidedly uncool to Cass.

"You all right?"

"I'm okay."

Scrolling through the technical manual as fast as she could, Cass tried to find a way to get the leak to stop. "How much water do you have in there?"

"Oh, it's not much, barely noticeable."

The manual and the schematics were tough to search for just one person who was unfamiliar with the machine's capabilities. "You're not lying, are you?"

"Cass," Rina shouted. She was pointing at the Lusca as it swung a group of its tentacles at the *Cudgel*. The impact knocked the machine backward a few steps, but it remained standing. Takis swung the left arm, but the blow barely registered with the monster. It lunged forward and knocked the *Cudgel* back, sending it splashing into the Pacific. The robot landed on its right side, applying enormous weight on the arm Ozzie was operating.

Alarms began sounding anew. The first warning screamed about the hull breach in Ozzie's compartment. It was worse, and the break had compromised the compartment's ability to rotate, leaving Ozzie himself on his side, while everyone else stayed with their heads up.

"Ozzie?"

"I'm okay." He went silent for a second while the sound of pouring water took over. "Uh... I'm stuck on my side and there's a lot more water coming in."

"Hang on." Cass cycled through the warnings again and found that Ozzie's compartment was blocked by some damaged panels and wouldn't auto-orient itself to make him level. "Okay I see the problem; I'm trying to find a way to fix it."

"We need to get up," Rina said. "That thing is coming in again. Ozzie? Can you push us up?" They'd been fighting in fairly shallow water, but it was still deep enough to cover most of the *Cudgel*'s arm.

The reply was garbled somewhat, with the audio cutting in and out. "I'll try…lot of water…and rising fast."

"Takis, see if you can get us up, or help Ozzie do it." Once again, Cass found her question too late as the creature dropped on them and began to encircle them with tentacles, more cautiously than last time, but the added weight was still forcing the *Cudgel* deeper down into the sandy bottom of the bay.

"Holy shit," Ozzie said. "The more weight… puts on us… faster the water comes in."

Cass saw the flashing warning. The water was backing up through the vent she had opened to help drain it in the first place. Additionally, sea water was coming in through the crack the Lusca had caused above the arm unit. "Just get out of there. Do you hear me? Ozzie? Just unstrap yourself from the arm controls and the seat and you can still push your way out through one of the hatches. The main one is above you right now."

"Ozzie?" Takis was suddenly alarmed, fully evident in his voice. "Ozzie get out of there and come over here with me."

Rina turned to Cass, her face pale in the flashing lights. "Ozzie?"

59

"It's chaos over there." Holli turned to look at the others. "We have to help them," she said. Tsui and Ornn could barely look up from the controls of the drones as they dealt with however many of the slags as they could. Ornn had confiscated a drone and began to imitate Tsui's strategy of smashing as many as he could. He was heartened to see that others in the shipyards had taken up the idea as well. They were doing a decent job of keeping the slags from getting beyond the beach.

This wasn't news to Linden. He'd tried to reason with Braun and anyone else he could reach, but no one wanted to unscramble the remote control signal and allow Linden's team to help control the *Cudgel*.

The open line filled the room with the shouts from the crew. "Takis, I'm going to check it out from here. Stay where you are, we need you to push us up." There was no response. "Takis, stay there."

It was horrifying for them all to hear what was happening, without being able to help. Linden paced near the door, kicking an end table as he went. There *was* more they could do. There *had* to be. "Tsui. Take control of *Mister Punchy* and attack the Lusca. Fly around the thing's eyes and ears. Just see if you can distract it."

"Ears? You see ears on that thing?" Ornn asked.

There was no way of telling if the beast had ears from looking at it, but Linden had hopes.

"I get what you're saying. It has auditory sensors," Tsui said. On the large screen behind him, *Mister Punchy's* view rose from the beach suddenly, still carrying three of the slags along with it. One of the fat hands clamped shut hard, squishing a slag easily. The two others fell off and out of the camera's sight. "It'll take a minute to get there."

"I'm going to go plead my case in person to Braun, if I can find him. If I'm not back in half an hour, I'm either in the brig or I decided to fight the Lusca with rocks and seashells." Out in the hall, Linden took a breath and turned for the stairs. Standing silently, not four feet away, was Lieutenant Johnson. "Jesus. You scared the crap out of me."

"I've been standing here for the last maybe three or four minutes."

Linden relaxed a little. "Yeah?"

"Yeah." Somewhere to the west, sounds of gunfire erupted.

"Any particular reason?"

"I've been trying to decide if I should give you this old slip drive with the new communications code for the *Cudgel*." Johnson held up a thin piece of plastic in her hands.

"That thing will get us back in control?"

"Yep."

"And you've been debating whether we should have it?" Linden couldn't help but stare at the tiny drive. "Why?"

"They left the first crew out to dry by sending them out in an ill-prepared craft, even though they knew what they were getting into." Johnson closed her fist around the drive. "But if they'd only sent a party to look for them earlier, if they'd just had the *Cudgel* equipped like it should have been, it could've handled this thing easily."

"That's probably true."

"And now they're fucking your people over, too." She took a few steps closer and handed the slip to Linden. "This'll get your communications back, and it will give you a little more control. It's the same basic control scheme that we used in training. The training officers used it to take over the ship when the trainees needed assistance. You can commandeer any and all of the *Cudgel* remotely."

The rectangular drive felt like nothing in his hand. "We could use your help. You know this ship better than we do."

Johnson was halfway down the hall. "I won't be responsible for another crew dying."

"If they die, we all do."

"Then make sure they don't fail." She hurried to the stairs and took them two at a time.

A door slammed on the floor below and then the little hotel was quiet around Linden. He looked at the drive again and hoped it was all she said it was.

"Stop everything and try this." Linden entered the room a little more dramatically than he'd intended. The group looked up in unison and then went back to their screens.

"What is it?" Ornn asked in his gruff annoyed navy voice. "We don't have time to stop everything."

Raising his hands in truce, Linden rephrased his request. "Not everyone. Just Holli."

She was clearly just as annoyed as Ornn. "What, Linden? I thought you were going to beg for mercy so we could help them. You were gone all of what? Three minutes?"

"Yes. But something just fell..." Linden caught a glimpse of the larger screen on the wall and was appalled by what he saw. "Is that *Mister Punchy* flitting around the monster's eye?" It was comical, like a gnat buzzing around a cow. Except, it wasn't as funny when he considered that gnat constituted the bulk of the nation's defense effort. "What the fuck?"

"I'm doing my best," Tsui said.

Before he could come up with a snide aside, Linden turned back to Holli and the more important task at hand. "I left, but the training officer was in the hall. She gave me this. Claims it's the training controls for the *Cudgel*."

"Training controls?" Ornn stood and quickly crossed to look at the thin drive. "She just gave them to you?"

"Yes. Remorse for the first crew, it sounded like."

Ornn turned it over and shrugged. "Could be anything. I mean, they're trying to shut us down, right? Could be another code entirely, that does just that."

Holli took the strip and held it next to the drive on her computer. "'Do we take the chance?"

They all looked back up at the monster on the screen that was pummeling the *Cudgel* while a gnat zipped around its face.

"I'm doing my best," Tsui said.

The rest of the group nodded and Holli inserted the slip into her computer.

60

With the *Cudgel* on its side, and the compartments in various states of orientation, it was a surprise to Cass when Takis lowered himself from the ceiling into the main control room. She was in the process of trying to unlock Ozzie's compartment when Takis dropped in and helped her turn the emergency release on the door.

"I still can't get any response on the com, and the cameras are out. I don't know what's going on in there." Rina came to the door as well and stood looking over Takis's shoulder.

The whole robot shifted as the Lusca began to wrap its tentacles tighter. The *Cudgel*'s frame groaned and crackled from the pressure. Cass thought about the fact that no one was at the controls except Jakob, who she hoped was still safe in the compartment with the leg controls.

Between the two of them, Takis and Cass pried the door open and lifted it upward on its hinges. Below them, there was a fairly small room with a twisted mass of metal beams and cables, and it was nearly completely flooded.

"Ozzie?" Takis whispered. He moved as much debris aside as he could and then dropped himself into the water without another word.

There was nothing else Cass could do but follow. She sat on the side and slipped over the edge, falling into the salty water and wires. She found Takis, trying desperately to move a panel that had fallen across Ozzie's chest. The compartment was large enough that she could swim around to the other side of Ozzie's controls. She braced herself against a wall and pushed with Takis, moving the metal piece from his brother.

It was obvious to Cass from the moment they uncovered him, that Ozzie wasn't moving. Nonetheless, Takis started tugging at the harness, trying to remove it. Cass's air was running out, but she didn't want to leave the brothers to struggle alone. She unlatched the shoulder harness as Takis unlocked the lap restraint and pulled his brother upward.

Cass moved to join him, but movement caught her eye. The crack where the water had likely poured in, was filled with the long thin legs of slags trying to get in. Above her, Takis and his brother were out of the entryway, so she opted to swim upward instead of engaging the slags.

When she pulled herself out, she turned and shoved the hatch shut. She turned the wheel to lock it and started to ask for help to make sure it was cranked tight enough when she saw everyone gathered around Ozzie. He was laid out near the consoles, with Takis giving him chest compressions, and Rina trying to breathe life back into him.

The *Cudgel* shook and it spurred Cass into action. She found the defibrillator and emergency kit by the main hatch and brought it back, starting the charging mechanism as she went. She got closer and Rina took it, hooking it up and placing the leads on Ozzie's chest.

As she watched the two work, she heard multiple voices in her earpiece. Jakob wanted an update, Holli had questions. As soon as she was sure she couldn't help with Ozzie, Cass moved to a spot out of earshot of the others, hoping they had taken out their earpieces. "The breach in our outer armor led to a similar crack in Ozzie's chamber."

"He's okay, though, right?" Jakob asked.

It took her a long few seconds to respond. "They're trying to revive him now."

"What?" Jakob said. "Revive him?"

Holli's voice came next. "Cass? Jakob? I need you to focus for a few minutes on the *Cudgel*, otherwise, you're all going to be crushed by this thing. Got it?" No one responded to her. "Guys? We're depending on you to help."

Cass looked back at Ozzie. "Yeah." She walked back and knelt down to take over CPR from Rina. Once she did, Takis stood and walked away toward the chamber they'd pulled Ozzie out of. Over all the other sounds, they could hear the scratching of the slags on the other side of the metal portal.

"You fucking monsters." Takis put his hand on the lever to open the door and grabbed Jakob's shotgun with his other hand.

"Takis, don't do that," Cass said. "You'll kill us all." She looked for a pulse on Ozzie and couldn't find one. There was a monitor on his other hand that Rina had applied and all the stats it showed had flatlined.

"Aren't we all going to die anyway?" His tears continued as he spoke.

"We don't know that," Rina said. "But your brother..."

"Don't say it."

Cass raised her hand to him to calm him down. "He gave his life trying to do something right."

"He's not dead." Takis knocked the shotgun to the floor. "He's a swimmer. He can hold his breath. He's a better swimmer than me." He stopped talking then, and sat himself on the floor with his back to the portal and the clawing beasts, and cried for his brother.

61

"I've got full control," Holli said. "It worked. It fucking worked."

If the drive didn't work, Linden was out of ideas. "Get them out of there. Get that thing back up on its feet and move it as far away as you can." Linden and the others had watched the screens helpless as the crew on the *Cudgel* screamed for help and shouted for Ozzie.

"Working on it. I'm doing everything myself here, no one is at the controls over there."

There was static on Linden's headphones, but he keyed the mic anyway. "Attention *Cudgel*. This is Linden. You need to get somewhere secure. You need to buckle in, we are taking over the controls." He waited but the group remained on the floor with Ozzie.

"Can I help?" Ornn stood up from his laptop. "Give me something to do."

"I'm sharing the control board with your workstation. Once I coordinate this thing enough, I'll have you fire up their thrusters and engines and take over the flight controls," Holli said.

"Perfect. That's right in my wheelhouse." Ornn started tapping his keyboard and moving the additional controls he'd pulled from his laptop-a joystick and a mouse-like square that Linden couldn't place.

"I have an idea, if we can get that thing upright." Tsui sounded confident.

Linden waved him off. "We need to get them out of there. That's the only idea we need."

Onscreen, the *Cudgel* managed to roll enough to push itself up with its good arm. The crack in the opposite shoulder was now obvious even from a distance. *Mister Punchy* swung around getting close-ups of the area, highlighting the swarm of slags that were prying and clawing their way in through the rupture. They were streaming from the Lusca, seeming to crawl right out of its skin.

It took nearly a minute, but the machine was finally upright. "Okay, go. Get them the hell out of there."

"We're working on it. Still have to lock in position."

"Don't take off. I have an idea." It was Tsui again.

"We don't have time."

"Grab the drone and see if you can pierce the Lusca's wound again."

"What?" It was almost in unison, everyone in the room.

"I read the drone's manifest. Everything from the supply list is automatically accounted for."

"So?"

"They seem to have loaded it up with a lot of explosives." Tsui sent the image to Holli. "We know the missiles won't pierce the thing's hide, but what if there was an explosion inside?"

It dawned on Linden what he meant, and it seemed as good a plan as any, but only if the *Cudgel* and crew could get clear. "How would you set it off?"

"That's the thing. There are some detonators listed onboard that drone, but I don't know how to get them to activate and cause an explosion."

"Someone might have a remote, or a password, or something, right?" Linden asked.

A voice came through the headphones. "Takis. He packed the explosives," Cass said. "I don't think he's going to be able to help." Linden wanted to ask what the situation was onboard the *Cudgel*. Cass's statement was the first response they'd received since everything started going to shit. "Jakob. Jakob helped pack them in." Cass's voice was strained. "Jakob? Jakob, are you there? Can you help?" There was a click on the line and some shouting. Alarms went off in the background and Cass became inaudible.

Ornn spoke up. "The longer we wait, the more danger they're in on that machine."

The sounds from the *Cudgel* prompted Linden to shout into his mic. "Listen, we can figure out how to do this on our own, you just take care of your people over…"

Cass's voice grew louder again. "His headset was off… Jakob, do you know how Takis configured the explosives back in the drone? Can you set them off, or tell us how to do it?"

"This is Jakob. The explosives? Sure, I can set them off. How the hell is that going to help anything?" He was out of breath as he spoke. Things were clanging in the background and the sound of rushing water was prominent.

"I am NOT going to risk these people's lives…" Ornn said.

"What about the lives of everyone that hasn't evacuated yet?" Linden asked. "Jesus, what about what's left of the original coast of the United States?"

Behind the two men, Tsui and Holli had begun talking to Jakob privately, attempting to get instructions without everyone else mucking up the communications line. Linden could hear them repeating Jakob's name. They were likely dealing with static and panic, trying to be clear of what he was saying.

"Look, the *Montenegro* was destroyed by this thing. You know what it can do. We have to stop it here, if we can before the Lusca can do even worse things," Linden said. He was gambling that the cheap reference to Ornn's former ship wouldn't anger him more. Both men paused, which gave Linden time to turn to the others. "Do you have it? Can you activate the explosives?"

Holli nodded and sat back down at her makeshift workstation. "I have the left arm control, Tsui has the drone."

"Bringing it up to you." It was almost a whisper from Tsui after all the yelling and arguing.

On the screen, the *Cudgel*'s left arm could be seen going through a series of tests, fist opening and closing, arm turning. "I wish that shovel hadn't been mangled so much."

"It'll still work." Linden hoped as hard as he could that he was right.

"Here goes." The *Cudgel*'s arm thrust forward and the blade glanced off the Lusca's hide. "Damn it."

"Just try again."

On the next try, Holli managed to time it just right, to stab the Lusca and land the blow in the center of the wound. Blood flowed out again, and the Beast roared.

Holli opened the *Cudgel*'s arm and Tsui deftly flew *Mister Punchy* into the palm. In a swift motion, the arm plunged back into the Lusca's open wound and Holli let go of the drone.

"Here goes." Tsui used Holli's code and set off the explosives.

The Lusca shook as the explosion shook the beast, black gore spilled out of the wound and the thing's eyes rolled up to look at the sky. It flailed its tentacles wildly and reached out for the *Cudgel*, locking on to the machine's waist.

"Holy shit, hang on," Holli shouted into her mic, but no one answered.

Linden tried next, hoping that someone was inside that ship that could respond.

As the *Cudgel* began to tilt, the Lusca's appendages slipped away and the beast fell to the beach.

It was too much to hope that it was over, so Linden didn't say a word. He was afraid to breathe, lest his expelled air knock the *Cudgel* over.

62

The buzzers and klaxons were still going off and adding to the chaos in the control room. Slags still climbed through the crack in the armor and into the arm casing that Ozzie had been in. The loud thuds when Jakob's shotgun went off, dispatching the creatures whenever their undersides were exposed. Takis's wails of despair still cut through it all. Rina wept silently next to Ozzie's body.

Just beyond the viewport, the massive body of the Lusca lay limp in the water. The tentacles swayed with the tide.

What would have been different Cass wondered. *Had they all stayed out of it? If they'd stayed with the Swansea or the Alba Varden?*

Drones came toward the frozen-in-place *Cudgel*. They flashed lights around the area, including directly at the control area. They couldn't see her, she knew, but she still looked away.

63

The television screen showed the Lusca was down and wasn't getting up, so Martin flipped the channel. The next station showed the same. None of the talking heads were saying anything about the *Cudgel* or the crew.

"They'll tell us what happened," Ben said. "Just as soon as they can sort things out."

The radios had all gone quiet just after Martin and the others transmitted the code to shut down the Lusca's energy draining capabilities. No one could call in or out via sat phone or anything else.

Martin sat back and tried to fight the urge to sleep now that everything was done. He put his hands on his chest and stared at the screen.

64

The chaos of the rescue workers and military vehicles was overwhelming to Cass, even after she'd spent hours in front of the controls of the *Cudgel* with lights flashing and warnings blaring. A few miles offshore, the *Adamant* was moving cautiously into port. Cass could see a medical drone speeding ahead of it, lights flashing, presumably with Martin onboard. According to Ben, neither he nor the rest of the crew onboard were allowed to accompany Martin, much to their consternation. They reported that he'd been in good condition, the bandages and paste that they'd used from the *Cudgel*'s medical bay had held and likely saved his life.

A similar craft had lifted off from the *Cudgel*, taking Ozzie away. The medical team had tried to keep Takis away, but that didn't go well for them. He shoved his way in, and planted himself next to his brother and snapped himself into a harness. The team decided there were too many people to help that day to waste time fighting a losing battle.

The carcass of the Lusca was stretched along the beach, smoldering from the open wound. Tentacles draped at odd angles, and dark fluids shimmered on the beast's side and hardened in the sand below. The coastline was fairly trashed, but the *Cudgel* and the drones had somehow managed to keep the Lusca from crushing or destroying most of the civilian buildings and roads. The naval base was not as fortunate, one of the huge shipyards to the north suffered a roof collapse, and a number of the barracks were obliterated by flying debris.

Kay-Tee's Ocean View Motel was quite safe, and turned out to be a good place to stay out of the way of the military for the time being. Takis had accompanied Ozzie's body back to the military hospital, with Rina and Jakob riding in the transport with him. Cass had been contacted by Linden as to his location and she decided to join his small team, even if it would only be for a few moments before she went to the hospital herself.

After introductions were made, and Cass managed to take a seat and breathe a little, they talked and informally discussed the last few days. She knew there would be a more stuffy meeting-days or weeks of them, even-but it felt good to be back with someone she was more familiar with.

"I don't know if it was the right thing to do."

"You really didn't have any choice," Holli said. "It sounds like they made you go along with it and you did your best to make it work."

It wasn't true, and Cass knew it. "No. I could've stopped it. Anytime. It wasn't like they held a gun to my head. I like them. I wanted them to succeed."

"The Lusca was defeated. That's important. The Oregon coast isn't currently glowing with radiation, that's a good thing," Linden said. He pulled a handful of beers from the mini fridge and offered one to Cass. She waved him off.

Tsui grabbed the one she didn't want and grabbed another. "Most importantly, I get sandwiches for the rest of my life." He opened one beer, chugged it, and tossed the bottle into the nearest garbage can, then opened the other.

It occurred to Cass that she had no idea who the man was. "How do you fit in here?"

"He's a scientist that we busted out of prison so he could help us." Linden nodded and raised his bottle to Tsui.

"I'm the one who helped get *Mister Punchy* into the *Cudgel*'s hand so it could be placed properly to explode with maximum grossness." Tsui smiled and waved his bottle around in celebration. "And effectiveness."

"You know that drone was mine? I was kind of attached to it."

Tsui looked to Holli and Linden. They nodded back at him to confirm she was being honest and not pulling his leg. "I was just trying to help. I mean, it was you that actually put it in place to finally explode."

Cass didn't even have the heart to mess with Tsui, on any other occasion she would have strung him along. "I think I'm going to try to catch a ride to the hospital. See how Martin is doing." She took a long drink of water and wiped her mouth with her sleeve. Manners and appearances had kind of gone out the window at that point.

"I have no idea what the higher-ups are going to say or do. My guess is they'll take turns yelling at you and then praising you," Linden said. "Either way, I think they'll keep things as quiet as possible about the *Cudgel* and play up the Lusca as the boogeyman here."

"They shouldn't keep it quiet, I got people killed. I used horrible judgement. If I'd done things by the book, this wouldn't have happened." She looked at the bed in the corner and suddenly wanted sleep. It had been too long since she'd slept more than a couple of hours in a row. If she even so much as sat down on the fluffy bed, she knew she'd fall asleep. Next to the bed, Cass pulled open the drawer on the night stand and pulled out a KAY-TEE notepad and pen. She quickly wrote a sloppy letter of resignation and folded it in half. After a deep breath, she turned to find Linden with his hand out. Cass shook it and nodded. She handed him the letter before turning to leave.

Linden looked at it. "I'm not sure this is entirely legal. I don't think I can accept it."

"It's legal. We had a deal."

At the doorway, Holli called after her. "Let me come with you. No reason to go over there alone. Maybe I can help get you through the security or something."

A quiet trip would give Cass a few moments to gather her thoughts and decide what to say to Martin and the rest of the crew. "I don't think that's…"

"I know, you'd rather be by yourself, but I'll be quiet; barely know I'm there." She scooped up her small tablet phone, disconnected it and slid it into her jacket. "I promise." She stood next to Cass, held the strap of her tech bag close to her chest.

It was hard not to roll her eyes, but Cass said yes.

"Okay," Holli said. She was way too enthusiastic for Cass's tastes. They started for the stairs, and Holli had her phone back out, typing away at the tiny keys. "Mind the steps," Cass said, genuinely fearing that the woman might fall and break her neck since she was staring at the screen instead of watching where she was going.

"Thanks." Holli was still looking at her screen.

They descended the staircase without incident, waved at the owners sitting in front of their bay window watching the tangled mass of ships and aircraft move through the harbor. They stepped onto the front porch and Holli stopped.

"Let's head up this way, the military has a station for non-military personnel to check in over in the main entrance." It took a moment for Cass to stop staring at the sea, the half-sunken ships, the dead slags that littered the beach, and the flames from destroyed ships. It was hard to overlook the giant robot less than a mile out to sea, or the smoldering carcass of the giant beast it was fighting. The aircraft and attack boats swarmed around it like bees on a honey hive.

"Hang on, stay right there." A jet of air and a high-pitched whine followed Holli's statement and Cass looked up to see a large drone coming down in front of their position. "What do you know? An ambulance on low power that needs to go back to the hospital to charge anyway, and it lands right in front of us." She slid her phone in her bag and stepped into the vehicle.

"You're quick with that tablet."

"Thanks."

Holli continued to tap away at her keypad as the empty ambulance lifted off. "I'm getting us clearance to land on one of the roof drone pads. We'll need to get out quick, once the doors open. I've set it to return to its regular programming thirty seconds after the doors open, then it heads off to recharge. You don't want to be there for that."

"Thanks," Cass said. She watched Holli zip across the tiny keys, listened to the minute clicks. The empty ambulance smelt of antiseptic and bleach, like a mini hospital room. "You work down the hall from Linden? I don't remember that we've ever crossed paths."

The tapping stopped and Holli looked up. "Yeah. I've been there for a couple of years. I don't get out of my cubicle much."

"Sound analysis?"

"Yep."

"Interesting work?"

"It can be."

"Hear anything interesting?"

"Usually just noises. Weird stuff that turns out to be nothing. A submarine engine can sound mysterious when it bounces off an undersea canyon or something. Whale farts. Crabs mating. Stuff like that."

"Whale farts? Sounds fun. Ever hear electronic sounds? Ever hear a watch alarm beep and have to triangulate the location?"

Holli looked up and set her tablet phone on her lap. "What?"

"I started thinking about this contact we have that occasionally helps locate bits and bobs from history, calls herself Subtle Bagpipe. I checked on the info she's passed on to the team. Just about all of her tips had one element of information gleaned from sound files. So many treasure hunters just use maps and rumors and whatnot, sound clues almost never play a factor. And yet here were dozens of clues based on hard to find sound files and reports."

"That does seem odd." Holli's cheeks became a light shade of red.

Cass just stared at Holli as the ambulance rattled in a sudden updraft.

"One minute to base medical," the automated voice's words came across in the usual soothing tone, not like the terse warnings Cass heard on the *Cudgel*.

"Whale fart," Cass said. "Maybe that should be your new code name?"

"Not the most flattering name."

"Subtle Bagpipe is kinda weird, too."

The ambulance landed with a slight bounce, jarring both of the passengers. A red light flashed over the door and it began opening. Cass remembered to gather her things and step out quickly before the drone had to take off again, following on Holli's heels as quick as she could. They stepped on the landing pad and moved for the door just as the ambulance hatch closed and the cool breeze of the rotors began to blow a breeze across the platform. They ran toward the auto-opening doors, dodging to stay away from the doctors and nurses wheeling the injured off other ambulances, all headed for the same set of doors.

Inside, it was more chaotic, more medical professionals, more patients, less room to maneuver.

Holli was staring at her phone again. "It looks like some of the crew are up with Takis, and the others are on the forty-first floor with Martin. Room four thirty-seven."

"I'll head to talk to Martin first. Why don't you go on up with the others?"

"I really don't know any of them all that well," Holli said. "Maybe I should come with you and wait outside the room?"

"You've known all of them longer than I have," Cass hit both buttons on the elevator bank, still careful to stay out of everyone's way. "Introduce yourself." The doors opened and the down light blinked. Cass entered and leaned against the back wall.

"How should I introduce myself? As myself, or Bagpipe?"

"Your call, but I'd seriously consider Whale Fart." The doors shut and Cass let her head thud against the elevator wall. Talking to Martin seemed to make sense, she betrayed the crew by being undercover and lying all that time, but she felt most sorry for deceiving him as the captain of the group.

She knew, however, that she wasn't ready to face the others, especially Takis.

65

The room was quiet, which surprised Martin. With the total chaos out in the harbor, he'd expected to awaken to a madhouse, and yet, it was just Ben waiting for him. There wasn't another patient recovering, no military liaisons, no navy nurses or physicians. "I thought we'd be lucky to get a room."

"You forget you're rich?" Ben asked. "As soon as your legal team found out you were injured, they sprang into action. You've got the closest thing to a private room, and you've got a civilian doctor. She was here volunteering to help, and apparently had gone to school with someone from your lawyer's cousin's son's class."

It wasn't something Martin had asked for. The possibility of someone else receiving lesser treatment because he had money didn't sit well. "That kind of sucks."

"It is what it is," Ben said. "You didn't ask for it."

A young lady in a loose white coat came in and greeted the men quickly. Her coat had small dots of red on it that Martin had to assume were blood. "Okay. These initial tests look good. The supplies that your crew used were a little out of date. That wrap technology has come a long way. Still, healing quickly, no infection that I can find, but we gave you antibiotics anyway. Blood substitute they used was a smart idea." She pointed to Martin's IV. "Pushing a fresh blood solution now."

"So, I'm good?"

"I think you'll be out in maybe a week if there are no complications," the doctor said. "We'll monitor everything extra closely for the next twenty-four hours. But, you lost a good amount of blood. Like, most of it? Yeah. I'd say you're not terribly close to being good just yet." She turned and quickly left, not bothering with niceties like a goodbye or a wave.

"She doesn't seem too impressed with you."

It wasn't a surprise to Martin. He wasn't terribly impressed with himself. "How's the *Adamant*?"

"It's fine. It might need a new coat of paint," Ben said.

"The *Alba Varden*? How's the other crew doing at the wreck site? Still bringing up treasures from the ocean floor? Anything unexpected?"

"Damn, Martin. I don't know. We've been in this hospital for what? Two hours or something? There are still some of those slag things fighting on the beach. I haven't really checked in with our treasure retrieval crew yet. I'm betting they stopped everything to see if their friends lived or died." Ben wheeled himself to the other side of the room, to the door. "You haven't asked about your crew. Jakob, Takis, Cass, Rina…Ozzie."

It wasn't something he wanted to ask, didn't want to know. "I heard what was happening over there. I know it got bad over there."

"Bad? Shit. That's… that's one way of putting it. You can't always focus on yourself, Martin."

"Focus on myself? I was slashed by some godforsaken beast that nearly killed me—you heard the doctor. I nearly died out there. I think I'm allowed to be a little self-centered right now." It hurt to yell, his lungs ached and his abdomen was tender, so he stopped. "I don't know what to say. They went onto the *Cudgel* to find supplies to help me. What would have happened if I hadn't been injured? If we would've just left that thing alone?"

"Jesus, Martin…"

"All of this is because of me. All of it."

Rina, and Jakob appeared at the doorway, interrupting Martin's chain of thought. "Everything okay?" Rina asked. "What're you two shouting about?"

Martin waved his hands and changed the subject as fast as he could. "It's fine. We're good. How is Takis?"

"He's upstairs. They're giving him some stitches for a cut he got trying to free his brother," Jakob said. "He's devastated about Ozzie. Theo and Angela are with him."

They were all broken up about Ozzie; Martin could see it on their faces, their movements. It took him a moment, but he realized Ben had the same look as the rest of the crew in the room. Ben had never been close with Ozzie, as far as Martin knew, but there it was—that same look on his face as he wheeled himself out of the room. "I can imagine."

Hakim picked up Martin's medical tablet and started reading the files. "Looks like you'll be fine."

"The doctor told me that, but thanks for the second opinion," Martin said.

"Yeah. No problem," Hakim said. "I think I'll sit with Ben. It's getting a little crowded in here."

"Jesus, Martin. That man is part of the reason you're still alive today. He reaffixed your dressings and monitored your…" Rina started in, but was cut off by Martin.

"I know. I was there."

The rest of the team began to file out, slowing down only to wait for Cass to step in. She'd been standing at the door, but Martin had no idea for how long. They all nodded, but said nothing to her.

66

"Seems like they're not too fond of you," Martin said.

"It's kind of a bad time to judge how people feel about each other right now, Martin. I think we'll be fine, given enough time and distance." Cass sat down with a thump on the plastic-covered chair in the corner. "It looked more like they had an issue with you. So thanks for taking the heat off of me just a little."

Martin laughed weakly.

"Looks like you're not dead," Cass said. "That's a good thing."

"Depends on who you ask, I guess." Martin adjusted himself in his bed and looked away from Cass. "Right now, this stuff they put on the wound itches like a mother. And…" He nodded toward the tiny IV stuck to his arm. "I still have to lug this thing around when I go to the bathroom."

"But you're going to be fine?"

"For the most part. They're growing some kind of tissue to make my abdomen stronger."

Cass stared at him for a moment. She had no speech prepared, no real questions, she just wanted to see him and make sure for herself that he was okay. "All right, well…"

"Yeah…"

"I'll see you. Take care of yourself." She gave him a wave and turned to leave.

"It's been suggested that I'm good at that," Martin said. "And I suppose it isn't far from the truth."

Cass nodded, not sure how to respond to that. It was true, but he also took good care of his crew, was generous with the splits he gave them of the treasure or finder's fees. He may have been self-centered, but selfish wouldn't have been the word she would have used.

"Thank you." Martin shifted in his bed, still not exactly looking Cass in the eye. "I wanted to say thanks for everything you did. I know that put you in a bad position. You could have said no and none of this would have happened." He quickly moved on from his apology. "Do you know what they'll do with you?"

It was a question that she mulled over all the way to the hospital, but really it was impossible to tell. "I don't know. They could make an example of me, but I would imagine they will try to keep as much of this as quiet as possible. I could be their hero, if they decide to make me one. There's been a job open in Geneva for some time. I suppose they could give me that position if they really wanted to sweep me under the rug for a while." Cass shrugged. "I turned in my resignation, but I'm not sure it'll be that simple."

She watched Martin nod a little, but he didn't say anything. "Well, I'll let you rest."

"I'm getting out of the treasure-hunting game... well; I'm getting out of the field at least. This was kind of an eye opener."

"I'll bet."

"Would you ever consider a less structured, more treasure-oriented position? One outside the agency?"

Cass laughed. "You mean would I like to be a pirate?"

"I was thinking more along the line of captain, but you could call yourself a pirate if that's your thing."

"Seriously?"

"I mean, we have to get a new drone to replace *Mister Punchy*. Someone will have to get that into shape."

It seemed like the least thought-out plan she'd heard since the crew came to her with the idea of stealing the *Cudgel*. And that turned out horribly in her opinion. "Are you honestly offering me a job right now?"

Martin shrugged.

Cass looked out the window at the mass of activity, drones, ships, people scattering to put out fires and help wherever they could. "What kind of drugs do they have you on?"

"Good ones."

The End

SEVEREDPRESS

CHECK OUT OTHER GREAT KAIJU NOVELS

KAIJU SPAWN
by David Robbins
& Eric S Brown

Wally didn't believe it was really the end of the world until he saw the Kaiju with his own eyes. The great beasts rose from the Earth's oceans, laying waste to civilization. Now Wally must fight his way across the Kaiju ravaged wasteland of modern day America in search of his daughter. He is the only hope she has left . . . and the clock is ticking.

From authors David Robbins (Endworld) and Eric S Brown (Kaiju Apocalypse), Kaiju Spawn is an action packed, horror tale of desperate determination and the battle to overcome impossible odds.

KUA MAU
by Mark Onspaugh

The Spider Islands. A mysterious ship has completed a treacherous journey to this hidden island chain. Their mission: to capture the legendary monster, Kua'Mau. Thinking they are successful, they sail back to the United States, where the terrifying creature will be displayed at a new luxury casino in Las Vegas. But the crew has made a horrible mistake - they did not trap Kua'Mau, they took her offspring. Now hot on their heels comes a living nightmare, a two hundred foot, one hundred ton tentacled horror, Kua'Mau, Kaiju Mother of Wrath, who will stop at nothing to safeguard her young. As she tears across California heading towards Vegas, she leaves a monumental body-count in her wake, and not even the U. S. military or private black ops can stop this city-crushing, havoc-wreaking monstrous mother of all Kaiju as she seeks her revenge.

CHECK OUT OTHER GREAT KAIJU NOVELS

ATOMIC REX: WRATH OF THE POLAR YETI
by Matthew Dennion

It has been fifteen years since Captain Chris Myers used his giant mech to draw the kaiju of North America into each other's territory to have them destroy each other. Once all of the kaiju had battled to the death only Atomic Rex was left standing. In Antarctica, the kaiju known as Armorsaur has entered the frozen valley of the yetis and attacked them. Devouring all but one alpha male yeti who was exposed to the kaiju's blood and left dying in the snow. The yeti awoke to find himself transformed into a kaiju with an obsession to destroy Armorsaur. Chris and Kate are forced to protect the people of their settlement by drawing Atomic Rex into South America where he will battle the kaiju there to usurp their territory and claim their hunting grounds as his own. As Atomic Rex enters South America from the north the enraged Polar Yeti enters the continent from the south. The two most powerful kaiju in the world will battle their way through a multitude of giant monsters as they are set on a collision course with each other!

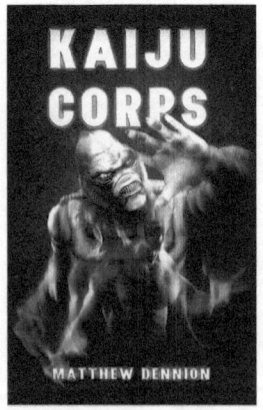

KAIJU CORPS
by Matthew Dennion

They are four soldiers who were genetically created to be mankind's last line of defense against potential world ending threats. They are soldiers who can transform themselves into gigantic monsters. They are the Kaiju Corps and they are facing a threat that is beyond the scope of even their fantastic abilities.

SEVEREDPRESS

CHECK OUT OTHER GREAT KAIJU NOVELS

KAIJU WINTER
by Jake Bible

The Yellowstone super volcano has begun to erupt, sending North America into chaos and the rest of the world into panic. People are dangerous and desperate to escape the oncoming mega-eruption, knowing it will plunge the continent, and the world, into a perpetual ashen winter. But no matter how ready humanity is, nothing can prepare them for what comes out of the ash: Kaiju!

RAIJU
by K.H. Koehler

His home destroyed by a rampaging kaiju, Kevin Takahashi and his father relocate to New York City where Kevin hopes the nightmare is over. Soon after his arrival in the Big Apple, a new kaiju emerges. Qilin is so powerful that even the U.S. Military may be unable to contain or destroy the monster. But Kevin is more than a ragged refugee from the now defunct city of San Francisco. He's also a Keeper who can summon ancient, demonic god-beasts to do battle for him, and his creature to call is Raiju, the oldest of the ancient Kami. Kevin has only a short time to save the city of New York. Because Raiju and Qilin are about to clash, and after the dust settles, there may be no home left for any of them!